BAPTISM of FIRE

ABRAHAM MORENO

Baptism Of Fire
Copyright © 2020 **Abraham Moreno**

All rights reserved. No part of this book may be used or reproduced by any means, graphic, electronic, or mechanical, including photocopying, recording, taping or by information storage and retrieval system without the written permission of the author except in the case of brief quotations embodied in critical articles and reviews.

Stratton Press Publishing
831 N Tatnall Street Suite M #188,
Wilmington, DE 19801
www.stratton-press.com
1-888-323-7009

Because of the dynamic nature of the Internet, any web addresses or links contained in this book may have changed since publication and may no longer be valid. The views expressed in the work are solely those of the author and do not necessarily reflect the views of the publisher, and the publisher hereby disclaims any responsibility for them.

ISBN (Paperback): 978-1-64345-468-9
ISBN (Ebook): 978-1-64345-666-9

Printed in the United States of America

To EAM

This story would mean nothing without your love. Thank you for teaching me how to love, and even though my love knows no bounds, it would be meaningless without the ability to express it in the most intimate ways. You succeeded where everyone else failed. You broke through barriers that no one else could. Only a soul mate can do that. I love you.

PROLOGUE

"Jeff!"

Fifteen seconds before the oil slick made an eloquent appearance, three-year-old Jeff disemboweled the second portion of relief. The poor little guy sat in silence with a blank stare, not knowing any better. Rodrigo unbuckled his seatbelt, only to reach back and unbuckle Jeff's as well.

"Can I use that shirt in the back seat?"

"Yeah, go ahead."

"I don't want him to get your seats all full of shit!"

Abraham laughed as Rodrigo placed the shirt under Jeff. He rolled down the window to allow the inevitable foul smell to escape. Rodrigo stuck his head out the window and yelled into the night, "Wild Zebra!"

The green Honda burst onto Highway 281 South, emerging from the downtown Friday night scene. Nightfall descended on the city of San Antonio, and the cool November evening deviated from the constant heat that swelled most of the year.

Eager to get the night started, delivering Jeff to his caretaker was the first order of business.

"My grandma should be home, so we'll drop off Jeff and then head to the strip club!" Rodrigo said, looking forward to carouse the streets. The life of a twenty-something, without a care in the world had its perks, but within a few seconds, that was all about to change.

* * * * *

The car began to drift, veering off to the right, nearly hitting the neighboring Toyota in the next lane. In a panic, Abraham slammed on the breaks in hopes to avoid collision. The highway curve, leading to I-10 west, further complicated the situation as an SUV closed in on him fast as it moved in from the left. Sandwiched between the two cars, he attempted to regain control.

The car swerved to the left with such ferocity that the concrete barrier presented danger rather than the safety precaution it was intended for. Rodrigo grabbed onto Jeff's shirt and clenched his fist, holding on to him for life. Unbuckling the three-year-old proved to be a mistake. His attempt to avoid feces reaching the seat from Jeff's soiled clothing didn't matter anymore. The perfect storm began taking shape.

With a head-on collision with the barrier, little Jeff unbuckled, Rodrigo holding on to his son for dear life, and a car impacting at 60 mph, left only a millisecond to brace for impact.

Boom!

The world stopped. The force knocked the wind out of him. It was like being in a crash-test dummy commercial, sudden and violent. A million thoughts flashed through his mind in half a second of time. *My life will never be the same.* Questions, many of them crept in as well. *Where do I go from here?* Uncertainty flooded in. *Will I live through this?*

Hope lingered, but there was not enough room for it to breathe.

* * * * *

The windshield cracked like ice. A thousand tiny pieces were ready to explode, but they did not shatter. The airbag deployed, grazing him on the forehead. The impact flung them over to what he thought was the grassy area beside the highway. After a couple seconds, he came to full consciousness. Upside down, the final resting place for the car was worse than expected. Unbuckling himself, he crashed to the floor.

Rodrigo yelled with urgency. He immediately escaped with little Jeff in tow.

The rear windshield had burst into oblivion. Debris scattered throughout the car. Abraham crawled out cautiously. He hunkered over the portion where the glass once held in the occupants safely. He noticed pavement as the car did not land where he predicted.

"Oh shit!" An African-American gentleman stood in shock as Abraham emerged from the wreckage. On his cell phone, he put his hand over his mouth. He was a heavyset man in his thirties, easily in position to help him out of the vehicle, but did not, as he froze at the sight.

"Ugh! Can't...breathe." He spit, tasting blood mixed with saliva. He couldn't speak freely and his chest felt heavy.

"Man, are you all right?" the gentleman asked with eyes widened. Abraham glanced over to his right. He didn't acknowledge the man as he focused his sights on a clearly injured Rodrigo and Jeff. Rodrigo cradled Jeff; his cries could be heard down the highway. He sat against the concrete barrier, opposite the one they crashed into, and he held Jeff like a baby, attempting to settle him down. His efforts were futile as Jeff yelled louder. Abraham crawled out sluggishly through what was once the rear windshield. Walking over slowly and dazed, he crept lower against the concrete as both men sat defeated.

"I called the police! An ambulance is on the way!" Shouts could be heard amidst the crowd.

Jeff cried unbearably. Rodrigo had a gash on the side of his forehead. Blood trickled down his leg, and both of his arms were cut up. None of that mattered as fear descended on both of them. Fear from a seriously injured Jeff and fear of a future unknown.

A young woman walked over calmly. "Is there anybody you want me to call?" Her voice spoke in a peaceful manner, unlike the rest of the crowd that began to build up.

"No..." he whispered as he did not want to alert Mom and Dad. They didn't need to know about this catastrophe. Mom and

Dad had Paulina for the weekend, and he didn't want her frightened at the sight of the mess unfolding. "Yeah…call…my mo…my brother." He gave her the number.

The wreckage spread across three lanes. Oncoming traffic onto I-10 West was blocked to a standstill. The car collided with the barrier on the opposite end of the highway.

"Man, you flew over two lanes!" a young man hollered. He couldn't have been more than twenty years old. With a baby face and weighing no more than 110 pounds, he shouted with no remorse. "I can't believe you walked out of that! That's amazing! This guy walked out of that! Hey, man, are you all right?"

Abraham ignored the young man. The red and white lights flashed with ferocity, and the crowd buzzed with speculation of the events that transpired. Traffic grew for miles and the center of attention remained on the three survivors.

"Excuse me, kid." A paramedic pushed aside the young man. He knelt down next to Abraham. "Sir, I'm going to check your vitals and put this neck brace on you. Are you in pain or hurt?"

The wind picked up. The concrete grew cold and uncomfortable. Abraham shivered. Being hot-blooded, he was not familiar with the bodily response. Naturally, the paramedic perceived him to be in shock as he reached for a neck brace.

"No, I'm fine…I don't need a neck brace."

"Are you in pain, sir?" the paramedic asked once more.

"No…just got the wind knocked out of me."

"Is it okay if we take you to the hospital just to check you over?" The paramedic looked him over with concern.

"No, I'm okay."

"Okay, just to cover our end, I'll need you to come over to the ambulance to sign off that we are not taking you to the hospital for medical attention."

Rodrigo and Jeff were escorted away into a separate ambulance. Rodrigo was put on a stretcher and hauled off.

The young woman, who offered help, approached him and helped him rise as his weakened legs moved slower than usual. "Your brother said he is on the way."

At that moment, Roy ran across the shut-down highway. He was not alone. Michelle accompanied him.

"I'm his dad, is he okay?" he asked the paramedic.

"He seems to be fine, but I need to take him over to the ambulance to have him sign off."

"Are you okay, Dad? I saw the car…"

Roy carried a different persona. He wasn't the usual dick Abraham had known all these months prior. When family members neared danger, Roy transformed to a point of unfamiliarity. Past altercations did not exist. A matter of life and death had a funny way of making it that way.

"Yeah, I'm fine." Abraham walked over with the paramedic. "What do I need to sign?" he asked, glancing over at Michelle. She spoke with an old friend she went to school with, who was now a paramedic. Even from a distance, he could hear the details of the crash as they briefed her. She turned to face him as he sat in the ambulance. Her eyes filled with tears. At that moment, his eyes welled up at the sight of hers, and he swallowed his emotions. He didn't want his voice to crack, so he remained silent, as he signed off on the laptop.

He hobbled over to Michelle. "I'll see you later at the house…" he turned away as his voice shook. "Donnie's on his way, and…I don't want Paulina to see me like this." He staggered away into the unknown. A set of taillights awaited him. If he didn't have a reason to get his life back on track, he had one now. The question was, where to begin?

* * * * *

"Is that the car back there!?" Donnie asked emphatically.

Abraham sulked in the passenger seat. "Yeah," he said in low voice. "Rodrigo and Jeff went to the hospital."

Donnie glanced over at him. Abraham had a faceless expression, and his emotions went numb. *This is serious,* Donnie thought. His brother was in bad shape.

"I'm sure they're gonna be all right."

Abraham didn't flinch. He gazed out the window into oblivion.

"You survived. That's all that matters."

Abraham absorbed the uplifting words, playing the events out in his head repeatedly. "You called my sister…no one was supposed to know about this…" he said in a monotone voice.

"I had to. Going 95 on the highway wasn't gonna get me there in time and I didn't want to take any chances, so I made the call." Donnie continued, "This is gonna change things…for the better. Everything from this point on will be based on how you decide to respond to this mishap…" Reassurance and encouragement were not his strengths, but he did his best to remember the pep talks he had been given. There were too many to count; nevertheless, he recalled the gist of such discussions and delivered a summary of what he felt was appropriate. *His words have never let me down, and I'm sure as hell gonna carry him through,* he thought. "Whatever you should decide…I'll be there with you."

He processed Donnie's words and for once, he was right.

"Don't worry, brother," Donnie reassured him, "I'm gonna stick till the end."

I
FIRE

Abraham walked and walked, slowly began picking up the pace. Running now, on his usual route, 2.8 miles long as he recalled. He ran as he did a thousand times before, like a well-oiled machine, around his alma mater. Burbank High School was but a distant memory. His presence there was simply because he used the school as a measuring stick of sorts, 2.8 miles from the moment he left his doorstep to the moment he stepped back on it. To him, the sidewalks, the steps, the track and all that was part of this place was just a training site now. The Class of 1996, he reminisced, was the last year he probably walked up and down these pavements on a daily basis. Now, seven years in the making, he trained on them, running up and down instead of walking. He gained nearly thirty pounds in the past six months, all of it muscle, going from a scrawny 130 to a strong 160.

Sweat trickled down his face. It glistened in the sunset as he stood alone on the track. He enjoyed watching the sun make its transition from one side of the earth to the other. During summer especially, he would take a few moments and cherish the last visible light shining down, and only in the summer would he thrive at night just as much as he did in the day. He recalled telling others on many occasions, "I thrive with the sun, I can't live without it." After all, being born on July 23 just barely made him a Leo, but nevertheless, he had the element of fire at his disposal. He knew that just by walking into a room, his presence was strong, as he would catch floating eyes look at him from head to toe. "You walk in like you own the place," that famous line echoing in his head, as he had heard it many times before. Standing only 5'7", fairly short, but probably average for a Hispanic, he looked fuller with the extra weight and probably taller than his vitals would indicate. His brown wavy hair was always trimmed down to a clean cut fade and his big brown eyes had the characteristics of both predator and prey.

He stood front and center on the street that would lead him home. The sun shot brilliant orange rays that gave a glow to his honey-golden skin. A cut-off shirt drenched with perspiration hugged the upper half of his body, displaying only biceps that were considerably larger than they had been weeks before. Silky royal blue shorts reflected the light as they rustled in the breeze with a baggy effect. On the verge of his twenty-fourth birthday, he felt fierce and untamed.

The fire, always burning inside him, made him look at least two or three inches taller. Being a Leo, as well as being confident, made for a firestorm of misinterpretations, which were usually upon a first impression. "Conceited" was usually a primary misconception to which Abraham would quickly correct. "Confident" was the term that he used to describe his sometimes dominant personality. The confidence was evident enough that he remembered girlfriends telling him it felt as if he was taller than 5'7". Jason, a close friend, believed that 5'10" to 5'11" predicted Abraham's height. Although Jason confirmed he wasn't buzzing at the bar, he tried to compare with a hand measurement that Abraham was in range of his six-foot frame. An optical illusion, or so it seemed, was an attribute that only the fire could manifest. The fire, burning so wildly at times, created a glow. Summer always made him feel alive, and it was only proper that *his* fire would become more intense during this time.

The energy emanated off him, and most people who were around him for a few seconds could feel the warmth. The smile and mystery behind the eyes puzzled others, yet they were drawn to him and would open up immediately after a first meeting.

His warm smile was the spark that would get your attention, his persona was the flame that made you look for his presence, his words were the fire that left you wanting more, and once you believed as he did, then you knew his life as a roaring blaze.

Souls that were drawn to him could feel the vibrant energy that coerced through his body. He considered himself a man of God, and whether or not people were attracted to him for that reason was up for debate. Faith had always been the root of his existence. Everything that surrounded him intertwined with the foundation built on this belief.

The Power to Believe

At thirteen years old, the belief of being "sent" rather than "born" began to make a definitive entrance. It was then that empathy and words became his allies and so, conversations with God from that point on were a constant. The 2.8 was no different. The training route required twenty-five minutes, enough time to talk to the Lord and so, it served as a form of therapy, evolution, and a further understanding of what it was to help people, despite attributes that were unexplainable. Adverse situations that were unique to his abilities were becoming more apparent, and in time, exchanges with the Lord were simply to seek advice.

The streets and sidewalks he had seen a million times, but the breeze carried a scent uncommon through the last leg, however familiar. The wind carried the scent and it danced around him. Unable to detect its origin, he let the fragrance flow through him. It took him to another place, another time, where problems didn't exist. At ease and relaxed, he looked around to the sidewalks, front yards, and finally to the trees. There in the breeze, he found the origin of the aroma that made him forget about running. The culprit turned out to be a bed of red roses. Not yet in full bloom, it was obvious that whoever lived in that house grew them regularly. He approached the property, admiring the flowers and the beauty they possessed. He took a few meditative moments and inhaled. The smell triggered memories, capable of transportation to a happier, stress-free time. Things had changed dramatically in the past year. "I remember…" he said to the Lord, "I remember what I said…that day…"

Noises blared in the distance. His attention remained with the calm presence of the roses. He touched one gently. His mind's eye recorded nine roses, days away from blooming. The disturbance grew louder. He caressed the rose. Its beauty could not be denied and its soft, smooth surface settled his soul. The noise finally overtook his meditative state, and he was transported away from the scent. His concentration broke, and the connection with the rose was severed.

He heard shouts and yells in the direction he was heading. Three men wearing all black surrounded the building, tactical clothing at best. Like a flock of birds, they flew toward a rust-bucket of a car across the street, sensing oncoming danger. They jumped in the convertible, and as they did, the roof of the liquor store blew high into the air with a balloon of fire and black smoke billowing out from it. The tiny structure swelled with flaming intensity. Windows shattered as the blast of energy reeled to escape.

The heat rushed onto his skin, and the sheer discharge knocked him to the pavement. Shingles, glass, wood, and bits and pieces of concrete flew onto the street and nearby houses within a hundred-foot radius. The mechanics across the street from the liquor store, who usually loitered at all hours of the day, stood silently in shock. Wearily gathering himself, he cleaned off the rubble. He noticed a piece of concrete the size of a tennis ball that missed him by centimeters, as it landed on the street.

He shot a look over at the flowers. His admiration for them delayed him long enough to stay clear of the blast radius. The beautiful smell that brought peace now faded away. From the ground, the bed of roses reacted to the events currently unfolding and, despite the disruption, stood in all their glory. He left their beauty behind and continued on to the burning structure.

But the flower wasn't done. The rose he touched seconds earlier began to open slowly. By the time he reached the scene half a block away, the rose was in full bloom. It breathed full life, setting itself apart from the rest.

A second blast came from the back of the liquor store. Training meant being mentally and physically prepared for the unexpected, but this surprise caught him off guard. Growing up, he emulated the tactics of the Dark Knight. His knack for checking his surroundings was a staple, especially in unfamiliar places. Observing exits in any place of business and the quickest way of escape was a practice that he prided himself on. "Never leave anything to chance," he reminded himself often. Detective Balderama recognized these subtle traits and even asked about his future plans. If it weren't for him running into the detective at the comic book shop, he would've never known that superheroes were something they had in common. Although detective work and physical training were parallel to the Dark Knight, Abraham was a Man of Steel at heart.

His instincts pulled him like a magnet to the busted and broken building. The old man, who owned the store, was presumably still inside.

In the air rang an aggressively deep voice. It blared throughout the streets as bystanders watched in a panic.

"Let's go! Let's go!"

II
THE GUN

The three men sped off in a vehicle that was an older make and model. The car had visible rust on it from years of fallen paint and most of the body had primer applied to it. Upon second glance, one of the men attempting the getaway was all too familiar. The giant figure towered over the other two men. It had been at least a couple of years since he had seen him, but nevertheless, he identified the gargantuan running amok. He had history with the leader of this tactical trinity. At six foot five, 230 pounds, he was a hulking presence around these parts. Inseparable at one time, his friendship with this man dissipated a few years ago. The mad man behind the heist was known around town as The Gun.

Abraham ran to the building, not knowing that danger still lurked near. Loud blasts were fired repeatedly, and it blared throughout the neighborhood. It took him a few moments to register that bullets were grazing past him as they flew too fast for him to react. His sprint never ceased as they struck the building.

The car faded in the distance. The only thing left to do was find the old man. The liquor store was a tiny structure, so small that his bedroom was probably bigger than the facility itself. The old man had to be in plain sight upon entering. Abraham stepped to the door, with it barely open. He pushed against it. Jammed!

The store was collapsing. He took a step back and charged at the door. Nothing. Boards fell, glass bottles broke, and the fire felt scalding hot. Doubt crept in. It was a test of mettle. *How strong am I?* Certainly, all this training wasn't for nothing. His resolve came alive. He stepped back once again and rammed the door with his shoulder with all his body weight. *Crash*! He broke through with just enough room for him to squeeze in. The newfound strength he recently acquired was put to the test, and on the second attempt, it did not disappoint. Blood streamed down his forearm. Impact caused glass to disperse everywhere. Cuts were visible on his right arm and above his right eye. The adrenaline made these insignificant injuries numb as he found the old man lying on the floor.

He knelt down beside him checking for vitals. The old man seemed like he was still alive, but he wasn't sure, and it didn't help that he didn't know what the heck he was doing as he checked for a pulse. With the fire raging, he was running out of time. He sweated profusely as the flames burned forcefully through every corner in seconds. Bottles of liquor busted with fury, and the facility was fast becoming an inferno. The glow of the fire reflected in his eyes, and it dared him to brave the danger as it danced around him. He propped the old man up by the arm. Sitting upright, he scooped him up and carried him out like a fallen soldier. The blaze surrounded them, and the door he busted down seconds earlier was now covered in flames. There was no way he could get by without one of them getting burned. He tried kicking the door aside. It didn't budge one bit. A piece of wood fell from the ceiling, hitting his arm.

"Aghhh!" he shrieked in pain, shaking his arm and nearly dropping the old man. Black ash covered a part of his forearm. He panicked.

The glass on the door shattered as the heat swarmed the structure, elevating his panic level. His strength wasn't enough, and he couldn't think clearly. As the smoke filled the store, clouding it with limited visibility, so too were their lives fading into the blackness. He kneeled, with the old man slumped over his shoulder. They were stuck. No one was coming to help, he thought. They would've done so by now. Fear, rage, and frustration consumed his mind. Together, these emotions brewed a ferocity in him that lay dormant. His fire trembled deep inside his core. The materialization of these emotions spewed out, erupting in a whirlwind that trumped the blaze before him. The power swirled upward vigorously like a tornado, taking the flames with it and clearing most of the black smoke, as it rose out of the gaping hole that was once part of the roof.

What the hell was that? he thought. Dazed and lightheaded, he was about to collapse. He wiped his nose as it dripped, and rather than the sweat that covered his face, it was a red substance that sprawled on his hand.

The door rattled and shook from the might. On the verge of being busted into oblivion, the door swung forcefully open from the outside, but it wasn't by his doing. "What the hell?"

A mechanic came from the body shop in a rescue attempt. "¡Córrele, córrele! *Run, run!*" The mechanic guided them out to safety.

Abraham scurried out as far away as possible from the blaze. The body shop across the street doubled as base camp until the paramedics arrived. The mechanics, all of whom but one, stayed clear of danger, as they assisted with the old man. They checked the old man to see if he was breathing. The three of them spoke Spanish, but it was clear that the old man would live.

"Está vivo, *He's alive,*" they said to one another.

His muscles ached. The old man was heavier than he looked. This was as real as it could get. No superheroes, no special stunts, no superpowers, only pure instinct saved the old man.

"Man, I'm tired," he whispered. *Am I going to be able to do this every day?* he thought. "What am I saying?" he said aloud. "God will see me through…He always does."

Resorting to his faithful thinking was a characteristic reminiscent of his predecessor thousands of years before him, and it was the only thing that kept him alive.

The old man owned the tiny liquor store with eighteen years of business under his belt. The parking lot, or lack thereof, could only hold two cars, and yet, business boomed. Every single day, the old man would sit in a beat-up faded lawn chair in front of the store reading the paper and gazing at incoming traffic. This was a ritual that had gone on for many years. After all this time, Abraham waved hello to this man and not a word was ever spoken and his name remained unknown. Swallowed by the inferno, the old man's liquor store was now burning to the ground. The wrath of Tommy Gun was evident.

What in the world is he doing in this area? he thought. Tommy was from the outskirts of the city, between San Antonio and Floresville. His presence there meant that he was desperate or perhaps something worse, expanding his personal crime syndicate.

The Gun was notorious for conjuring up a criminal career in robbery. It was like a hobby for him, and he often referred to it as his weekend job. He was highly susceptible in getting himself involved with crimes that carried large sums of money. Nevertheless, he felt the need to keep up his reputation for packing heat. The shots fired were not to harm, but for show. The Gun, however, had no history of taking casualties, but felt that it was necessary to show off his vast weaponry. A showcase also engineered to strike fear as well. The day was fast approaching when luck would run out and Tommy Gun would take his first casualty. Until then, the city was safe from Tommy's bullets, but robbery was another story.

Officer Ramirez arrived on the scene and calmly did his job, blocking off incoming traffic to detour vehicles from getting too close to the inferno. He placed red safety flares, blocking off the street from cars and spectators alike. Traffic slowed on South Flores with cars refusing to turn on Glenn Street next to the fiery ruckus. Fire engine sirens went blaring through the neighborhood streets. The sidewalks flooded with an audience witnessing the blaze. The show officially began.

The fire department arrived hosing down what was left, but there wasn't much to salvage. Abraham did everything he could. His first experience saving a life didn't go so well, but the old man was alive and that's all that mattered to him. He continued his training exercise. The old man was in safe hands.

"Who got him out of the building?" a paramedic asked curiously of one of the mechanics.

"El chavo que se fue corriendo. *The guy that left running.*"

Words were never spoken between Abraham and the old man. Things had remained the same.

III
QUESTIONS

I have so many questions…

Twilight fell upon him. With his training exercise back on schedule, it was just him and the concrete trail. Running the last leg of his route, questions of what he was meant for still lingered. Saving the old man foreshadowed things to come.

What is my destiny? Why am I here?

Thoughts were always speeding through his head during the twenty or so minutes of peace that he labeled the 2.8. Like the pebbles before him, his thoughts were scattered everywhere. Some of which remained far away and undisturbed, while others stayed close. The beliefs of being "sent" were no strangers at this time of the day. The burdens and advantages, the success and sacrifice, the consequences and repercussions, the trials and tribulations, the triumphs and tragedies, the gift and the curse, he knew very well, for there is no good without evil, no dark without light, and in spite of it all, these gifts were for a purpose. God's plan was obviously deliberate, but the reasoning remained uncertain, at least here on earth.

Am I meant to do this? Save lives?

God did not leak too much information at once. His career path was up for debate, and this recent debacle raised lots of questions and much uncertainty.

Why did You send me?

These anomalies, I know they are from You, he thought, *and the mission, is what I need to figure out.*

Death came to visit seven months prior, but in Death's case, it didn't go so well. Surviving meant that God had something greater in store. What it was, he didn't exactly know yet.

Why am I so different? I don't understand…

There has to be others, he thought. There was Wendy, but she was half a world away. If he could just band together with his kind, then he would feel at home, understood. Until then, a secret it would remain.

I need your counsel…

There was nothing that could keep him from his goals. He was relentless and proved to be many times over. Relentlessness had always transported him to great places.

Just like the time when Ms. Villarreal said that he couldn't graduate high school early, he did it anyway. When Dr. Dom told Abraham he couldn't graduate with a degree so soon, he did it anyway. When he was the first psychology graduate from Texas A&M Kingsville System Center San Antonio, they left him off the list. He walked the stage anyway. Training to be one of San Antonio's Finest was a feat he could accomplish single-handedly. The only person who could bring him down to failure was himself.

Thank you, God, for this beautiful day…

You have given me so much, he thought. *Thank you for another day of life and thank you for guiding me, and, in time, I know You will show me what I am here for.*

Even at eight o'clock in the evening, he sweated profusely, thanks to the humidity. The summer weather in South Texas was unforgiving, and despite the sun setting, the temperature remained in the 90s. But that didn't matter; he was on a mission.

The sweltering summer heat in San Antonio carried the most spectacular days, nevertheless. Training became an event as birds chirped and skies remained blue as the sun shone down on the earth. The Lord laid out plenty of opportunities; Abraham wanted to be sure he chose the right ones.

That last six months of his life were intense. Sculpting his mind and body proved to be a tedious task, which required much determination, and he wanted to be ready for whatever mission he was meant to take on.

IV
GRANDMA MARCELLA AND THE DANCING DIVA

"Damn, I'm late!"

The doorstep was only seconds away as he turned the corner. What was supposed to be a typical training day turned into a circus of events. A thirty-minute run became a one hour and fifteen minute affair, and Grandma would surely be waiting for him, peeking out the door periodically. He jogged straight to the front steps and began the stretching rituals. Sure enough, Grandma stood on the other side of the screen door. At seventy-three years young, she was still full of life.

"¡Apenas! *Barely!*" she spoke in a loud voice.

"Yes, Grandma, I was running."

"¡Todavia! *Still!*" Grandma Marcella exclaimed.

"Yeah, there was a lot of commotion."

"¿Como que commotion? *What do you mean commotion?*" She gave a puzzled look. "¿Ya comiste? *Did you eat already?*"

"Grandma, I'm already late, I gotta get in the shower."

"¿Ya te vas otra vez? Cuando vas a comer? *You're already leaving, again! When are you going to eat?*"

"I'll pick something up on the way," he said, trying to escape her clutches. She eyeballed the side of his face as she studied him like a hawk.

"¿Estas sangrando? *Are you bleeding?*"

"No, Grandma, it's probably dirt."

"¿Porque estas todo mugroso? Que pasó que hay tanta lumbre?" *Why are you so dirty? What happened that there is so much fire?*"

"The liquor store at the corner caught on fire—"

"¿Se quemó? *It burned?*"

"Sí. The bomberos ya vinieron. Ellos están apagando el fuego. No te preocupes. *Yes. The firefighters already came. They're putting out the fire. Do not worry.*"

"Bueno. *Okay.*"

* * * * *

He darted to his room to prepare for the adventurous evening. A shower, a light shave, and a restroom break took all but fifteen minutes. Hunting for a set of garments appropriate for the special event got sidetracked by a browser left unchecked. The screen presented a tempting treat of chat room cheer. Only a few days old, the laptop came to life, and it stayed that way as Grandma's house experienced a technological takeover. With vast knowledge at his disposal, he surfed the web freely and frequently. The username *Superman78204* made its presence known the last few nights.

There was a guest in the chat room that stood out from the rest. Her face graced the screen with the unsuspecting username *21shortydiva03*. Her eyes caught his attention. Beautiful and light brown, they spoke volumes. Her smile was innocent and somehow familiar. He was certain they had never met, but her aura radiated on a frequency he'd known before.

He clicked on her call sign. A bright green dot lit up next to her name. She was online! Without wasting a second, he sent one word to see if she would respond. Immediately, the mystery girl responded, "Hey."

Immediate reciprocation was a good sign. *Now what?* he thought. Before he could even think of what to say, she sent a message that he did not expect.

"I'm logging off, but here is my e-mail, *nydancediva@hotmail.com*. Add me on messenger."

The timing was flawless as he was running behind schedule. Had she wanted conversation, he may have missed out on the engagement at hand.

Stepping out of the bedroom, a voice boomed that was loud and unruly. His safe haven had been breached. Silently, he let out a dreadful sigh, knowing he had to encounter the visitor who came for a late dinner. A dark cloud suddenly loomed over him. The oncoming exchange was going to be exhausting as usual. The conversations were brief and consistently billowing with tension. He decided to step out and face the music as this visitor would take his time eating, and he desperately needed the newspaper in his hands. He reluctantly made his presence known as he stepped in the kitchen to get the confrontation over with.

Without a second to lose, the visitor spoke harshly.

"Hey, boy, I'm going to need you tomorrow…to paint the house."

Abraham knew his father well. Unemployed since graduation, he was forced into slave duty in the 100-degree summer heat. Manual labor consisted of sawing off branches with a twenty-foot saw, to transporting dirt in a wheelbarrow, to painting the house, which happened to be the current project.

"I can't. I have an interview downtown?"

"Is this another Mickey Mouse job?" Roy asked with a condescending tone as he devoured frijoles. It was the frijoles and rice that brought him over for a visit, as if living next door wasn't close enough.

"It's retail…"

"When are you going to get a real job?" he scolded.

"I should start the Academy in October."

"Well, I hope you make it. You're already twenty-four, and you've never had a job yet," Roy said mockingly, adding insult to injury.

"I don't turn twenty-four until next month," Abraham countered, correcting Roy.

"Same difference, what's another month…you're practically twenty-four already, Abe! Shit! Get a real job, already!" In turn, Roy responded by raising his voice with a sarcasm that filled the house.

Abraham shook his head, avoiding an unnecessary argument. Up to this point, anything he did was never good enough for his dad.

"Well, when you're done with that I need you to come right back and start on that, you hear me?"

"Yeah."

Growing up with Roy wasn't easy. Living with Grandma for the last eight years was a relief. Even though it was only next door, a different roof made all the difference.

Abraham grabbed the newspaper and immediately reported back to his room. Flipping through the pages, there was one ad that caught his attention. Plan B needed to get off the ground fast, and although it wasn't his first choice, Michelle urged him to give it a try.

"Never leave anything to chance," he mumbled to himself.

He folded the paper with the headline face up: "Pre-K Teachers Needed." Wasting no more time, he pressed a pair of khaki pants that served no purpose for the past year and prepped a maroon button-up. Within minutes, he was out the door.

V

THE VOLCANO

"Moreno!" Detective Balderama shouted. "I need you to be ready this week. I've got you scheduled for the next step of the process. You'll be getting further instructions in the mail on where to report. How are you doing? Hanging in there?"

Abraham wasn't quite sure how to respond to the detective, being that it was a Saturday night; he had no reason to pester him on the weekend. "Yes, sir. I'll be ready. I'm good, just ready to get to the academy."

Phone calls with the detective only lasted a minute or less. He found it odd that he called for no reason.

"All right, Moreno, sounds good. We'll be in touch."

* * * * *

He jumped into Honda 2 and she shined beautifully. Fresh from the car wash, along with her brand-new parts, made her glittery green gleam. She survived their last trip together, and it was nearly a total loss for them both. It took many prayers and a promise to God, and unlike her predecessor, thankfully, she came back to life.

Rodrigo lived down the street in a neighborhood the streetballers called inner city. The speakers blared en route to Rodrigo's house.

He waited eagerly on the sidewalk. His style of Timberland boots and baggy jeans were complemented with a striped polo. He preferred a thin beard at all times and was sometimes mistaken for a white boy. There was a New York feel to him as he wore urban style clothing and his khaki hat was a signature item. He felt the disguise of a hat was necessary in a dance club.

"What up, playboy? Man, Honda 2 is lookin' nice! You just got her back?"

"Just yesterday, it feels good to have her back in my custody."

"It would've been a shame to lose her so soon, especially after Honda 1…may she rest in peace."

"No joke! Thank God it wasn't us resting peacefully. How is little Jeff?"

"He's good. All healed up and…get out of the way, you old bag of shit!" Abraham slammed on the brakes as Honda 2 came to a screeching halt. An elderly woman walked in the middle of the street. She chased Rodrigo to the car.

"You forgot to clean out the sink!" she yelled.

Rodrigo carried no remorse, not even for his grandmother. "I left the sink full of hair. Fuck it, we're late. I got my pills and forty bucks, we're good to go!"

"You can still drink and take those?" Abraham asked, as he noticed the little round blue pills.

"Yeah, I'm used to it."

"You know who I saw in our neighborhood earlier, who also needs crazy pills? No offense." Abraham couldn't keep the joke to himself, as well as tell the story of the day's events and more importantly, the villainous acts of an old friend.

"Who?" Rodrigo asked calmly, preparing himself for a response that could possibly involve one of his many women.

"You'll never guess!" Abraham engaged Rodrigo in a guessing game, curious of what wavelength he was on.

"Ummm. Sabrina?"

"Nah."

"Christina?"

"Negative."

"Steph?"

"No, man, think Palo Alto, from the gym." Abraham redirected Rodrigo's train of thought.

"Richie?"

"No…Tommy Gun," Abraham finally gave away the answer.

"Tommy! That big piece of shit from Palo Alto that used to hoop?" Rodrigo had to be sure, but both men had only known one person by the name of Tommy Gun.

"Yeah."

"I hate that motherfucker! He would talk a lotta shit. I ran his ass and Grasshopper, they couldn't hold me. Nobody could hold me at PAC. Fuck those dudes!" Rodrigo did not hold back when it came to basketball boasting and wasn't shy from expressing his feelings with a barrage of expletives.

* * * * *

It was only nine o'clock and the parking lot already had a few recognizable cars.

"This party is starting early," Rodrigo chimed in.

Abraham looked over at Rodrigo for confirmation, "You ready?"

"Yes, sir, let's do this!"

As Abraham and Rodrigo made it to the entrance, the bouncers greeted them, "Y'all are late!"

A heavyset man sat in a wooden barstool at the entrance door. He was in his late twenties and worked the door every weekend for the last five years and, in that time, had developed a relationship with the regulars that entered the facility.

"Gene, how's the wife? I haven't seen her in a while," Abraham inquired.

"She's doing good! We're expecting! She's fourteen weeks now."

"Congratulations, man! You're bouncing days are numbered! I doubt the wife will have you working at this crazy place!"

"Yeah, I'm gonna have to retire. Don't worry about the cover charge, just go straight in," Gene motioned to the door.

"Boss man, Gene in the house! Thanks!" Abraham said, shaking Gene's hand upon entering.

They walked in the facility greeting friends, partygoers, and fellow regulars alike. Balloons attached to tables floated above in the area sectioned off, and each of the tables carried the name of the man of the hour. A bottle of champagne sat on the table awaiting the birthday recipient.

Walking into the Volcano on the other hand was like walking into hell. With the darkness at every corner, tiki warriors, and flames flaring red and orange around the ceiling, it portrayed an uncanny environment of the underworld.

"Abraham, what up?"

A familiar friend shouted, "What up, Rodrigo?" Buck was the first to greet the duo.

"What up, Buck?"

"Still ballin?" Buck asked curiously.

"Always, fool. How long you been here?" Abraham responded, catching floating eyes.

"We've been here as soon as the place opened. We got a gang of drinks at the table. They're on special for another thirty minutes, so get your drink on!" Buck escorted Abraham and Rodrigo to the table where glasses were filled to the brim.

In the sea of people, a collection of basketball players from Palo Alto College overwhelmed the club. Different characters came together on this night in honor of a basketball comrade and a good friend. Grasshopper was in attendance, along with Boobiez, Double H, Ciro Torito, Transporter, Dave Yugo Jones, Edward Stark, Big Benz, Jose The David, Ricky B. Sticky, Jake the Snake, and the Diesel.

The crowd encircled around one particular table. It was evident that a most popular person occupied this area as smiles and drinks splashed the scene.

The masses sensed a presence among them and the partygoers parted like the Red Sea.

"He's here!" a few girls whispered louder than intended.

"Finally!" another voice said, not so secretive.

Rising from the table, with an empty sparkling champagne glass in his hand, was the man of the hour. With both arms raised in the air and a smile that the alcohol boasted, this man spoke two words, "About time!"

His name was unlike any other and, without a doubt, even rarer than his newfound brother. He refused to be called by his true name, and so, a variation of it came to exist.

Abraham shot a look over at the birthday boy, "Donnie, happy birthday, brother!"

"Abraham! Glad you're here!" Donnie chimed in, as the two embraced each other. He stood two inches taller than his brother, but somehow they seemed to be at equal stature. "It's the S everybody!" He held two drinks in his hand, and it was clearly evident that a few, if not many, shots of Patron had been ingested already.

"What's up, Abraham?" Friends greeted him, and it was his ritual to greet everyone individually upon entering.

"When are you going to pop open that bottle of champagne?" Abraham questioned eagerly.

Donnie gave a sharp smile at his friend, "We were waiting on you, brother. You know I had to wait for my main man! As you can see, they were running out of patience, but that doesn't matter."

"Word!" Abraham took a liking to that answer.

As Donnie poured the first two glasses of champagne, he couldn't help but smile, "Man, I'm having a good time. I love you, man. I'm glad you came."

"Are you buzzing already or what?"

"Nah, man, I know what I'm saying. I'm just happy that all my people are here, you know. I mean how many times are all of us in the same place at the same time, besides on the basketball court."

"Yeah, I know what you mean."

"So who did you roll with?" Donnie wondered.

"Just Rodrigo and I," Abraham gulped some champagne.

"You're super late. I was beginning to think you weren't gonna show!"

"Sorry, ran into some heat earlier. Anyway, you know better than that! Of course, I was gonna show…better late than never."

"We've been waiting for a while and I didn't want to crack this bottle until you got here, and now that you're here…the party is complete."

"Hey, we forgot to toast!" Abraham interrupted and Donnie stopped as well. Donnie pointed to his temple and then pointed to his brother's. "I like where your head's at!"

Both men raised their glasses.

"To my friends or rather to my family forever," Donnie said genuinely, with a nod to his friend, as they touched glasses, "And the night officially begins. I love you, man, I really do. And I'm proud of you…graduating with a bachelor's degree and now a police officer, that's awesome!"

"Thanks, but I'm not a police officer yet." Abraham couldn't help but smile. He didn't get a whole lot of praise for his accomplishments.

"Man, whatever! Like you're gonna fail!? You're already one of San Antonio's Finest as far as I'm concerned. You got everything going for you, bro! And the degree…none of these people, *our* people, don't even have that!"

"They're on their way. Everyone here is still in school, well, almost everyone," Abraham said, motioning to Boobiez, "they'll get there."

"They're on the eight-year plan," Donnie laughed. "I'm on that train, too! I wish I could be done like you, with a degree."

"It doesn't have to be that way," Abraham intervened, "You still can, you just have to believe, I mean, it's all in your head. I can cook you up a plan, you'll be finished in a year and a half tops. You know I always have a plan. We'll get you started with easy classes and then work your way up."

"I don't know, it seems so far away," Donnie said, looking to the dance floor in deep thought.

"*What* seems so far away?"

"All these classes, all this time…time that I wasted."

"What's bothering you? I know it's more than school. Lucy, isn't it? Have you talked to her today?"

The uncanny knack for Abraham to sense someone in distress sometimes bothered people. Donnie knew he wouldn't be able to hide it for long.

"How did you know?"

"I just know. Your eyes gave it away. The eyes never lie." Abraham read his pain and anguish. He used the booze to cover it up, but the alcohol betrayed him as his feelings became apparent.

"I talked to her earlier. We got in a fight and…she's not coming. We've been fighting for a long time now," Donnie said somberly as his brown eyes looked away and then down at the floor. The short spikes of hair resembled sharp blades ready to strike at any moment. When his eyes wandered off, it was then that Abraham knew his counterpart was truly affected.

"It'll be all right. You know what? Two weeks from now, the both of you will be together again, and we'll be laughing about this shit! I guarantee you, by the time my birthday rolls around in exactly a month, we'll all be here having a drink. It's your birthday, man, let the worries go." Abraham hoped to inspire his friend with existentialist words.

"Yeah, you're right! What is it that you always say…I can't remember it. Falling hard on your ass and then dusting it off or something…"

Amused at the effort, Abraham chuckled, shaking his head in disappointment. "No, no, no, old friend. It doesn't matter how hard you fall, all that matters is how you respond."

"That's it! I remember, now. Man, you had a rough year last year. A falling out with your dad, psycho girlfriends all over the place, and a near-death experience are just the ones that come to mind. You were on the dark side. You reminded me of me back in LA," Donnie teased.

"Don't remind me. The only highlight of last year was getting a bachelor's degree. Other than that, 2002 was a year to forget." Abraham did his best to shelve those memories on a whim.

"But you made it, and you're here. You had a few setbacks, but you came out on top. You're the one that made it out of the hood."

"Haven't made it yet, but I'm working on it."

"Out of our whole entire circle of peeps," Donnie reiterated, "you got more than anybody else at this point, let's face it. Real talk!"

"Real talk, huh? Just like your real name. Abb—"

"Don't say it. Please."

"All right then, let's get back to the task at hand, us having a great time!"

Abraham's tactic worked like a charm, and the subject changed on a moment's notice.

"Yes, you are correct!" Donnie agreed.

"Well, then, let's get to it! It's your day, now act like it!"

"You're right! Let's paaaaaaaaaaaaarty!"

"That's what I'm talking about! It's time to celebrate!" Abraham reassured him. "Hey, I got some great news! Jackie is looking to hire help at Top Sports, and guess whose name went to the top of the list!"

"Are you serious? You're gonna hook me up again? It's not what you know, it's who you know! Thanks, brother. How can I ever repay you?"

"Let's start by not getting fired."

"All right, I'll see what I can do...not making any promises. That dough is gonna be rollin' in between these two jobs, and we're gonna be at Wild Zebra every weekend with all the strippers at our table! Believe that!" The excitement Donnie held was mostly due to the three previous vodka cocktails, as he took another sip of his current drink.

"Calm yourself, you haven't even been hired yet!"

"Coasting down Commerce on Saturday night, cruising on Military Drive on Sunday night and hitting *all* the clubs on Loop 410 in one weekend, that's the life right there! 2003 has already been a great year, and we are only halfway through! It's gonna get even better, best believe that!"

"Donnie, it's minimum wage, not a six-figure salary!"

"All right, all right...back to reality...hey, is Avril coming?" Donnie asked after chugging the rest of his champagne.

"Yeah, I think so. I don't know. She said she was going to come later," Abraham responded uninterested.

"She's like a Mexican Beyoncé, with curves like an hourglass." Donnie gave hand movements illustrating imaginary curves.

"Yeah, but she can get a little crazy too. You know what I mean?" Abraham quickly reminded his friend. "Hey, I gotta tell you something…"

"What is it? Don't tell me…she's pregnant?"

"Hell no, that is not even funny! Why? Are you ready to be an uncle? Talking crazy like that…"

"Well, what is it? Is it good, bad, ugly?"

"I kinda…I kinda met somebody," Abraham chuckled.

"Who? What do you mean 'kinda'?"

"Yeah, like…I mean…we chatted a bit…and she seemed cool."

"That's good…that's great. Where did you meet her?"

"Well, I was checking out a…chat room…and…"

"A chat room? You met her on the internet? What the hell! So you haven't met her?"

"Shhhhh! Not all loud! Nobody knows, and no, not yet…not officially…not face-to-face, I mean."

"Dude, seriously…only desperate people do that! That's for people that can't get girls, like your boy Boobiez over there. Look at him…he's trying to talk to girls that are seventeen years old…that's desperate."

Peeking over, Abraham noticed Boobiez talking to girls with glowing wristbands and the backside of their hands with a huge M written in permanent marker.

"Now, you know I'm not desperate like that…I was just checking out the chat room and saw her and that was it…it may not even be a thing…you know?"

"Okay, so how many girls did you hit up in the chat room?" The booze was kicking in for Donnie. His eyes sparkled like the glass he was drinking out of.

"She was the only one…no lie."

"Well, is she hot? Like this fine ass girl right here?" Donnie eyeballed a voluptuous female as she pranced by.

"Hi!" the young woman responded with a flirtatious smile. Donnie shot a look at Abraham.

"Did you see that? I'll be back, gotta go to work…you can tell me about your internet fling later!" Donnie whisked away, and Abraham receded into the shadows, admiring the eye candy.

Liv came to mind. His interest piqued just talking about her. How he wished she would show up unexpectedly to continue their conversation. Highly unlikely, he resumed his attention to the party at hand.

He looked over at Buck, who was babysitting his drink. Double H dared Ricky to chug his cherry vodka sour, and he did. Davey "Yugo" Jones and Transporter guzzled down tequila shots in unison.

Ciro Torito, Jose the David, and Diesel courted a group of girls at the entrance and Edward Stark and Big Benz sat at the table guarding the booze. Boobiez showed off his cornrow braids in a last ditch effort to impress the girls to no avail.

Drifting off to the bar, Abraham observed the activity from afar. A few regulars showed at their usual time, but the nightclub mostly had students from Palo Alto College.

Over by the restroom, three figures loitered in a dark corner. Suspiciously, they waited. As the festivities flared, a presence remained undercover. An uncomfortable feeling settled over him. A presence he had known before.

Emerging from the shadows was an old friend. One that he had seen hours earlier, yet their paths were destined to cross once again. A huge figure appeared from the darkness, complemented by two smaller silhouettes that followed. The rays of light finally gave way unveiling the mystery man. A clean-cut fade and facial hair, followed by a smile that stretched from ear to ear, displayed the characteristics of a man treading too close to the realm of darkness. An outstretched hand belonged to the one known as Tommy Gun.

"What's up, Superman?" Tommy surprisingly was happy to see Abraham.

"What's up?" Abraham expressed much displeasure derived from the unfortunate events hours before.

"What you been up to these days?"

"You're a fuckin' dick you know that! You almost fucking shot me, and you almost killed that old man too!"

Tommy had a confused and awkward look on his face. He did not expect such a response from an old friend.

"What? What are you talking about?"

"Your liquor store robbery!"

"Oooooh...that was you? I almost popped your ass. My bad! Shit, my bad!" Tommy laughed hysterically, outstretching his long arm once again. Abraham reluctantly shook his huge hand.

"You almost murdered my ass and you're laughing about it? That's messed up, Gun!" With that, The Gun couldn't help but laugh harder.

"Dude, my bad! Let me buy you a drink. Come on, Superman. Anyway those bullets would've just bounced off you."

"Yeah right!" Abraham agreed sarcastically. Gun whispered an order to the bartender as he flashed a handful of hundreds. Within seconds, shot glasses lined the bar.

"Hey, did you see that fire out there? It was an inferno, I didn't think it was going to burn that fast." The Gun spoke with pride about the incident. "And you were quick. The fire was burning all right and not even a bullet could touch you!" Tommy handed over a clear substance in a huge shot glass, "Here you go!"

"What is it?"

"Just drink it, I got you two. You ready?"

"I guess so."

"My bad, Super One," Tommy apologized as the two men touched glasses as a toast of forgiveness. Tommy smirked and said a phrase he hadn't said in ages, "From the Gun to the One!"

The liquor solidified the apology. The Gun gave a wave to his two bodyguards and then pointed in Abraham's direction. "This is the guy who gave me the call sign...the one who started it all! This career would not exist without you, Super One! This calls for a toast!" Originally, the name given was Tommy Gun, which eventually evolved into just simply The Gun.

Their relationship once rivaled that of Abraham and Donnie but at a different time. During their run, Tommy coined this particular phrase as they backed each other up countless times. Donnie joined up with Tommy's new crew from time to time but felt it was better to stay away from the temptation of his escapades.

"Hey, remember when we used to go out? You took me to my first club and then my first strip club and remember when you got me my first shot? I got totally wasted that night and didn't remember jack in the morning. Those were good times!"

"Yeah, I remember Gun. Those were great times…and that was before you had your new career," Abraham reminded him.

Tommy laughed and just shook his head in agreement. Abraham never approved of Gun's second career, and their once tight relationship became a memory of the past. They remained friends, and the more Gun's career thrived, the more their friendship drifted apart.

"There's a rumor going around?"

"Oh yeah, what's that?" Abraham asked, raising an eyebrow.

"That you're gonna be a cop."

"I'm supposed to be already, but it's taking a while. I've been passing all the tests so far. I'm just waiting and watching."

"Well, cheers to the Gun, to the One, and to you becoming a police officer. And you better not arrest me once you make it."

"Just don't shoot me or rob me or I'm gonna have to!" Finally, Abraham smiled in the presence of The Gun.

"So do you think you're really gonna make it?" Tommy Gun questioned.

"Well, it's not really up to me…"

"Who is it up to then, if not you!?"

"Gun, let me tell you something. God has three answers to prayer: yes, not yet, and I have something better in mind. I have no worries, Gun…in time, I'll find out which one."

There was no shortage of faith on his part. He prayed for the answer to arrive. Deep down, he had no need for doubt because one thing was certain, he had God on his side.

VI
THE TEST

Donnie kneeled beside the bedpost. He reached under the bed. His hand was playing a guessing game searching for the object of interest. He grabbed a box that had layer after layer of dust on it. Fingerprints were evident on the box, but they, too, had one less layer of dust. Many months had passed since he opened the box, and before that, many years. He did not have a need to use the contents that remained hidden in the box. Five years prior, he thought that he would pick up the life he had left in Los Angeles, but much to his surprise, his new home existed in a different world than the one he knew before.

With a heavy sigh, he placed the box back in its place. He stood up and pulled out a book from a small two-shelf bookcase. He wasn't much of a reader, but coming to San Antonio changed things. At Grandma Josie's insistence, it was his first gift upon his arrival in San Antonio. The offering was symbolic for him: new city, new circumstance, new life in the Alamo city. He sat on the bed, his head down and eyes closed. He did not open the book but placed his right hand on it like he was being sworn in to the presidency.

Don't mess up…don't mess up!

The book had a bit of dust as well, but nowhere near what the box carried. The pages were old and faded and the cover was rather worn. A decadent dark red made the book stand out and its gold-lettered title barely visible. In its heyday, it might have looked completely elegant, but now, it was tattered down to a relic of yesteryear printmaking.

Things are going good, don't mess up now!

He placed the book on top of the bookshelf, never opening it, as he felt the need to refer to it more than ever. Before walking out, he made sure not to put it back in its place, for its presence would make all the difference. A time of testing was coming.

VII
SNAKE WITH LEGS

Lord, I love You. Please give me the guidance to do what I need to. Please, Lord, give me a sign of what I'm supposed to do with my life. Am I supposed to be a police officer? Give me a sign please if I am meant to be that. In the meantime, please help me find a job. It's what I really need right now for the summer. I know in the end everything will be all right. I love You, God. Amen.

Some time passed since he prayed for a sign, and he remembered the prayer well. To hold him over, a job popped up for the summer, but not without conflict.

"So do you have any tests coming up?" Emma asked pleasantly.

"No," he said with a sigh. "The applicant process was put on hold. Hopefully, I'll report to the academy in the fall."

"Is that why you're here? I mean, you know, working here for the time being."

"Unfortunately, Emma, the San Antonio Police Department and I have the same problem. We're both low on funds, so to answer your question, yes," he laughed heartily.

It had been fourteen days since he walked through the door of Top Sports and Jackie was not what she seemed. Tensions ran high. He was set to meet the girls for inventory and their urgent request to speak to him was daunting.

He had become fast friends with the girls that worked there as he picked up the store procedures rather quickly. Inventory brought all these characters together, with the exception of the boss.

"You don't know yet, do you?" Emma began her questioning. She served as the veteran at Top Sports. She knew the store from front to back and could practically run it single-handedly. Then there was Pam, who at only eighteen, was the youngest of the crew. Last but not least was Justina, who provided great backup. Emma, Pam, and Justina served as the glue which held the store together. They were valuable assets that Jackie could not afford to lose.

"Know about what?" Abraham asked puzzled.

"Jackie, the things she does around here. She does what she wants."

"Well, she's the manager, she should be able to, right?" Abraham tried reasoning with Emma.

"She does nothing here, Abraham. Nothing! When Tim, the district manager, comes to visit, she tells him that she does the whole store display when it's us who do it all the time. The last time she made Pam do it all by herself, and when Jackie didn't like the display, she made Pam do it over."

"Really?"

"Yes. And whoever opens the store with her in the morning does all the morning duties while she reads the paper, drinks coffee, and rides the clock. Abraham, why do you think I don't want to be assistant manager or keyholder? She takes all the credit herself. That's why there is no assistant manager and why she hired you as a keyholder instead."

Justina jumped in, backing up the statements made by her coworker.

"We think the reason she hired you as a keyholder was just so she can take her vacation."

He sensed a bull's-eye on his back.

"What do you mean?"

"Once she gets what she needs from someone or something, she disposes of it, or them, like a piece of garbage."

"So you're telling me she is going to dispose of me once she returns from vacation?" Abraham couldn't believe the news he was hearing.

"She is threatened by you. We think…" Justina looked over at Pam and Emma. "…that she is going to fire you when she gets back."

"She's stupid if she fires you, Abraham." Pam couldn't help herself any longer.

"I don't understand. Why? How can she fire me? I've done everything she has asked me to do," Abraham questioned.

"Well, we are not saying that she is, it's just what we think she might do. She has done this before. She's just not a good person, and she'll take advantage of anyone when she has the chance." Justina clearly felt relieved telling Abraham the truth.

Rumors surrounding Jackie's work ethic were no secret now. He could feel the fight or flight response brewing up inside like he was entering a bout. Caught in the crossfire, he needed to make a choice and he felt the girls were trustworthy enough.

Why would they lie to me?

He believed them, but at the same time, Jackie put on a good show. She never faltered in his presence. Her act included the academy award for the hardest working retail manager on the planet. Her methods were too extreme. The girls accused her of being cruel, lazy, unfair, and robbing the time clock, yet she presented her persona as the all-American Top Sports manager of the year. Jackie took her vacation as planned, but with all the accusations against her, Abraham contemplated a counter attack. *If what they say is true, I need to prepare,* he thought.

"Why haven't any of you called her out on it or complained to upper management?"

"Abraham, we are scared to do that because she will fire us in a heartbeat! Justina just returned from maternity leave and I'm paying for school," Emma said disheartened.

With his gut feeling assuring him and the evidence coming to light, there was no doubt that Jackie had a deceiving way about her. In the last place, he imagined confrontation; he knew a battle was coming.

She wasn't quite what she seemed, and in time, he knew the truth would reveal itself. A plan to counteract her was in the works. With the girls help, dispatching her would be smooth and quick. It was only a matter of time before she would set her sights on beating him to the punch.

He looked at the time. Nine o'clock sharp. *Time to close up.* With that, he locked up and counted the till in record time.

The churning commenced in his stomach. He loathed confrontation but loved it at the same time. The combative nature of warfare tested his character. It kept him sharp. The adrenaline rush made him feel alive, and every time he felt scared going into battle, it was the fear that would drive him.

The sports bar next door was not only convenient but tantalizing, as his mouth watered for a drink. His best friend, and only true friend at this point in time, sat on a barstool inside. The scene was still and a drink would do the trick of getting his mind off the coming storm for sure.

"Abraham! I got the job!" Donnie was not shy about celebrations. His theatrics were evident in any establishment he occupied and he made his presence known nonetheless. Once, he requested everyone to attend a celebration because he got fired from a job. Another time, he celebrated for holding the record of having a job for the least amount of time, one hour and fifteen minutes. He even celebrated with the news of getting offered three different jobs in one day, only to claim that he was not going to take any of them.

"How long have you been here?" Abraham took a quick glance around the bar, only to find two other poor souls who looked suicidal rather than celebratory.

"I came here the minute after I got hired! Which would be…" He checked his watch, focusing his eyes to read it. "Approximately five hours ago!"

At that exact moment, Tommy Gun emerged from the back restroom. His hulking stature cast a shadow over half the bar.

"Super One! You came to celebrate! You're about four hours late!"

"Five!" Donnie corrected.

"Tommy, I'm surprised you're not shooting up the place. You like blowing up places with liquor, don't you?"

Abraham had a knack for showcasing humor, sarcasm, and a shot of truth, all in just a few words. Tommy accepted the remark with a grin, offering his hand to greet Abraham.

"One has jokes today!"

Abraham shook Tommy's hand with a firm grip, although his hand did not make a dent in a hand that was nearly double his.

"I'm going to take off right now. I got to give y'all a chance to get out of here before I come back and blow up this place, oh, and rob it too, but not in that order."

"All right, Gun, be cool!" Donnie gave his farewell to an old friend. Abraham shot a look over at Donnie with an eyebrow raised in wonderment. His smirk faded quickly and was replaced with a serious expression.

"Super One, I'll get at you later. B, I'll call you tomorrow."

* * * * *

Donnie let out a sigh. Abraham whipped out his first and most important question, "What the hell is going on? You're not going rogue on me, are you?"

"He just wanted to hang out, that's all!" Donnie laughed.

"Yeah sure."

"I'm serious!" Donnie giggled a little harder. "He just wanted some advice."

"On what? How to steal?"

"Nah, just everyday stuff. I'm offended by that comment! I'm a changed man!"

"Oh, so you're a counselor now or what?"

Donnie finally let out a full-fledged laugh. "Hey, we just came to celebrate and hang out, so come on and have a drink with me! It's a celebration, bro!"

Donnie detected seriousness and the stone-faced look on Abraham confirmed it. His smile faded and the celebration took a detour for the moment.

"Look, in all honesty, nothing or no one can come between us. Air tight! He knows my loyalties run deep and that we're blood. The Gun may be an outlaw, but he respects that you and I are family. He, among others, may not like that I favor you over everybody else, but you know what I say, 'Fuck everybody else!'"

"Had I gotten killed on any one of those dates with death, you would've been rolling with him right now! Best believe that!" Reminiscing of the year before were memories Abraham did not want to revisit.

"Are you serious right now? When is the last time we went a whole day being incommunicado?" Donnie challenged in defense.

"I can't remember."

"Exactly. It doesn't happen! If that ever happens, it's because I'm sick or something."

He knew what to say to change the subject to a lighter topic. His persona was like a Jedi mind trick all in itself. It was clear Donnie wasn't going to give up information regarding Tommy Gun, so Abraham let go of the suspense and opted to change his topical course.

"So what did Jackie tell you?"

"She loved me, man! I got the job on the spot!" Donnie rejoiced.

"That's great news! You're probably going to replace me."

"What? What are you talking about?"

"The girls told me just now that they think she is going to fire me soon."

"That doesn't make sense! She relies on you, doesn't she?"

"Not for long. I can feel it, she is not a good person." Abraham pointed at Donnie's drink as he let out a deep breath. "I'll have what he's having." The bartender nodded and fixed his attention on conjuring up the cognac treat.

With a dejected gaze at the bar top, Abraham fell silent. Donnie sensed the conflict brewing in his counterpart. He took a sip of whiskey, waiting for Abraham to continue, but even after taking several sips of cognac, he remained mute.

Drawing up comforting words to say was never his strong suit, especially in times of distress, Donnie broke the silence. "You know what I think…she's a snake with legs." He shook his head as if he was having a conversation with himself.

"A what?" Abraham glanced over at him, wide-eyed and confused.

"Yeah, bro…a snake with legs. It's just like the devil…he seduced, deceived, and corrupted Adam and Eve as a serpent. People do the same. Snakes with legs."

Surprised at Donnie's attempt to uplift his spirits, a reference from an unlikely source caught him off guard. Abraham inquired further, "I thought you didn't read the Bible, much less know any stories from it!"

"Yeah well, I picked up some bad habits from somebody I know. I won't name any names. You know, God is always working in your favor, brother, even when you think He is not. He may be doing something now or has done so already. Something or someone special may just come into your life. You just never know. Wow! Does that sound familiar?"

"All too familiar…didn't I use that speech on you last year?" Abraham questioned.

"Yeah well, like I said, I've been picking up some bad habits from you. Just have faith like you're always telling me…you may be on course for something better that has yet to unfold."

Both men raised their glasses in unison. As they clanked together, Abraham commented with sincerity, "Cheers to that, brother."

VIII
SOUL SEARCH

1998

    She wrote carefully. Every word, she chose meticulously, as was the entire letter itself. One day, she would meet him, and her letter would buy her that much more time. An introduction to her other half at thirteen years old was not exactly suitable in her mind, but her faith cautioned that she was only a few years out. The letter would suffice for now as she wrote to the most omnipotent being the universe had ever known.

    Please let me meet him when I'm a little bit older. I know he is out there…allow me to find him, but not just yet.

    She inked her last words, folded her letter, and sealed the envelope indefinitely. Her course had been set and she was ready to wait. With one final gasp, she kissed the letter gently and closed her eyes.

    God answers prayers.

    It was only a whisper, but her other half could hear it.

IX
SOULS MEET

He strutted excitedly into the food court. Ten minutes early, he waited for her anxiously. After several phone conversations, some lasting into the wee hours of the morning, he had a voice to go along with the girl he quickly began forming a bond with but no face to go with it. She wouldn't be a mystery girl for long. He made sure that he wore decent attire for the meeting. A beige short-sleeve button-up, jeans, and wheat Timberland boots were presentable enough, he thought. He looked for a table to sit as he waited for her. *What if Donnie was right? What if I am just desperate?* he thought. It didn't matter now, as she was surely walking to the rendezvous point.

She turned the corner. *It had to be her,* he thought. She wore relaxed clothing and kept it simple: jeans, v-neck t-shirt, and black shoes. She was working after all and was courteous enough to meet him on her lunch break.

He stood up and smiled at her. "Hello there!"

"Abraham?"

"You guessed right."

"I'm meeting my boyfriend here, too, if that's okay?"

Boyfriend? he thought. He was sure not to miss a beat. "Sure, it can be the three of us."

"You're okay with that?"

"Yeah, I don't mind. We are just having a friendly meeting is all, right?"

He is too calm, she thought. *Maybe he's not really into me like I thought,* she wondered. "Did you want to eat here?" she asked.

"Sure. Subway?"

"I was just going to ask you that…so am I what you expected?"

"Ehhhhhh."

"Really? That bad, huh?"

"I'm just kidding. You look a little different from your picture, more like four foot ten."

"Good different or bad different? And I'm four eleven."

"It's a 'I didn't know you wanted a threesome on our first date different.'"

"I thought it was just a friendly meeting?"

"It is."

"I was just kidding. I don't have a boyfriend."

"Me too."

"You don't have a boyfriend either?"

"No, not that…about this being a first date."

Pound for pound, she held her own. *She is amazing,* he thought.

"So is it a good different?"

"It's a good different. So do you have calves?"

"Do I have what?"

"Calves…you know, like the muscle?"

Liv busted out in laughter. "Are you serious?"

"Yeah. You see, if a woman has calves, then she'll look amazing in high heels."

"You must be a leg guy."

"You could say that…among other things."

"Other things?"

"Yeah, you know…other things."

"Tell me."

"You first…calves?"

"Possibly. And you…breasts? Booty?"

"Possibly."

As she ordered her sandwich, he studied her. She had a beautiful complexion and wore no makeup. *She didn't need to,* he thought. Her eyes were a beautiful and innocent light brown.

"Your turn." She turned to him, and he glanced quickly in the opposite direction so she wouldn't catch him gazing at her.

As he ordered, he could feel her eyes penetrating his flesh. His peripheral confirmed it, as she, too, skimmed his stature.

He understood the protocol of a first meeting and studying each other secretly when the opportunity presented.

"How long have you worked here at South Park Mall?" he asked as he grabbed the sandwiches.

"I've worked here for about two months, right after I graduated from high school."

"Wow, you're just a baby."

She smirked at the comment somewhat amused. "Let's sit here," she said, as she pointed to a table for two in the middle of the food court. "And what year did you graduate, mister?"

"A long time ago…in a galaxy far, far away, I'll just say that."

"Are you like one of those nerds that like Star Wars and Spider-Man?"

"Star Wars, yes. Spider-Man, no."

"You probably like the Incredible Hulk."

"Wrong again. I'm more of a DC guy than Marvel."

"Huh?" she asked puzzled.

"You know, there's DC Comics. Batman? Superman? You know? And then there's Marvel with Hulk and Spider-Man."

"It's all the same to me."

"Wow! You are going to have to undergo some serious super-hero training if you're gonna be rollin' with me!"

"You're too funny! No, I will not be participating in any kind of training," she giggled. "So seriously, what do you do for a living?"

"I am actually in the process of becoming a police officer."

"Oh, impressive. A real-life superhero, huh? Why?"

"Why what?"

"What made you want to become a police officer?"

"Well, it's actually a step toward what I really want to be…"

"And that is?"

"A detective. I'm really good at figuring and finding stuff out. I'm good at hunting people down."

"You sound like you've done that before."

He took a bite of his sandwich. She paused for his refutation. He looked up from his sandwich at her as she sipped her soda and studied his eyes.

"Well…" she said, "I hope you make it. I'll pray for you."

"You pray?"

"Yes, is that a problem?"

"No, not at all…that's great! I do too."

"What do you pray for, Mr. Abraham?"

"Well, I pray for a lot of things…guidance, strength, and people…for the most part. What about you?"

"I pray for my family, my friends, and peace in the world."

"The world is a big place."

"That doesn't mean it can't be saved."

"When heaven comes to earth, then it will be."

"You say it like we can't do it ourselves."

"It's not impossible. Difficult, yes…I never give up hope."

She smiled. *He is amazing,* she thought. He didn't have an age, it seemed, and, he existed without an identifiable perception. His eyes couldn't be read, and she was curious to what was behind them. They told stories and they had her full attention.

"You eat fast. Were you in the military or something? They usually eat fast."

"No, I'm just hungry."

"Well, I have to get back."

"Your lunch break is fifteen minutes long?"

"Actually, I didn't get a break today. I left to come meet you."

"I'll walk with you. Is that okay?"

"Sure."

As he escorted her back to her store, she stopped in the middle of mall, reaching down to her shoe.

"What's wrong?" he asked curiously.

She lifted up her pant leg and turned to look up at him.

"Wow, you do have calves?"

"A little bit. But you're not seeing them in heels just yet. I'm not that easy."

He laughed. "In due time."

X

THE DREAM THIEF

"Where are you at, homeboy?"

Donnie hadn't seen Abraham in two days. He felt the need to check on his brother as they had communicated strictly by cell phone in the last forty-eight hours.

"Hey, brotha…I'm heading into work right now. What about you?"

"I'm working the game tonight at the SBC Center. Lakers are in town…you know what that means! I'll be suited up just in case they need a sub."

With his hometown being Los Angeles, Donnie was a huge Laker fan and an even bigger fan of Kobe Bryant.

"Well, you're going to be standing behind the bench suited up for a while then because they don't need another ballboy."

"Why don't you come out here? I'll tell Dale to get you into the arena."

"Wish I could but I'm actually going into work right now myself, but I'll call you after."

* * * * *

He had a couple of minutes before clocking in. Hearing her voice would make the hours go by faster, so he dialed her number. The lunch date with Liv brought him smiles the second he left her presence and he craved more.

"Hello?" she answered sweetly.

"Hey there, how is your day going?"

"Eh, it's going…how about you?"

"I'm doing better now that I'm talking to you," he said with a smile.

"That's good to hear," she paused.

"What's wrong? You don't sound like you."

"Nothing."

"Nothing? Well, how about if we hang out tonight? We can go eat a late dinner or catch a movie…we can even go to the—"

"Abraham, I don't mean to burst your bubble, but I have plans already."

"Oh okay, we can go after—"

"My ex-boyfriend wants to talk and…he wants to work things out."

"Oh," he spoke quietly. "Is that what you want?"

"I…I don't know."

Stillness followed. For once, he dove in head first and took a chance. It wasn't his style to pursue but rather be pursued. "Okay…well, I hope it works out…for the both of you."

"Do you think…" she hesitated, "do you think I should give him a chance?"

"If that is what you feel, then go for it."

"I'm sorry, Abraham."

"Hey, no worries, we are just friends, right?"

"Um, yeah, you're right…we *are* just friends. Don't forget to keep in touch."

It's okay, it wasn't a thing anyway, he thought. "We're gonna have a great day, nevertheless!" Positive self-talk worked amazingly well despite failed attempts.

* * * * *

Abraham walked in the door and noticed Pam at the register. She rang up a customer and gave off an awkward look.

"She's back."

Jackie had just returned from vacation, which was dreadful to say the least. Confused, he waited until the customer left to begin conversation.

"Hey, Jackie is in the back waiting for you. I think she wrote you up."

"She wrote me up? For what?" He stood puzzled.

"I don't know. I think it was something about you being off on the till."

"Hey, how did Donnie do the other day? Did he do all right for his first day?"

"Yeah, he did well. He is a cool guy and funny too. Where did you find him? Y'all act the same I swear." Pam gave a hint of attraction.

"He is my brother, I mean not for real, but we are really close, you know what I mean?"

"Yeah, he was fun to work with, but Jackie was getting impatient with him. She said he moves too slow."

Abraham laughed at her remark. "It's because he doesn't like to work."

He approached the stockroom, and there she stood waiting.

"I need you to sign these." Her voice turned to ice.

Jackie slid three papers to him on the cluttered desk. All three detailed different alleged violations. The last had a reprimand that simply stated, "Termination."

She beat him to the punch. He had no words to combat her allegations. Taken off guard, he could barely skim the words she scribbled.

"I'm sorry, Abraham, I have no choice but to relieve you from your duties. After you sign these, you can clock out."

Within a split-second notice, he was transported back to the day they met. His gut spoke the truth. He should've known better.

The store was quiet. It was filled with sports memorabilia from nearly every era of professional sports. There wasn't a person in sight, and in the background, a jazzy tune came to life. Doubts came to mind, and suddenly, he felt as if this endeavor was not meant to be.

A young lady popped up from behind the counter. She was rather goofy looking and stood about 5'5". Her long black straightened hair matched the dark frame of her glasses. She had a thin physique and sported a Top Sports t-shirt perfectly tucked into her khaki shorts. She didn't notice him walk in and seemed to be in her own little world.

"Hi." Abraham spoke first. "How are you?"

"Good!" she said in a startled voice. "Can I help you with anything?" Her voice and smile were uneasy as she attempted to recover from being caught off guard. Instantly, both parties sized each other up as if going into battle.

"Yeah, I saw your ad in the paper and I was wondering if I could apply."

"Okay sure, let's go talk in the back. I have an application that you can fill out back there. Pam? Can you come to the front please?"

A very young-looking petite girl came rushing from the back. She had a baby face and couldn't have been more than twenty years old. She had short hair, a bob cut of some sort, which complemented her chubby cheeks well.

* * * * *

"I worked in this place believe it or not. I mean before it was Top Sports. It was Sports Fantasy back then, but it closed down in 1998, and after that, they opened Top Sports about three months later."

"Oh, so you're familiar with this place."

"It's a little different, but yeah, it was fun working here. Maybe I will again, right?"

"Yeah, that's crazy. By the way, I'm Jackie. I'm the manager here."

"I'm Abraham. Nice to meet you."

"Abraham? Like Abraham Lincoln?" Jackie laughed.

BAPTISM OF FIRE

"No, not really. It's Moreno actually," he said clearly not amused.

"So Abraham Moreno, are you working right now?"

"No, I'm in the process to become a police officer right now, but it's kind of taking a while."

"Oh, so you plan to use me, huh?" Jackie snickered. He smiled, not knowing how to respond. "Sorry…the stockroom is a mess right now. We've been really short-handed lately. It's only been me and two other girls working nonstop. I haven't had a day off in three weeks and I'm supposed to go on vacation soon."

The stockroom was tiny and cramped with shirts, boxes, and junk that hadn't been tampered with in some time. Jackie sat on a chair that served to be part of a desk. Abraham looked around and noticed there was not a chair in sight.

"Oh, hmm…you can go ahead and have a seat on that box right there. I'm sorry, we don't have any more room back here."

"It's okay, I understand. You all must be really busy."

"Yes, we need help. So you have experience you said."

"Correct. Like I said, I've done retail—"

A loud ring interrupted Abraham. The business line rang loudly in a stockroom with no breathing room. A cordless telephone sat on the wannabe desk filled with scattered paperwork.

"I'm sorry, hang on a sec." Jackie picked up a walkie-talkie and spoke to Pam who was in the front.

"Pam, could you get that? I'm busy doing an interview, help me out a bit, would you." She resumed back to the interview and switched back to her tea party persona.

"Sorry, about that, now you said you've worked here before."

"Yes, a long time ago. I've done retail for a few years now."

"Really?"

"Yeah. My last job was at the Spurs Shop, running the downtown store before it closed down. By the way, if you need good help, a friend of mine who worked with me at the Spurs shop is looking for a job."

"Oh, yeah? Is his name Tony Parker?"

"I wasn't talking about that friend," Abraham laughed, "although he has accumulated a hefty debt of shipping charges while I managed the shop. Packages to France, Arizona, and Chicago and all over the world, have certainly rung up the bill, so yeah, he owes me!"

"Although we *are* desperate for help here, I don't think Tony Parker is!"

"I do have someone in mind though, if you really want an extra person. He can put in a few hours here to help out."

Abraham thought about Donnie. If Jackie was in dire need of help, then she would take Donnie in a heartbeat.

"Okay, tell him to come by."

"All right, will do."

"Abraham, I think we're going to work well together."

"So when do I start?" Abraham questioned with an "I'm just kidding" smile.

"How about Friday?" Jackie answered with a semi-serious tone.

"Really? That was easy."

"To be honest with you, I want to hire you as a third key. I think you'll be able to handle it."

"Wow, that'll work."

"I'm going on vacation in a couple of weeks, but I think you can get the hang of it by then. Oh, you know what, I didn't realize that Friday was the Fourth of July. You didn't have any plans, did you?"

"Ummmmmm." Abraham wanted to say yes. Popping fireworks for once was in his agenda, but he couldn't pass up this opportunity.

"No, it's fine. I'll be here." With that, the two shook hands. In that instant, a horrific feeling buzzed through his body. She wasn't trustworthy. Her cold smile was snakelike and her darkened eyes spoke lies. Her body language displayed confidence but it was a false confidence, he sensed.

Abraham left but not without a wary feeling.

Abraham grabbed the pen and out of nervousness began to ink his signature. He paused.

What the hell is happening? I can't believe she is firing me. I've never been fired before. What is she trying to do?

"No," he said forcefully. His reserve restored to full power, instantaneously. "No, I'm not going to sign these. I'll clock out, but I don't agree with this."

"What? What do you mean? You have to!" She was surprised at his rebuttal.

"I don't have to do anything." Abraham threw the pen on the desk and left Jackie pondering.

A shocked Pam observed in awe. He punched in a few numbers on the register and ended his affiliation with Top Sports.

"I'll see you later, Pam."

"Abraham, you're leaving?"

She swiftly made her way around the counter and gave an embrace. Confused, her face displayed a number of emotions.

"It's okay, I'll see you later."

And with that, Abraham walked out of the store for the last time. He remained shell-shocked at the turn of events. It symbolized a historic day for him. It was the first time he had ever gotten fired. There was now a blemish on his resume. Upon further consideration, an even more detrimental blow yet awaited. The dream was over. Jackie single-handedly and with no remorse destroyed the hopes of him becoming one of San Antonio's Finest. Once Detective Balderama received word of this catastrophe, Abraham only needed to hear him confirm his worst fear, and as all hopes were sealed with despair, he had one question brewing in the moment.

What am I going to do now?

XI
FIRE RISES

Abraham sat, slumped over in his chair, disheartened at the latest turn of events and exhausted at the emotions spilled onto paper. A black journal lay on his desk. The ink in his pen unleashed the bombardment that begged for release. He poured his thoughts therapeutically on paper.

No matter the circumstance, there is always a choice…rise or fall. God administers a test for a reason. There is no success without sacrifice. People often give up and say, "Why did this happen?" Rather, there are those that say, "Despite their situation, what am I really made of?" The division and recognition between the two is a key element of evolving.

No man or woman can make plans against God's plans…whichever way it goes is because God has a reason for it…

He felt numb, useless. The future, his future, one that he was once certain about, now drifted toward uncharted waters. Dismissal from the processing detail meant that the bright future he expected now seemed dim and dark. He glanced over at the picture of him and his fellow students on graduation day. The headline was farthest from the truth.

Where dreams come true.

But the dream was over. As of today, that degree stood for nothing. He earned it to contribute greatly to the community and the world, to serve others for good. For now, it didn't matter.

How did I let it get this far? he thought. His conscience was under attack. Guilt began making its presence known along with anger, resentment, and last but not least, retaliation. *No, I can move on and forget about this whole thing.* Coaching usually worked, but inside his core, he knew it was only going to hold off these feelings for so long.

His concentration wavered. *I need to think clearly,* he thought. Countermeasures seeped in. The phone calls from the girls last night were short-lived as they inquired about a possible return. He gave a convincing response—there would be no return. The damage was done and the girls made it clear they stood with him.

Bitterness looked for an opening to clasp onto him. The unfortunate situation caused these side effects to manifest. *I should just let it go.*

Adversity tests a person; it builds their character. The anomaly is complex; nevertheless, it is a worthy opponent.

Uncle Phil once told him something he would never forget. "It doesn't matter how much pussy a man can get, how much ass he can kick…what makes a man is how he handles himself in a crisis."

Dark forces began swarming. He feared the day that darkness would have a legitimate chance to overtake him and prevent him from seeing the light permanently. He had been acquainted with it once; an occurrence that adversity spawned.

God has an interesting way of testing…the consequence of choice/ free will. The devil tempts and attacks from all angles to see what the soul will decide. It is always darkest before the dawn, and at the peak of greatness, the devil puts on the darkest show. God's greatness is only decided when the heart and soul turn away from the light or when these elements are drawn toward it. Only the strongest reach deep down inside when all hope is lost, when the light ceases to visibly exist, and it is only then, that a fire deep within will ignite. In darkness, it is evident to all who witness that a fire rises.

Confusion began to burrow in, conflicting with his current thought of counteraction. Business with the sergeant was set for 9 a.m. and this was the last chance to remain a candidate with San Antonio's Finest. Deep in his subconscious, emotions rattled and swayed. A fire was brewing…

XII
BACK THE BLUE

"Do it, brother, do it! You've worked too hard to not fight for this!" Donnie took a bite of his burger. "You got this," he said with a mouthful of fries.

Abraham nodded. Rosita slipped him a plate of tacos. "Thank you, Rosita."

"De nada. Un taquito de chorizo con huevo, barbacoa y carne guisada con queso. Algo mas? *You're welcome. A sausage and egg taco, barbeque and stewed meat with cheese. Anything else?*"

"No, gracias. *No, thank you.*"

"Bueno, Abraham. Si necesitas algo, no mas di me! *Okay, Abraham. If you need anything else, just ask.*" Rosita smiled and checked on her other guests.

He focused on Donnie's words. "Donnie, you're right. I need to give it one last go and see what happens from there."

"Of course, otherwise, it wouldn't be you if you didn't. You know I don't like cops, but I'll support you, no matter what."

"So you'll back the blue?"

"You know I back the blue, just not the police kind of blue."

"What other kind of blue is there, brother?"

"The Superman kind, brother…I back that kind of blue."

"Word!" He laughed at the sentiment.

"Hey, Abe, how long have we been coming here?" Donnie looked around at the orange, pink, and turquoise colored walls of the restaurant.

"Five years, why?"

"Are we the only ones that don't speak Spanish, here?"

"Hey, I can get by. I don't know about you."

"Rosita may not know what I am saying and I may not know what she is saying, but it's all love. I love this place. And when you're a cop, we can eat here for free!"

"We already eat here for free! Most the time anyway! Let's not get ahead of ourselves. The odds are against me today, so I'll need prayers."

"You know I don't do that."

"Well, you better start. I'm counting on you. What was it you said, 'Support me, no matter what,' is what I heard."

Donnie laughed hard. "All right, all right...thy will be done." He shoved the burger in his mouth.

"Dude, this is a taco place and you always order a freaking burger. Maybe you should try ordering some tacos at least, hence, Patty's Taco House!"

"That's why I love this place! We eat like kings here, and I can order whatever I want. If it weren't for you, I wouldn't be stuffing my face at this fine place. I got the tab this time."

"Of course you do! It's next to free! I'll take it, though. I just have to get through this morning, and I'll know what lies ahead."

"Great things, believe that!"

"Donnie, this time, I hope you're right." Abraham devoured a taco, contemplating the meeting that could change his life.

"Whatever happens, you'll bounce back fast. That's a good policy to have, you know, your recovery method."

"Recover within twenty-four hours...I'm surprised you remembered that one. This one should be no different. I almost forgot," he said as he made the sign of the cross.

"You make me nervous when you do that," Donnie chided.

"This meeting got me all discombobulated...I forgot to pray before I wolfed up that taco. You should be used to that by now." He grabbed the chain around his neck and kissed the cross that dangled on it.

"I don't think I ever will," Donnie reiterated.

"God, I know you won't let me down," he whispered.

XIII
COUNTERMEASURES

Abraham took a deep breath. He read somewhere that breathing helped calm the nerves. It did not work so well, but being that he arrived twenty minutes early, he sat in the car for a couple minutes to gather himself. In a few moments, he would have his answer, but right now, his future hung in the balance. He emerged from the car like a ball of confidence. *I can handle it.*

Wasting no time, Abraham sat directly in front of the sergeant. His office was a good 15×15 but carried very little in it. He had seen the office many times before when he had his weekly meetings with Detective Balderama. As plain as a room could get, the sergeant had no pictures on the wall, the paint was white, and Abraham occupied the only chair in his office, which was also an uncomfortable one. Clearly, the sergeant never had visitors or maybe it was just that he didn't want any. The sergeant stood over six feet easy and towered over Abraham. Pushing at least 6'3", he had a deep commanding voice to go with his stature. Nevertheless, Abraham was not intimidated. Even though he only boasted a 5'7" frame, he was not one for intimidation especially from a bigger man. The only person that had ever put thoughts like that in his head was his father, Roy. As a child, he remembered those feelings when his father came crashing through every door in the house to talk Abraham down and whip him occasionally. Evolution taught him to deal with the commanding soldier-like personalities, such as that of his father, and every time another man tried to intimidate him, he would look him in the eye until the other looked away, regardless of height. He trained himself to fear no one and the sergeant was no different.

"Moreno! What brings you here today?" The sergeant spoke in a firm tone. He was an older Caucasian man in his late 30s or early 40s and carried about 240 pounds of mass. Whether it was muscle or just dead weight was questionable under his loose-fitting uniform. He had what looked like light brown hair as it was shaved down to a flat top.

"Sergeant, first of all, thank you for seeing me today. I just wanted to meet with you and see if there is anything that I can do to get back on the processing detail as a candidate."

"Well, Moreno, it doesn't look good. First of all, you failed to update your status with the detective. He had no clue that you were employed at the place you just got fired from."

The sergeant was right, and fifteen seconds into the meeting, he had the odds severely against him already. "Second, as I mentioned, you got fired from your place of employment. When a candidate is terminated by an employer, they are automatically dismissed from candidacy."

"Sir, I understand that, but this is the first time I have ever lost a…gotten fired and it just so happened to be during my candidacy. I'm ready for the academy! I just need one shot to show the department that I—"

"You've had chances, Moreno! I'm sorry, but it's over…you are deemed permanently unsuitable by the department."

His eyes widened for a second and sat stunned in the uncomfortable wooden chair. Not once did the sergeant sit in his chair, but paced back and forth behind his desk placing files from shelf to desk. Within two minutes, the meeting was over and the sergeant stood firm. Realizing he would not waiver, Abraham accepted that this was the way it was going to be. He regrouped quickly as to not show weakness in front of the sergeant and spoke confidently.

"Sergeant, thank you for taking the time to meet with me today."

"Good luck to you, Moreno."

Abraham stepped out of the office swiftly. Directly to his left was the cubicle of Detective Balderama. *What the hell,* he thought, *it wouldn't hurt.* He marched over surprised to find the detective sitting at his desk overlooking paperwork.

"Detective?"

"Moreno, what can I do for you, sir? Did you speak to the sergeant?"

"Yes, I did. He told me that, that…this was over." He paused. "I just stopped by to say thank you for everything you've done for me. I really appreciate it."

"I'm sorry things didn't turn out the way you planned. You were one of our top candidates. I'm sorry to see you go. Maybe…" the detective hesitated, "…maybe I can talk to the sergeant and—"

"It's okay, Detective…it just…wasn't meant to be."

With that, Abraham walked out of the office and into the unknown.

💣

"It's over."

He left the processing detail better off than what he originally thought. Tears should've been pouring down his face, but he couldn't cry and he didn't know why. Astonished at the news, Michelle questioned him with concern, "Oh my gosh, Abraham, what happened?"

She had been gone for almost two months. This failure reminded him of how far away she actually was. He couldn't go home and wait for her as he once did. Living hundreds of miles away changed things dramatically and so the phone call would have to do for the time being.

"I got fired from my summer job, and now I'm permanently unsuitable for the police department."

He was ashamed to tell her. He wanted her to know the truth, so he felt the short version would suffice.

"You got fired? How can you be permanently unsuitable for that? Do Mom and Dad know?"

Her interrogations always sprang off with multiple questions.

"I don't know Michelle…that's what they said…that I was permanently unsuitable. Nobody knows yet…just you."

He started losing focus. Talking about this failure was draining enough. He wanted to get the disappointment off his chest as quickly as possible without giving her too much detail.

He drove away into what seemed oblivion. His actions for the moment ran on autopilot as he swerved through lanes taking the street lights home rather than the highway.

"Abraham, I've been telling you to apply at Head Start. They need male teachers for the little kids. They would hire you in a heartbeat!"

Michelle had been adamant about him teaching young children. She hoped for some time now that he would change his mind and become a preschool teacher, and each time she tried to persuade him, the conversations got shorter and shorter.

"Michelle, I know nothing about little kids, much less trying to teach them. I wouldn't even know what to do!"

"Abraham, just try it out! Give it a chance to see if you like it."

"I just don't think I'd be good at it."

"They will all be little like Paulina…you're good with her. It'll be cute. You would be a great role model. Abraham, I'm your sister…I know you will be a good teacher…trust me."

"All right, fine! I'm dressed like I'm job hunting anyway. What's the worst they're gonna tell me? No?"

"Abraham, maybe something bad would've happened to you like getting shot or killed. It's better this way. Okay, let me know how it goes. It will be okay. I love you."

"I love you. Thank you, Michelle."

She always made him feel better. Her aura was calming when she wanted it to be and she could talk Abraham into or out of anything. Her assertiveness was a force to be reckoned with, and luckily, she used it for all the right reasons. Gray did not exist in Michelle's world, only black and white, and she did not waiver. As polar opposites, they complemented each other well.

He trusted her as she guided him to his next destination, and so, to the Head Start main office he headed.

In the meantime, he continued to replay the events over in his head. The victim of sabotage, Abraham walked out of the door of Top Sports defeated and he despised that feeling. Jackie won. There were no two ways about it, and the more he thought about it, the frustration grew stronger.

He inhaled and exhaled slowly, taking deep breaths as he did. He reached a stoplight and closed his eyes. "Justice," he whispered, "Justice needs to be served."

He made up his mind. Jackie had a fight coming and he needed to prepare for battle.

If he chose not to counteract, she would go on coasting through her position of superiority, her manipulative ways, and her entire life not knowing what it was like to be dispatched unwillingly. He was capable of saving the girls. They are good and honest people, he thought, and they don't deserve this.

"It's time," he said to himself.

He focused on the training of strategy and tactics. The forthcoming battle had to be approached differently. As discreet as she was, he needed to do the same. Unlike the many confrontations he faced against Avril, Jackie displayed drastically different procedures. He replayed his interactions with her off the top of his head and had no trouble recalling the characteristics he encountered while in her presence.

Exploitation, he thought. If she was going to get rid of hardworking innocent people on a whim, then he wanted her to feel the same.

An ounce of sickness was brewing. After several bouts with Avril, he was fresh off from dancing with the devil, and it was a dance floor he did not care to return to.

He didn't mind the battling; it seasoned him to be the tactical powerhouse he was becoming.

He held off sinister forces one year ago, and walking the line of evil scared him deeply. He was not confident enough to stage a standoff with that kind of wickedness, just yet. He needed to get closer to God in order to stave off the heartless nemesis; otherwise, it would come with a cost. He wanted to reunite with the Lord fully, so he needed to tread carefully.

Justification came in the fact that it was justice, rather than vengeance, in planning this attack, and the girls from *Top Sports* would agree.

She could use a taste of her own medicine, he thought. How to deliver the remedy was another question. Options came to mind with a high degree of success, however, he was going to need help.

Trained inadvertently to be relentless, he reminisced to where it all began. Dispatching her was a tantalizing and fulfilling thought, but the degree of difficulty was rather poor. *This was easy compared to what I've been through,* he thought. The challenge of disposing a full-fledged opponent with psychotic tendencies rested with none other than Avril Vasquez.

XIV
APRIL RAINS

September 2002

    His capabilities were extraordinary in instances such as this. What made this unlike any other experience was that it was not for someone in distress, but for his own purposes. He did not consider himself one to rely on his talents and knowledge for personal gain and definitely never for misuse, for they would lead to a doorway with origins of the dark side. This time, however, he would override the code of responsibility that came along with his extraordinary talents, but rather use them for a personal vendetta. His mind was clouded so much that feelings of the light side, feelings that always flowed from the Lord, feelings of love, compassion, faith, hope, and everything that encompasses of how a servant of God should be, were all but missing. Instead, in its place were fear, anger, aggression, and feelings that Abraham never felt so strongly before and never knew that existed within him. The "perfect" Abraham that everyone once knew was no more. This new concoction, however, was filled with hate, frustration, jealousy, and rage: all of which combined perfectly to help him begin the fall from grace. Everyone, including the Almighty Lord, watched him in an unfamiliar state. A state in which he never thought he would see himself, and yet everyone he ever loved and cared about watched helplessly. He was falling.

He was semi-aware of the state in which he was in. Emotions filled with darkness clouded his judgment. His tactics as a detective were becoming unprecedented, but it was his inner power that began to take on a new form.

He walked to the car whispering to himself, "It's not over, I'll find her." He drove furiously, his plan premeditated. He knew exactly what he needed to do to find her and just exactly how much time he needed to pinpoint her location. Instead of taking his usual highway route, he chose I-35. The normal route would cut off options in finding her and he would lose valuable time back tracking in case he needed to.

Avril knew how to push his buttons and would retaliate with such mind games that challenged his own. He considered himself a master of psychological warfare and had bested Avril several times before. But each time would be a little more challenging, and each time would bring him that much closer to the dark side. Avril was not fully aware of the descent he was in either, her concern was merely matching him blow for blow on the psychological level.

She coasted confidently down the street, driving casual as if she had won the battle. Little did she know, a rematch was coming and she only had a few precious minutes left.

Abraham reached I-35 in approximately sixty seconds. On a typical night, it would have taken three minutes, but this night was far from normal. From this point, he had two options: the first, he could catch her by taking the highway that led to her house. The second, he could veer off right and take Highway 90, exiting the ramp leading to his house in a backtrack attempt just in case she was still in the area. She could've been anywhere, but he figured one of two things: she either traveled home or stayed in the area. He already knew how she operated. Even though she failed to give him her exact location, he would have to rely on his abilities to find her. He narrowed it down to two as he neared the point of no return.

He began the process. He searched for her with his feelings. Avril did not fully understand his abilities. It spooked her out. He had performed a mental breach on her many times before without her knowing, and this time would be no different. He knew he should just let her go and move on from this tragedy. His heart spoke, but the darkness overshadowed its cries.

Nearing the entrance ramp of the highway left him with ten seconds to track her. There was no time for error and he would have to feel her presence quick. He closed his eyes and concentrated.

Eight seconds. The mental breach was successful. He walked in fairly easy. *It's pretty busy in here*. There were a lot of things going on at once. Most of it didn't make sense, but that was Avril, strictly running on impulse with nothing making sense. Everything seemed to be working overtime. There were flashes going off like cameras in a packed stadium. He stood on a slope of what he considered a hill comprised of pink soft tissue. It was like standing on a grassy knoll watching the night sky light up with fireworks. It was the best seat in the house.

Five seconds. He could feel her close. He scanned everything in the chamber, and then he saw it. There was one flash that shot off creating a light brighter than the others. In an instant, he was gone. As fast as he probed, he emerged without her noticing. There was no way she could have ever felt him. He found his answer in that bright flash. She was near.

One second. In an instant Abraham veered off to the right. She hadn't gone far, and he would catch her sure enough.

* * * * *

He took the Probandt exit, backtracking to his vicinity. He could feel her presence lingering in the area. He drove slow and cautious, like an officer on patrol looking for suspicious activity. His strategic skills and tactics were very much sharpened in the many battles he had with Avril. Like a telepath, he would thrive on anticipating her actions, giving way to psychological victories. He became a cunning warrior, thanks to her challenges, but it came with a price. In this case, the price of psychotic warfare was not what he expected, much less what he was even aware of. He had become a predator, so much so that when it came to Avril, he vowed to never become her prey. His descent into the dark side was in full swing.

Abraham approached the stoplight and looked over at the gas station to his right. There was a lot of activity for it being a weeknight. As he looked over the perimeter, there she stood pumping gas into her car. The gas station was literally down the street from his house, and she stood as if everything was cool on her behalf. He slowed as he turned left at the stoplight.

Across the street was a parking lot, which was vacant due to early closing hours of the Silverado. The local bar was usually busy on any given weeknight but this night was drastically different. He parked, turned off his lights and waited and watched. He dialed her number on his cell phone.

Ring. Ring. Ring. Ring. Ring.

No answer. She left her phone in the car. After a few seconds, she finished up. As she entered her car, he dialed once again.

"What?" she answered harshly. Avril proceeded to drive away, and much like an officer on a stakeout, he began the pursuit.

"Where are you?" Abraham responded with the same tone that she answered him with.

"I'm going home." Avril said every word convincingly, but he saw the truth for himself. She was driving back to his house, and her lies were tactics she used as a psychological edge. It might have worked with any other ordinary man, but in this situation, he was anything but. Being a step ahead of her actions and counteracting her every move was a sickness he prided himself on. On the other hand, she challenged him like no other person had before.

"No, you need to come back to my house." Abraham spoke in a different manner now, knowing he regained the psychological edge from the heated argument earlier.

"Why? So you could yell at me! I don't think so!" Avril responded with confidence, oblivious that he was trailing her and watching her every move. Finding her and luring her back to his house was not for reconciliation, but for a sinister purpose he was not clearly aware of. He wanted to finish the fight.

"Just go back to my house so we can talk." Abraham tried to reason with her.

"If you start yelling at me, I'm leaving and I'm not going back, you hear me!" Avril finally gave in to the request.

"Fine," Abraham agreed, giving false reassurance.

He was a few seconds out from finishing the confrontation on his terms.

Don't do this. You don't need this. Just let her go.

He tried to reason with the sickness.

Balance, remember. Bring balance to your inner self.

He tried to talk his way out of a situation that was way out of control. The darkness began eating his soul. The anger had poisoned his entire being, and now his pep talks were futile efforts.

Balance…the balance between good and evil. Since the beginning of time, the essence of our existence has always been the struggle between the dark and the light, one constantly striving to prevail over the other, with the soul choosing to ultimately claim allegiance to one of these forces. Although battles are often fought in remote corners of the earth, the greatest battle is the conflict within. What makes a hero are the villains that they face. The consequence of choice…

Two there are, but only one can be made. Like the yin and the yang, each carries the seed of the other in a never-ending cycle, and yet they coexist within each other. Two separate worlds, one dominated by the light and the latter by the dark, cultivated as one constant entity. Segregation from these two worlds is impossible, for both exist within us. Thriving and beating like a heart, dispersing love and hate, light and dark, injustice and rage, and liberty and peace, they beat as one.

It was no use. The venom infiltrated the blood flow into every region of his body. His heart could barely cry out as it had been overtaken one too many times.

They both pulled up to the curb seconds apart. The street light had been out for several weeks now, which made visibility poor. Like a lion closing in on unsuspecting prey, he made sure the disposal was all his.

She stepped out of the car and realized the inevitable. "You were following me, weren't you? I can't believe you! I knew I should've gone home!"

He approached her car and commenced the rampage. "Yeah, I knew you didn't go home. You thought you were home free, but I was watching you the whole time."

Avril knew the mistake was hers. She tried to inch her way back into the car but met resistance.

"Oh no, you're not leaving until you hear what I have to say!"

"Abraham, let go of my door!"

She pleaded with him. She sensed the fight escalating. This time, Avril was about to witness a wrath she had never seen before, one that would see him and his abilities for dark purposes.

"I'm not! You're staying here until I'm done!"

"Abraham, stop! Leave me alone!" She desperately tried to yank her door closed, but he was too strong.

"Let go!"

"If you leave, I'm going to break this motherfucker!" Abraham raised his fist in a threatening manner and aimed it at the driver's side window.

"If you do, I'm calling the police!"

Eager for a getaway, she started the car and pressed the gas. He refused to let go. Infuriated, he cocked back his arm.

"I'll run you over if I have to!"

He closed his eyes. His fist froze in midair. His anger wanted to drive it through, but a tiny ray of light urged him to stop. The window began to show visible cracks.

"Avril, don't make me fuck it up!"

Halfway down the street, she pressed further on the gas. His boots slid on the pavement as she hesitated to drag him. He concentrated on his destruction as the cracks ran deeper. He placed his hand on the window and yelled into the night sky. Unbeknownst to her, the crackling sound of the glass grew louder.

"Leave me alone!"

"No!"

He cocked his fist, ready to finish what he started. Just as he was about to swing, the glass shattered every which way, as if a bomb exploded within the car. Avril let out a scream and pressed on the brakes.

"You motherfucker, I can't believe you just did that!"

"I never touched it!" He came to consciousness, with adrenaline pumping at full throttle. He finally let go of the car, in shock of the destruction he had just caused. It was the first time he used his power to create such devastation. The sudden pause had been equivalent to waking up from a nightmarish sleep. He awakened. As quickly as the shockwave hit him, he fought the evil as it failed to relinquish its grasp. "Fuck you! You shouldn't have driven off. All you had to do was stay here."

"Fuck you! It's over! Go back to your whore, May!" Avril sped off into the darkness. Her taillights faded to black, and she was gone.

Furious at the outcome, he was far from satisfied. A roar of frustration rang down the street, as he craved destruction.

"Ahhhhhhhhhhhhhhhhhhhhhhhhhhh!"

XV
JUSTICE

Abraham closed his eyes slowly. The process had become second nature. He began his method as he had done countless times before, and after all these years, he grew to enjoy the tactical edge. He sensed her feelings and, as he did, took a deep breath.

Both nervous and cautious, her paranoia kept her on edge. She asked the girls endlessly if he had been by the store at all. He wondered if it was because she had done wrong or because maybe deep down she knew trouble was coming her way or worse yet, both. In any case, he anticipated her next move. She counted on him making his presence known.

Foolishly believing that Donnie would help her was a grave mistake. She feared retaliation. He found what he needed to know.

He no longer had a reason to tread in the garbage she called her thoughts, and in the blink of an eye, the connection had been severed.

"I called Tom. The only thing I need is for all of you to back me up and then it will be over. She only has two ways out…she will either be terminated or she will resign and that's it. You'll be all right."

Emma's eyes widened. "This is happening too quick! What did he say?" Emma asked surprisingly.

"You are going to get a call from him today. Within twenty-four hours, Jackie will no longer be affiliated with this place and you can run this store the way you see fit. You will finally get the credit you deserve, all of you. As for what I told him…only what he needed to know."

He extended his hand to her, but the shock caused her arm to delay as she slowly shook his hand.

"When it comes to revenge, you're not to be messed with." She half-smiled, trying to take in this unexpected turn of events.

"I thought about that, Emma…and it wasn't revenge…it was justice. There is a huge difference. I'm glad you stood by me and backed me up, and for that, I'm grateful. Good luck to you…and thank you."

He emerged from the store and from the wreckage Jackie caused. As he walked along the Riverwalk, with its restaurants and stores, operating as they usually did on a Friday, he realized that this would be the last time he would have a Mickey Mouse job, as his father called it.

The scenery was unlike any other, hand-crafted for tourists while maintaining a San Antonio feel. Mariachis played familiar tunes outside for all to hear beside the river. The overflowing audience took up residence on the tables, chairs, and the steps surrounding the mariachis in their outdoor arena. Even riverboats made their way through the amphitheater-like portion of the outdoor area of the mall, as they made their customary U-turn to venture into the rest of the downtown area, unaware that a man with a broken dream walked in their midst.

The NBA All-Star game, the NCAA Final Four, and the many fiestas were now archived in his memory, and all those experiences of a young man making his way through college were part of an era that just met its end.

✟

The director welcomed him into the office. The anxiety intensified as he journeyed into the unknown. Never before had he taken on a position that he absolutely knew nothing about.

Ms. Mendoza was all business. Her inability to crack a smile meant that he needed to be a quick learner. The social worker, Rita, and the assistant director, Trisha, sat at their desks as they greeted him. The atmosphere remained quiet and rather relaxing, for them at least, as he sat in front of Ms. Mendoza's desk.

She said but three words upon his arrival and it became increasingly apparent that she was hard to impress. "Come on in" is where she left the conversation for the time being. Checking over his paperwork kept her attention and then she finally spoke.

"Do you have a third letter of reference?"

"No, I was only able to get a hold of two."

She turned to her assistant and, without hesitation, made a simple request. "Trisha, can you please write up a reference letter for him?"

Without skipping a beat, Trisha opened the drawer to her desk and retrieved a pen and paper and began writing immediately. Much to his surprise, Trisha had the opportunity to ask him any questions about anything, but she did not. He sat within close proximity to her desk and wondered how she could write a letter of reference about someone she didn't even know at all.

"Mr. Abraham, let's go to the room you are going to be in, and that way I can introduce you to the other teachers as well." Ms. Mendoza led the way to his future classroom.

"Okay," he said and smiled as he always did no matter the circumstance. *Mr. Abraham,* he thought. No one ever addressed him as mister and it sounded bizarre.

They passed through a few classrooms, and he made sure to observe everything going on. Some children were just waking up from nap time in certain rooms and others were empty. One child waved to him and he waved back. She was about three years old with light brown hair in a ponytail. She had a light complexion with brown eyes and her round face squeezed out half a smile. She looked on with such innocence, and he could tell that she wondered who he was. She continued setting the table for snack. One cup and one napkin per chair and as she walked to the next table, he noticed her overall straps fell off her shoulders and her pink undershirt matched her pink and white shoes. After walking past three classrooms they arrived at an empty one, which apparently was the one he would be a part of.

"Well, Mr. Abraham, I think they are outside already." She proceeded to walk farther down the hall as he followed. The last classroom bathed in total darkness. Ms. Mendoza flipped the light switch to let the teachers know what time it was. "Ladies, nap time's been over for fifteen minutes already. Wake the children up for snack."

At the end of the building were doors leading to the playground. They stepped out together and, with eyes widened, smiled nervously at the chaos. Four-year-olds ran amuck. Yelling, screaming, fighting, and crying in every area of the playground. *This is a total mistake,* he thought. He felt overwhelmed at the sight of preschool children to which he was desperately outnumbered.

"Mr. Abraham, what do you think?"

Was she serious? he thought. *She's just fooling with me to see my reaction,* he concluded.

"It's…uh, it's good."

"Okay, let me introduce you to Ms. Marissa, who will be a co-teacher with you. Ms. Marissa? Let me introduce you to Mr. Abraham, your new teacher."

A young lady with long black straight hair strolled over to him. "Hi, nice to meet you!"

"I'm Abraham. It's nice to meet you too."

"Mr. Abraham, I'll leave you with Ms. Marissa so you can get a feel for the class."

"Thank you."

Ms. Marissa had a nice smile to her. Her personality seemed pleasant. "Have you taught before?" she asked.

"No, never…I'm not gonna lie to you. I don't have a clue about teaching at all, much less teaching little kids."

"It's fun. Every day is different. It's a lot of work. We follow a schedule every day and we have to make sure the kids wash their hands, brush their teeth, serve themselves food, and oh, there's a lesson plan with all sorts of activities for them to do. Licensing requires us to—"

"Whoa, wait a minute! This is too much. You're gonna have to take it slow with me. I'm a rookie, remember?" he said with a laugh.

"Okay, I'm sorry. We'll take it slow, Mr. Abraham." She giggled sweetly.

A little girl ran past them, cutting in between them. She was being chased by a little boy. Her expression was neutral. A harmless game of tag, he thought. He turned to follow the pursuit. The little boy pushed her, and she slammed into the fence as he ran off. In distress, she yelled at him, "Stop!" Her brow crinkled. She frowned and walked off to the side of the building to sit on the steps alone.

"Justice!" Ms. Marissa called out to her. "Come over to the playground so we can see you."

"I'll get her," he reassured Ms. Marissa. He walked leisurely to her. She had her arms crossed and her head hidden away in her lap. His instincts kicked in and the counselor in him responded.

"Hey there, what's wrong?" With her head still concealed in her lap, he continued. "What's your name?" he asked as he sat next to her.

She elected to raise her head. He wondered if it was curiosity that piqued her interest of an unrecognizable voice or if he actually made a connection. Calmness came over him. Her brown eyes resonated with such innocence. She stared at him silently. She studied him, and as she looked him over, he experienced an immediate caring for her. She sprang up and ran to the playground. *That was weird, she didn't even talk,* he thought. "Great job, Abraham…you probably scared her," he said quietly to himself.

This job was different. Michelle was right; it was nothing like working in retail. He gave her his word that he would give teaching a chance.

Dispatching Jackie was the right thing to do. His gifts allowed an advantage against her, and he could live with the way he handled things this time. Evolving to become better not just for himself, but for the world. Using such power for destruction was not what God intended and the memories of misuse called. But that was all over now. He was entering a new phase in his life, one that had innocent children.

XVI
MAP

Mom left a voicemail that had him curious. *She never leaves messages or bothers me, even when I want her to,* he thought. "Isn't that what moms are supposed to do?" He would often ask of her. She made it clear that her parenting style was more rigid than loving. She was high on rules and low on love. "I have to make sure your ass is straight!" She would say as she never let a chance escape to tell him those words since the day he was born. Her voice and persona were soothing and caring on the outside, but on the inside, her inner force was militant. Her submissive personality fooled many, but she could pack a punch when she needed to deliver.

It became obvious why she invited him as soon as he entered her house. In any other event, she would've have come to him at Grandma's house or asked for him on a night when Roy played darts at the local bar. She knew better than to get her son and his father in the same room for too long.

He made his way into the living room where the much celebrated guest and Roy had been in conversation. Her beauty went beyond her physical appearance. Her voice carried throughout the house in a joyous celebratory tone, and her sneakiness could not have come at a better time. He missed her dearly.

She clearly spoke of her experience in medical school in a tone of excitement.

"I've already opened up a cadaver and saw what it looks like post-mortem…we are already getting hands-on experience there, whereas, other schools don't let you get into that stuff until your third year."

Her story sounded exhilarating, but he had to interrupt his beautiful Michelle.

"Hey, I didn't know you were coming!"

"Hey! Well, surprise! I'm only here for one day, though, so nobody knew I was here, and plus, I wanted to surprise y'all. I haven't seen Grandma yet, hopefully, she doesn't have a heart attack!" She let out a heartfelt laugh.

"Are you on vacation or what?"

"No, there was a two-day conference that we had to go to and there happened to be one in San Antonio! I chose this conference so I could come home and visit."

Meanwhile, Roy wasted no time. "Hey, boy, where were you today? I could've used your help with the privacy fence!"

"I had to go to work today."

"When you gonna start living on your own? What happened to being a police officer? It's been a long time already…and nothing." He began his rant as usual and the hostility even more exaggerated in Michelle's presence.

"It doesn't start until October, right?" Michelle intervened.

"Yeah, I have a couple more months to wait."

"Roy, not so loud…Paulina is asleep!" Gloria reminded Roy as his voice began to carry.

Michelle changed the subject to avoid all-out war. "Ok, well I'm gonna go see Grandma next door. Mom, call me when Paulina wakes up."

"Give this to Grandma. It's a piece of cake I made yesterday and tell her not to eat the whole thing all at once," Gloria said.

The pair made their way out the front door. Abraham shook his head in disgust. "See what I mean, Dad is such a dick! That's why I don't come over here anymore!"

They walked ten steps over to Grandma's house and entered the safe haven.

"¿Mijo, eres tú? *Honey, is that you?*" she questioned. Grandma walked to the front room and in much surprise, smiled happily.

"Mija! Cuando llegastes? *Honey! When did you get here?*"

"Grandma! Llegue a hora, pero solo voy a estar aquí esta noche y me voy en la mañana. *I arrived today, but I'll only be here tonight and I leave tomorrow morning.*"

He let Michelle have her time with Grandma. He made his way to his room in the back and sat in his chair, comfortably waiting for the conference that was soon to take place. Within fifteen minutes, Michelle entered the room. She sat on the mini couch beside his bed and made herself comfortable. Abraham swiveled around in the computer chair to face her.

"Michelle, they called me! Head Start!" he exclaimed.

"That's good, Abraham! I'm glad they called you! I told you they would!"

"I had an interview with the director of the center I'm going to work at. It's crazy, isn't it?"

"Think of it this way…they've seen your application, they know you don't have a degree in education, and yet they were still interested. They must like something about you on paper, and I know that once the kids meet you, they're really going to love you. Just keep an open mind about it."

"I'm trying to, but if I'm working with kids all day, what am I going to do? That part freaks me out!"

"You'll be fine. They probably called you because not that many males apply. They always want males for the little kids that don't have a dad and stuff. You'll be a great role model, and plus, they will all be little like Paulina."

"Yeah, but Paulina is *one* child, I will have like twenty in one room…it's different!" Abraham shook his head nervously. "I don't know…I'll give it a shot, I guess."

"You have to look at it this way, this is happening for a reason. Think of all the jobs that you have applied at, and finally, these people call you pretty fast. Perhaps this is God's way of saying that He wants you to really make a difference rather than just working retail. Anyone can sell a hat…it takes a special person to make a difference in the life of a child."

Abraham paused the moment those words were spoken. As always, she put everything in perspective. Her persuasive words were for the better, and his leap of faith had been solidified by the key phrase, "Make a difference."

"I have to say…this is the first time that your words put water in my eyes. You are right about everything you just said. I feel like I'm having a conversation with myself because after hearing those words…it's something I would say."

"Wow, that's good to hear. I know that I have been trained well, as you say. You should hear some of the things that I have had to tell Garrett. You would be proud, and I don't say those things just to sound good or smart. That is the way I really think about life now. I don't know when my perspective changed, but I'm glad it did because I know now that when I talk to him, I make a difference and I help him to see things differently and get through tough times."

"You still talk to Garrett?" Abraham inquired in shock, as Garret was believed to be a thing of the past.

"Okay, I just told you how much difference I made in someone's life and that's all you got."

"I thought he had been dispatched a long time ago is all. I didn't think you still talked to him. Either way, thank you. Your words made me feel better. You *have* been trained well. At least I have an idea of what to expect and your right, I have to look at it that way. Kids are special. Having Paulina has drastically changed my perspective on kids and anybody can sell a hat, but hats don't need guidance. I start next week, so I'll let you know how it goes."

"I'm glad you feel better and I'll be praying for you. Did you tell Mom or Dad yet?"

"Heck no, Dad still thinks I'm working right now. They don't know about anything yet…not about Top Sports or the police department."

"Well, you're going to have to tell them sooner or later. Hopefully, you'll like this job at head start. You're gonna be fine."

"I hope so, Michelle."

"So tell me what's going on otherwise. How are all your friends? How is Ricky and his family?"

"Pretty good, I guess."

"Y'all don't talk anymore?"

"Once in a while, we don't talk like we used to, you know that."

"Have you forgiven him?" Michelle asked.

Abraham sighed heavily. "Yes, I have. I told him face-to-face and he apologized."

"He is like your brother…"

Michelle spoke the truth. and Abraham delivered an even harsher reality. "He is, but sometimes family can do some fucked up things to you. You, above all people, know that."

"Yes…I do." Michelle said somberly, but being quick on her feet, she asked about the rest of the team.

"And all of the other guys?"

"Well, that's a long story. You got time?"

Michelle sprang back with a confused on her face. "Just gimme the short version."

"Okay, Jason got married and lives in California, John-John went into the Air Force and is stationed in Japan, Johnny is busy with his girlfriend and doesn't like to go out, and Chris just disappeared."

"What? What happened with you guys? Y'all are all over the place!"

"Life just happened. The League is not what it used to be, everyone is gone, just doing their own thing. We'll all come back together again one day. Just watch, it will be historic. I never give up hope, remember?"

"Yes, I remember, before I left, you all were close…a lot has changed since I've been gone. And Avril? Are you still with her?"

"Eh, sometimes." Abraham laughed.

"Abraham, if she is still acting crazy, you need to leave her. I'm serious."

"I know, I know, chill! I actually met someone though."

"That's good, hopefully she's not a psycho and don't be getting all crazy either, you little girl." Her humor seemed to emerge in unassuming moments.

Abraham laughed. Michelle was certainly made aware of his psychotic tendencies when being pushed too far.

Just as he was about to change the subject, Gloria came in right on cue. She brought a guest that Michelle had not seen in months.

"Paulina! Hi, what are you doing?"

"Hi, Shell." Paulina ran over and sat in Michelle's lap as she hugged her.

"I was sleeping. Ham! Hi, Ham!" Paulina said happily.

"Between the two of you, you both help me to find my way, and when the three of us are together…that is my map."

"Your map?" Michelle inquired.

"Yes, my map. Michelle, Abraham, Paulina…M-A-P, you see?"

"You're such a dork! Geez! Does Grandma still make you breakfast in the morning?"

"Sometimes. Does Mom still send you money?"

"Sometimes."

"Michelle, you know Grandma took care of me and Mom took care of you. Mom even said so herself."

"Shell, I was playing with your Wonder Woman toys," Paulina said.

"Did you take them out of the box?"

"No…yeah, Ham told me to."

Michelle turned to Abraham with a cock-eyed look. "Abraham! Those are mine to keep, not to open!"

"Hey, I didn't know if you wanted them anymore. Plus, I got them for you, so in a way, they're kind of mine too!"

"Shell, do you like Wonder Woman? I like Wonder Woman. You're Wonder Woman and I'm Wonder Woman. Two Wonder Womans." Paulina rambled on. Michelle and Abraham laughed at her words. They both thought she was the cutest thing in the world.

"See, Abraham…the kids will all be cute, like Paulina."

"Yeah, until they start throwing tantrums…but not you Paulina…you're a good little girl, right?" Abraham motioned to Paulina.

"Yeah, I'm a Wonder Woman girl," she said to them in a serious manner.

"Michelle, do you know what I call us?" he asked her.

"What?"

"When the three of us come together, I like to think that we have the power to change the world so, I like to call us…The Triad Thunder!"

"You're an idiot, I swear!"

He enjoyed her mockery, and he laughed uncontrollably. He missed her terribly, and today, it was just like old times.

XVII
JULY 18

"It's the midsummer night party! We can't miss Edward's annual gathering," Donnie insisted.

"I know, bro! I'm here, ain't I?" Abraham said adamantly, as the duo walked to the backyard through the driveway.

"I thought you were gonna bail on me!"

"My sister is in town. If she didn't go to bed so early, I would have."

Abraham and Donnie strolled into the driveway. Edward was notorious for house parties with unlimited booze and debauchery.

"Hey, what happened to that mystery girl from the internet?" Donnie inquired.

"I haven't talked to her lately…we've both been real busy." Abraham attempted to bend the truth.

"You should've invited her to the party."

Abraham was relieved to see Edward approaching. He didn't want to divulge any more information regarding the embarrassment of being rejected.

"What up, homie, G dawgs! Glad y'all could make it!" Edward met them in the driveway and led them to the backyard.

"Edward! We wouldn't miss it, bro! Just lead me to the booze!" Donnie exclaimed.

"What up, Edward? This party is popping already…this could be the best midsummer bash to date!"

"It's looking like it…we got people from all over the place. That group of girls over there just graduated high school!" Edward pointed over by the fence where a few girls huddled taking shots of tequila.

"You're robbing the cradle, Ed!" Donnie said as he took a shot of his own.

One of the girls looked at Abraham in awe. He smiled at her. She left the group without hesitation and approached him, shaking her head, smiling from ear to ear. "I can't believe it. Out of all the places and I find you here!"

"What are you doing here?" he asked her, unable to hide his huge smile.

"I came with my cousin and a couple of friends that knew of a Palo Alto party," she said happily. "Abraham Moreno…I never thought I'd see you again!"

They gazed into each other's eyes, and their smiles could not be wiped away. "I can't believe you're here," she repeated, "and you don't even have a drink yet!"

"We just got here as soon as you saw me walk up…does it look like I need one?"

"It wouldn't hurt. Come on, I'll show you where they're at." She grabbed his hand and held on to it as she led the way. She maneuvered through a horde of students surrounding the keg. "Can I get one, please?" she asked the boy running the keg.

"Sure. Here you go. I poured it with love," he said.

"It's not for me. It's for him." She turned to Abraham and gave him the beer.

"Oh," the boy said disheartened.

Abraham giggled quietly as to not embarrass the boy any further. "Thank you, doll." "You're welcome, baby," she said with a twinkle in her eye.

"I take it the tequila has taken effect?"

"No, it hasn't! I'm fine!" She placed both of her arms around his neck and smiled, looking into his eyes. "What is behind them?"

"Behind what?"

"Your eyes…"

"Liv, you *are* getting toasty! I can see it in your eyes. They're beautiful, by the way."

"You like them?" she asked giddily.

"I do. I never got a chance to tell you before," he took a sip of his beer, "before you ended up getting back with your boyfriend. Is he coming?"

"No," she said, tilting her head with attitude, "we are not together. He decided he wanted to be a player."

"I'm sorry to hear that."

"I'm not. Anyway, now that you're here, we can—"

"Liv! We have one right here for you!" a girl shouted amidst the crowd.

"Abraham, this is my cousin, Corina, and my best friend, Evelyn."

"Hi, Abraham!" they said in unison.

"Hi there!"

"Abraham! Who are these hot girls you're with!?" Donnie glided over to meet them.

"Liv, this is my brother, Donnie."

"Nice to meet you, I've heard so much about you," she said, shaking his hand.

"Likewise. He won't shut up about you."

Abraham laughed with embarrassment. "He's a joker…I haven't mentioned you in days."

"More like a few minutes," he chimed in. Liv blushed as she smiled at Abraham.

"Looks like your man called you out, Mr. Abraham."

"Oh, shit! They don't know about that!" Donnie shouted as he glanced at the shots lined up.

"That is dangerous!" Abraham warned Liv.

"Woohoo!" the girls yelled as they took another round of shots.

Abraham and Donnie looked away, knowing it was a matter of time before the effects would start taking place.

Liv returned to him and placed an arm around his waist. He reciprocated the gesture by placing his arm around her. They studied each other in plain sight, with the other not giving an inch. Shyness and embarrassment ceased to exist. The adoration was evident. *She's going to kiss me,* he thought. She leaned in and pulled him by his neck, moving him closer to her. She closed her eyes and swooped in to get her kiss that she had long awaited. With her lips closing in on his, she diverted course as she bent over holding her stomach. Liquid spewed out onto the dirt. "I'm so sorry," she said, trying to catch her breath.

"It's okay. Come on, let's go to the street." He held her hand guiding her, as she slumped over walking gingerly. "There's nobody out here…it's okay. You took too many shots in a short amount of time. We weren't lyin' to you…that stuff is dangerous."

"I'm so sorry…" She discharged the liquor uncontrollably.

"Here, sit down." He opened the door to his car and directed her to the passenger seat.

"I'm so embarrassed. You should be having fun and not having to take care of me," she said with her head facing the ground.

"It's gonna be okay. I wasn't feeling the party anyway. It's nice and quiet out here on the street." He held her soft hair back. It was long and the ends were curly. He caught a whiff of her shampoo and her perfume. "Your scent smells amazing," he whispered to himself.

"Thank you, Abraham," she said quietly in between gags.

"I'd rather be out here taking care of you than in there boozing right now. This is the greatest time I've had in a long time."

"You're such a liar," she said with a half-hearted laugh.

But it's the truth, he thought. Little did she know that the evening alone with her was the best part of the night and even if she didn't remember, he would have an opportunity to remind her… when the time was right.

XVIII
HERMANOS DE SANGRE

Abraham slowed as he neared the end of the court, beating everyone to the other side. Donnie dribbled toward Abraham and broke through a double team that met him at half-court, evading the defenders with a spin move. He sped down to the free-throw line, and at the last second, Abraham went backdoor on his defender on cue. Donnie read the play perfectly and fired a bullet pass that met Abraham under the ten-foot rim.

Abraham elevated with force. A defender rushed in from the opposite side of the backboard to meet him at the rim. Tall and lanky, he was more than capable of slapping the ball out of bounds. The defender forged his hand between the ball and the rim and Abraham maneuvered abruptly. He brought the ball back down and like a windmill, reversed it on the opposite side of the glass. Game over.

"Yeah, baby! Another one!" Donnie shouted.

"Yeah, yeah…just got lucky," Jax said with an annoyed tone.

"I wouldn't call five in a row, lucky. Go on home! I'm tired of beating on y'all anyway."

"What the fuck? You ain't shit…you ain't nobody." Jax stopped dead in his tracks and approached Donnie. He towered at six foot one and was used to inner city confrontations.

Abraham trailed Donnie as tempers flared.

"We run Concepcion Park! I'll beat your ass off the court too!"

"Let's go then, motherfucker!"

Jax grew up in inner city, and his demeanor didn't put up with trash-talkers. Abraham wrapped his left arm around Donnie. "Be cool. It's not worth it, man."

"Nah, fuck this dude!"

"Donnie, don't…we don't need this…"

Jax returned to the court in a threatening manner. Donnie held his position, his resolve unwavering. Some of the players stayed and surrounded the two. Buck circled over to Donnie's right and stood firm. "Come on, man…be smart, let it go."

Jax stood face to face with Donnie. His words, vigorously spoken, spurred Donnie's anger further.

Donnie swiveled his head and looked at Abraham calmly before erupting.

Jax continued to instigate. "Listen to your boys and—"

Donnie swiftly swung his left elbow, striking Jax in the mouth. Jax fell silent and hit the floor.

"What the fuck!" Pete, a member of Jax's crew, stepped up. He was new to the park and his ties to inner city were fresh.

"Back the fuck up, Pete. It's over, everything's cool…let's leave it at that," Big Rue intervened. Being a veteran park player, Big Rue stood up for his longtime friends and his peaceful demeanor was not one to be reckoned with.

Jax's group began to withdraw and survival on the south side proved successful. "Thanks, Rue," Abraham added.

"I got your back, AB. We'll see y'all tomorrow. Be cool, Donnie."

Donnie and Big Rue shook hands. "Thanks for the backup, Rue."

"I'm out too. Never fails, I always catch southside drama," Buck joked.

"You're done, too, Buck? This was just warm up! Let's run one more," Donnie chided.

"Nah, I got class in the morning. Catch you later, S. All right, Donnie, see you in class tomorrow."

"Later, Buck."

The duo walked back onto the court. Donnie meditated discreetly. "Sorry, man. I had one of those moments."

"A past life experience?" Abraham asked, but he already knew the answer.

"Yeah, blame it on the day job. Well, the old day job. For a second, it was like I was back in LA again."

"Don't worry about it. You had a nice recovery though, despite the elbow. A little too violent for me and unnecessary, but that meditation thing was good."

"I learned from the best," Donnie smirked. "It could've gotten more violent, though. Sometimes, Abraham, you just have to be ruthless. If you can get into someone's head, then strength and skill stand for nothing."

"Duly noted," Abraham acknowledged.

"You have a million nicknames here, bro. I still lose track of who's talking to who around here…" Donnie laughed, "S, AB, SOB, I just can't keep up with all your call signs."

"SOB, really? Hating on me ain't gonna get you a good nickname. We need to come up with one for you. Hmmm, let me think… oh, I got it. How does The Destroyer sound? It has nice ring to it, and it makes sense too."

"I don't catch your meaning…"

"It makes sense, Donnie. Your past life, and let us not forget your real name. You remember it, don't you…Ab—"

"All right, I get it…I get it. That's enough of that. You know that I hate my name. Besides, that life is gone."

"Are you sure? It didn't look like it a minute ago with Jax."

"Mental lapse. I'm not perfect like you, S." Donnie grinned jokingly.

"It's okay, I forgive you," Abraham responded. "Seriously though, you're right. The destruction you caused was another city ago, another time ago, and another life ago. You're rollin' with me now and the S is about good things…and so are you."

"That's why I'm here, brother. A second chance at life…" Donnie took a moment of gratitude, "I never thanked you. You and my grandma saved my life."

"That's what family does," Abraham reassured him.

"Blood brothers stick with each other no matter what. No one is going to mess with you as long as I'm here. That's a promise. Have I ever let you down?"

"No."

"You remember when I picked you up that day?" Donnie questioned.

"Yeah, I do," Abraham answered in a serious tone, recollecting the particular events of that day.

"I said I'd always be there…you've never let me down…so I sure as hell am not gonna let you down…especially after everything you've done for me."

"That was the day I decided that I was gonna make something of myself and be somebody…and now, I will be. It's not what I planned, but God's plans are always greater," Abraham said, reaffirming his thoughts.

"God is definitely on your side. You should've died in that crash. I saw the car…you took all the damage on your side…and there's no way a person not protected by God would've survived that mess."

"You know what I've been thinking, Donnie…since I'm here…survived something that should've killed me…I think about these Pre-K kids. These kids are good kids…and I don't know what the heck I'm doing…I don't know if I'll even be good at it, but I feel…it's where I'm meant to be…"

"Of course it is! You're the smartest person I know. You have a lot to offer and everybody sees that. They say you're great and you *are* great."

"I've heard that before…"

"All these abilities are not—"

"Normal?" Abraham questioned. He had grown used to hearing his uniqueness as an abnormality.

"Ordinary. You just have a little extra. Extra…ordinary."

"It doesn't mean anything…if I don't know what I'm meant for…" Abraham countered.

"In time, brother…you will. Only you can find that out…I wish I could help you, but I can't."

"My mom said that to me once," Abraham recalled, "when I was thirteen and the one person who could help me didn't."

"Your dad?"

With a blank stare, Abraham focused on the white lines on the court. The silence was deafening.

"Do you think you could ever give your dad a second chance?"

"I've given him plenty of chances…it's not about the chances. It's about him changing."

"I know you won't give up on him…just like you haven't given up on me," Donnie spoke with confidence.

"I love my dad, I mean…he will always be my dad. He has been my cross to bear in this life, but I never give up hope." With sincerity in his voice, he prayed for that day to come.

"You'll find a way," Donnie reassured him.

"How do you know that?"

"You always do."

"I don't know, Donnie. This is different. This is a challenge on all fronts…"

"A challenge, huh?" Donnie questioned curiously.

"I've never faced one like this before."

"Your cross to bear, possibly…but I see a different obstacle that you haven't faced yet…one that will change your way of life," Donnie pressed on with a gut feeling.

"Meaning?"

"What you have…is something that people usually don't have…it's like…you really have some sort of…I don't know…superpowers."

"But I don't!" Abraham barked.

"But you do! God wouldn't give you these things if he wasn't going to test them or test you."

"If I really flew or had heat vision, okay, yeah, then I would agree, but I don't," Abraham attempted to reason with Donnie.

"Abe, that's fiction, this is real life and what you have…is as real as it gets. It's crazy because I know you can feel me when something is wrong, and it's weird because sometimes I can feel you…and the thing about the oil slick, how you told me you saw the crash before it happened and when you found Avril, twice! She could've been anywhere in the city and you felt her out and found her, so you tell me, can normal people do that?"

"I can't answer that. I guess I don't know what normal is," Abraham said, calming himself.

"Before I knew you, I didn't believe in that kinda stuff, much less see it for myself. You know, in a way, it helped me to believe that God is real…because if He sent somebody with these gifts, somebody who is good, who has a good heart, then I know He is for real. It's helped me, you have helped me…to believe that there is good in the world and the crazy thing out of all this…is that it's helped me to believe in Him."

"Finally, you admit you believe in Him. I could see some changes in you and to finally hear it with my own ears is great. Of all these things that I can't explain, I am actually glad these abilities have helped you to believe, and if nothing else, at least they did that much for you."

"It's called saving lives. Superhero, I tell ya," Donnie laughed.

"Is that what you would call it?"

"Being able to feel when people are hurting or are in danger? Yeah, I *would* call it that." Donnie did his best to persuade his friend of his existentialist nature.

"There is this…connection that I develop with certain people…people that I'm close to and I don't know, I can't explain it," Abraham struggled to find the words, "I'm just glad it helped you, bro."

"And…that's why you're gonna do great. Those kids are gonna love you. You have the ability to change the world…" Donnie gazed at the trees in the distance, "and those kids are gonna know…that heroes are for real."

The park ceased to be paraded with partygoers. The birds continued on with their chirping as they nestled in the branches for the night. The last family packed up their barbeque fixings and called it a day. The basketball competitors were long gone, tired, and beaten. Only two souls sat on the bench at midcourt. Dusk fell on Concepcion Park, and what was once an area infested with conquistadores now had a new era of less violent domination.

"We had a good day today. We ran those fools, didn't we?" Donnie boasted happily.

"Yeah, we did. We ran them four or five straight?"

"It was five! Five straight, don't get it twisted. Today was too easy…when we are on the same team, its total domination. I kinda like when we are not on the same team, sometimes…"

"Why's that?"

"Because it levels the playing field."

Abraham laughed at Donnie's cockiness.

"You did good today. Your jumper was on, I think you got quicker," Donnie complemented.

"Blame it on the training. I should've been in the academy right now, but instead, I'm ballin' with you fine people."

"You have to look at it this way, things could've gone wrong. You might've gotten killed. It wasn't meant to be and that's a good thing. I don't know, but maybe you're meant to be a Pre-K teacher like you said and just maybe, you're meant to be with that girl from the internet…this is the life that you should be living. Not the one you could've had." Donnie raised both eyebrows in amazement, "Wow! What the heck did I just say? You definitely are rubbing off on me, brother!"

"You, sir, are absolutely right. Rubbing off on you, huh? Well, you're welcome!" Abraham said sarcastically. "Speaking of Liv, we've been going out. She's really cool. I'm glad you got a chance to meet her at the party."

"She seemed cool. Tell her that blood brother Donnie approves! I didn't even know y'all were going out already."

"I ain't gotta tell you everything! Relax, don't get all jealous. You're still my number one girl," Abraham prodded.

"So are you going to be my wingman tonight or what?" Donnie asked excitedly.

"Can't, brother…Liv and I are going out tonight."

"What? Are you serious? That's wacked out, man…you're going out with her instead of your main man? Never mind, I don't approve!" Donnie said jokingly.

"Calm down. Maybe we can all meet up."

"Nah, I'm all right. Go do your thing, I'll fly solo. I don't wanna be a third wheel!"

"Come on, don't make me feel bad. There will be plenty of other times, trust me."

"Your cell phone is ringing. It's probably your wife calling. It already begins."

Clearly not amused, Abraham answered it. "Hello."

Donnie mocked him, pretending to kiss his arm. "I'm so in love with you," he said, caressing his forearm.

"Hey, is it cool if I bring Donnie with me?"

Anxious to know who Abraham spoke with, he went silent.

"Okay cool. We will be there in twenty."

"What shenanigans are we getting into tonight? Was it Liv? Does she have a super-hot friend?" Donnie asked curiously.

"Ricky wanted me to go over to have dinner with his family and I asked if it was okay to bring my sidekick."

"Sidekick? So you're taking Liv then?"

"Ha! Funny! Come on, let's go. I told him I was bringing a princess named Donnie."

"Yeah, we'll see who gets there first Mr. I Think I'm Cool Because I Have a BMW Now!"

"First off, I was cool before the BMW, and second, the M3 will wax that little pony of yours."

"There's too much muscle for that Beamer of yours too handle. As a matter of fact, I bet you'll be three cars behind."

"All right, let's put that to the test. As soon as we hit South Presa, we take that road all the way to Rick's. Are you in?"

"Always!"

* * * * *

The mechanical beasts made it to the stoplight of Military and Presa. The remodeled '69 Mustang was revamped to perfection. The engine roared and prepared to do what it always did best—race. The '02 M3 was sleek, sharp, and sported a silvery glow. The aerodynamics looked both intimidating and impressive, and its driver was confident, nonetheless.

The evening had just overtaken the city. Side by side, the two vehicles took after a set of paternal twins, related with a small bit of resemblance, but drastically different. The angel eye lamps were like two sets of eyes that signified some relation, but the personalities were all their own.

The false sense of zero traffic on South Presa was deceiving at best. The long and curvy road only had two lanes for traffic, one for coming and one for going. The danger of going head on with innocent bystanders was imminent, but the thrill of the challenge clearly outweighed that of safety.

Testosterone flooded out of both machines. The engines revved, seemingly to never end, and the sound of them roared down the street they were meant to ride on. It was a test of vehicular muscle and neither driver gave an inch.

"No backing down now! You ready?" Abraham spoke with confidence and excitement, but inside, he was as giddy as a little boy with a brand-new toy.

"On green, we'll find out! When the light turns green in your rearview, it's go time!"

The stoplight lit up the intersection a quarter of a mile behind them and in front of them was a road stretching for a few miles with no streetlights and trees on both sides of the roadway. Darkness descended quickly, and within seconds, South Presa blazed with smoky roads.

XIX
LUCY IN THE SKY WITH DIAMONDS

Lucy remained skeptical amidst the forty-minute drive to the epicenter of downtown San Antonio. Assurances from her boyfriend were not easy to take in as he ranked in the 50/50 ratio of keeping his word. A special occasion, or so it seemed, she could only wonder. The intricacies of the night so far were perplexing, as she struggled to hide the nervousness. Her knees shook steadily and she made a conscious effort not to make it so obvious to her counterpart. If he asked, she would just say it was simply the vibrations of the muscle his car boasted. Slightly excited but more worried than anything, she hoped her dress and high heels took his attention for the most part. She chose the color scheme to complement not only his style, but the black and red vehicle as well, and like the muscle car, her black dress hugged her body and the red designs flowing from top to bottom showcased wavy red roadways, further enhancing her voluptuous body. She looked stunning. Her candy-red heels topped off the entire outfit and theme for the evening, as eyes were stuck to her like bees on a hive.

She studied his outfit from the corner of her eye. She wanted a closer look. What possessed him to wear black slacks and a maroon button-up shirt, she thought. Inconspicuously, she glanced at his dress shoes, which were also black, a style unlike his current trend. But what was most bizarre was the fact that he had his neatly pressed shirt tucked into his pants. A tie, had he worn one, would have just been mind-blowing. At a loss for words, this was not a normal evening on the town.

Her eyelashes were curled to perfection and a very light application of blush were enough to bring out her natural beauty. Her dark hair, which was naturally curly, fell straight on her shoulders and back, and because of her dark-colored hair, it made the red lipstick stand out in a rather elegant way. The perfume she chose for the evening flowed throughout the Mustang. Sweet enough to taste like candy and fresh smelling like stepping out of the shower, it caused him to twinge with excitement.

He pulled up to the venue. "Have you ever been here?" he asked.

He parked next to the tallest standing structure in the city, the Tower of Americas. It stood a proud 750 feet above the ground.

"She was built in '68. Ten years before I was born." He motioned to the tower.

"For the World Fair," she added, "and twelve years before I was born." She smiled.

For thirty-five years, she overlooked the city and its inhabitants, surpassing all other structures in the vicinity.

"I love HemisFair Park…it's the heart of the city," Lucy said.

"And that's why we're here, honey…without the heart, love cannot thrive."

"That's deep, even coming from you, Donnie. Why are we here, exactly?"

"You'll know in about," he glanced at his watch, "thirty minutes or so."

"Full of surprises today. Aren't we?"

Donnie grinned. Normally, he felt uncomfortable during intimate outings, but this time, he felt calm and in control. "I've heard that the observation deck is amazing."

"As far as the eye can see." She was rather excited and his vibes were soothing, for once. "When I was little, my parents brought me here. We ate in the restaurant and it rotated three hundred and sixty degrees and we could see the whole city from every angle. The bar was nice, but I was too young to enjoy it," she giggled.

"Bar 601? My brother told me about happy hour up there… said it was the best happy hour the skyline had ever seen." Donnie reached for her hand and she held his. "I've lived in San Antonio for five years and I've never been here. This will be the first time," he said happily.

As they entered, a young gentleman stood guard by the elevator door. He gave the couple a half-smile. "Going to the restaurant I take it?" he said.

"Yes, we are," Donnie replied.

"It's going to be a few minutes until the elevator comes back down."

"Okay, not a problem."

A gift shop caught his attention just over to the left. "Let's see if we can find a memento!"

As soon as the two walked in the gift shop, the young man attending to the elevator shouted to Donnie. "Sir, the elevator will be here in a few seconds, I can hear it coming down now."

"Okay, thank you!" Donnie picked up a small statue by the register. The tiny structure had a bluish color to its mere two-inch status.

"Ma'am, I'll take this, please," he said to the cashier. Donnie paid for it and gave it to Lucy. "I want you to have it. So you can remember this special night and our time here together."

"Thank you, I will treasure it always."

Lucy blushed, and she remembered moments like this that made him special. He treated her with a tender gentleness that was genuine. She had her sights set on disposal, but he was quickly making a comeback.

Together, they ran into the elevator, entering the chamber that would take them to the skies. Along the way, the view was spectacular. Rising above all they had known dearly at ground level, like a bird they had taken flight.

"Wow, look at that!" Donnie said to Lucy.

"Beautiful," she whispered.

Still rising, more structures came to life. Rivercenter Mall made its appearance, along with the Marriott hotels, the Tower of Life building, St. John's Church, La Villita, Alamo Plaza, the old Pioneer Flour Mill, and as they rose even higher, the roller coaster at Sea World in the far distance.

They rose to the heavens, and in the sixty seconds of bliss, they watched the city take its current form in amazement. Unwillingly, they were pulled from the moment. The elevator went black for a second, and the lights illuminated the glass cylinder that housed them.

"Sir, we are here at the restaurant," the young man said to them as the doors opened. "The hostess will take care of you."

"Thank you."

Lucy felt closer to him as tension and uncertainty were replaced with comfort and calmness. The ride up the tower changed the perspective of the night to come. In only two minutes, they appreciated life more than they had on ground level, and it was only proper that they felt that way approaching heaven's door.

As the pair made their way to the table, dusk fell on the city below.

"What do I owe this surprise to? You have never taken these measures before," she said lightheartedly.

"I don't want to speak to soon, but things are just going really good right now. I'm high on life for the first time. I mean, I have never felt this way before, and I don't want to make any more mistakes. It's a great feeling, but also a scary feeling."

"You need to control your temper, Donnie. That is what gets you into trouble."

"I know, and I'm working on that. I promise it will be better. I mean look at us...I have the best-looking girl in the city, we are dining in the clouds, I have the best friends in the world, my grandma's alive and well, and I got a job!" Donnie couldn't wait any longer and blurted out his latest achievement.

"You got another job? I'm so proud of you!" Lucy said, amazed.

"I know! I'm gonna do things right this time. As a matter of fact, I'm going to start right now." He reached in his pocket and, as he did so, reached for her hand on the table and held it with his.

"Please don't get on one knee! Donnie! I know you're not proposing to me. We are in no condition to make any serious, I mean *serious*, commitment right now!" She felt better to tell him before his gesture went any further.

He laughed at the onslaught of caution she threw his way, but he made sure to laugh it off in a kind way and not in a mocking manner. "No, silly girl! I'm not going to propose, don't worry, of course not…I mean, not yet. I mean…no, it's coming out all wrong…just let me explain it to you."

"Donnie, I don't understand…we fought last time we saw each other and we ended up in a shouting match and then a texting war. I just can't…" she turned, staring at the sunset dwindling away, "I can't do this anymore."

He listened to her truthful words. Speaking his side before she finished talking was definitely a habit he strived to break.

Maybe he has changed, she thought. Her decision about being with him hung in the balance. Much to Lucy's amazement, he rose to the occasion. She was curious about the setting he chose for his last stand, but naturally, they discovered a new comfort for one another.

"I just want to give you a gift. Is that okay?" he asked politely.

"I don't know, I'll see. It depends on what it is," she warned.

He placed a small box on the table. It had a red color made of felt and she was certain it housed a ring of some sort. She smiled excitedly with innocence, but also with caution.

"Before you open it, I just want to tell you why I got this for you. I know that I haven't been the best boyfriend and the transition here has been hard for me. I want you to know that I *do* appreciate you and all that you have done for me. Thank you for putting up with me and giving me chances, even when I didn't deserve them. I do love you even when you think I don't, so I hope you like it."

She listened to his words. He spoke with such sincerity; it caused her eyes to tear. She wiped them away, maneuvering her fingertips to avoid smearing her eyeliner. She believed him and proceeded to open the box.

She sighed heavily as her mouth dropped to ground level. As she opened the gift, there sat a circular object, the last rays of sunlight flickered off the shiny mineral. Out of the tiny box, she pulled the most beautiful diamond ring she had ever seen.

"It matches your style," he whispered.

"It's small, but not too small. It's perfect." She wasn't the type to bring too much attention to herself. She slipped it on her finger. "It fits amazingly perfect…size six and a half! So you were paying attention when I told you what size of ring I wore!" She laughed. "White gold?"

"Fourteen karats," he said, smiling.

"The diamonds are so beautiful! Why three?"

"Past," he pointed to the little one on the left, "present," he pointed to the little one on the right, "and future," he pointed the big diamond in the middle. "One day, I hope to be with you forever… if you'll have me."

"Well," she sighed with a big smile, "this is a good start."

He never knew what it was like to have a life that brought happiness, and for the first time, he had goals and ambitions and Lucy was the most important. He caressed her hand, admiring her ring. "I like being up high above the city. It reminds me of being back home, being so high up. It is only appropriate that my love is up here with me, now. My Lucy in the sky…with diamonds."

XX
SOUL MATES

He pulled up to her house slowly. A normal date would have ended at this point, but this was just beginning.

"When I talk to you, it's like I'm talking to God."

"Trust me. I'm not God," he laughed quietly, shaking his head.

"I know, but it's weird. I feel like when I am talking to you it's like I am praying," Liv smiled. "Are you close to God?"

"Yes…or I should say, more than I was a year ago…but not where I once was a long time ago." He could feel the power energizing his aura, and she could feel it as well. "I feel…like I'm running on full throttle these days."

"I can see it. Our lives revolve around God, He is our foundation, and when we are together, I feel like we are linked through Him."

"I feel it too. You don't seem like you are eighteen years old. You seem older than that, like an age gap doesn't exist between us."

"I've never told anybody this but…" she trailed off hesitating with slight embarrassment, "when I was 13, I wrote a letter to God. I asked him to let me find my soul mate…but not too soon. I was young and didn't want him to come right away, so I asked God to send him when I got a little bit older…when I was ready to receive him."

"That's sweet. So who is it? I mean, have you met him yet? Anybody I know?"

"I think I might have already," she said, smiling, "You might know him. He's a great guy."

"Perhaps one day I will meet him."

"Oh, I'm sure you will. I call him Superman."

"Sounds familiar," he said with a laugh.

"Okay, so tell me three things about you that nobody knows. I told you one about me."

"Are we really playing this game? I'm not one to share a whole lot…I'm a private person."

Her laugh boomed in the midnight air, "Let's be real here. You are so not shy!"

"All right, fine. I'll play, but you tell me your three first since you started this game."

"Let me see…okay, in high school, I was the 2003 Honey Bear of the Year…"

"Which means?"

"The dance team, you know, like the best dancer on the team."

"Got it…Honey Bear threw me off a little. I wasn't sure if it was a camping award. So what you're telling me is that you're a really great dancer, huh?"

"The best! Maybe you'll see firsthand when we go to a dance club. You won't be sorry."

"That can be arranged. As long as you wear heels, we can go this weekend. I'm sure I won't be disappointed!"

"I bet."

"I'm sorry…a little off-track…continue."

"Yes, let us refocus, shall we?" she asked giddily.

"Of course! My apologies."

"We are on number three. Oh, I remember what it was. When I grow up…I want to be…a nurse."

"Wow, that is great…I can see that. You're very nurturing and a natural healer. Your presence is so soothing. I always feel better around you."

"Really? How come you never told me?" Liv giggled excitedly.

"I just did!"

"What else haven't you told me?"

"Lots! But we'll stop there."

Liv swung her arm on his chest. "You jerk! Okay, now your turn…three things."

He sighed. "Where to begin…why can't we just go on about you? I'm sure there are at least ten things I don't know about you."

"Really, Abraham? You know a lot about me and you never talk about you! It's only three things, come on!"

"Okay, only three! Let me think." He took a few seconds to retrieve old memories. "All right, I got one. You're not gonna believe this, but I reached the top of the Eiffel Tower before I had been to the top of our very own Tower of Americas."

"How the heck did that happen!?"

"I have no idea, but I've been to the observation deck on the Tower once…two years after the Eiffel Tower experience. Anyway, number two, hmmm…I'll let you in on a secret…you can't tell anyone."

"Okay, I won't!" she said with excitement.

"Water is my Kryptonite. I don't like it, don't like to be around it, I don't swim, I don't know how to swim, not even enough to save my life and I especially hate it when water gets in or around my ears."

"Kryptonite, huh? So if I wanted to kill you, I can just spray you with water? And you'll melt or what?"

"No, not melt, but I stay away from large bodies of water."

"And the ears?"

"That's a long story. I'll save that one for another time. Let's see, one more, huh? I'm thinking…hmmm…oh, there is one that nobody knows about. I've never even said it out loud."

"Well, what is it?" Liv was eager to find out. *Perhaps he'll confess feelings for me,* she thought.

"Are you ready?"

"Yes!"

"Okay, here it goes," he paused, leaving her in suspense, "I talk to God every morning before I get out of bed. It is the first thing I do before I even talk," he said, exhaling as a weight had been lifted of his shoulders, "and that starts my day."

"That's a great way to start your day." Her light brown eyes gazed upon him, falling more in love with him with each word he spoke. "What made you become that way? Talking to God every day?"

"I don't know really. It just came to be, but it's always been the foundation…"

"Foundation of what?" she asked.

"My entire life."

"Is it also the foundation of your relationships too?"

"It is or I try for it to be. People are on different spiritual levels, so it doesn't always correspond well."

"Do you think we 'correspond' well?" Liv hoped for a confession.

He admired her attempts, but he did not want to reveal too much, just yet. *I need to keep it to myself, but I don't want to,* he thought. She looked on him with a heartfelt grin.

"I've dated a water sign before," he pointed out.

"How did that go?" she questioned curiously.

"It was good. I mean, it was probably one of the best relationships I've had. She's a good person and we got along well."

"So what happened? No, forgive me, I'm sorry, I'm being nosy," she tried not to pry too much.

"No, it's okay. She went off to college and it fell apart. Long distance relationships are tough."

"Would you do it again? I mean, a long distance relationship?"

"I don't know. Maybe, it just depends, I guess."

"Depends…on what?"

"It would probably depend on the person, the situation, and whether or not if the girl is worth it…" he paused, noticing her light brown eyes turn away. "And to answer your question…we 'correspond' amazingly well. Our frequencies are on a level all their own."

"We do and they are." She lit up from the somber expression a second before. "Since you're a Leo, do you know what that means?"

"What does it mean?"

"That you are my direct opposite…fire and water, the sun and the moon, a lion and a crab."

"Most people usually confuse the two *greatest* complementary forces that God created. Can you guess what they are?" he said, fully engaging her in a spiritual contest.

"Ummm…" Her smile was innocent. She desperately wanted to get the answer correct to impress him. "The sun and the moon."

"Nope! They are…" he stalled, attempting to build suspense.

"Tell me!"

"Man and woman."

"Awww, I didn't think about that one! For a moment, I thought they might be fire and water."

"Well, since I'm fire, you might think twice about playing with me because you might get burned."

"If I was any other element, I would be at your disposal, but since I am water, it will be no contest. Water puts out fire!"

"Even if it's a—"

"Roaring blaze? Yes!" she cut him off with extreme confidence.

"Touché. Fire is a radiant force, while water is cool and soothing. I like that." He nodded, admiring her logic.

"That's who we are…in perfect balance."

She intrigued him. The connection went beyond the normal realm of just two people getting to know each other. Her soft skin was like silk and her complexion was as beautiful as any, with zero blemishes to boast.

"I've never met anyone like you. Spiritually and intellectually, you're unlike any girl that I've ever come across. It doesn't even feel like you're eighteen years old." Abraham admired her savvy nature.

"Even though we are six years apart, I don't feel like there is an age gap either. You're a man who is mature and knowledgeable… sometimes I wonder why you even bother talking to me, I mean, a young girl."

"It's because you're just as mature and knowledgeable. Do you think I would waste my time on someone way younger who didn't intrigue me?"

"No, not at all…I'm surprised I keep your attention."

"My attention is kept because even though, you may be eighteen, your soul is not. It corresponds to mine."

"Corresponds," she giggled, "just like our last names do, Abraham and Liv Moreno."

"Whoa, easy now! That sounds like a marriage."

"Sorry, I didn't know that would make you feel uneasy."

"Actually, it doesn't. It sounds nice."

"Have you ever talked about marriage with anyone you've been with?"

"Never. This is the first time." He jerked his head quickly in her direction. "I mean, you know, not that we're together or anything but just speaking of marriage in general. It's the first time, yeah."

She blushed. *I think he does like me,* she thought. "You know if we ever get married, I won't have to change my name. I hate my last name."

"You hate your last name? I love my last name or *our* last name."

"I wish I could change it. If I marry you, I'll be stuck with it!"

They both laughed at the idea. There was no pressure, and he liked the fact that she gave him room to breathe. In the past, suffocation brought him to the verge of relinquishing serious relationships, but she was resurrecting a new hope.

"In case you're wondering," she further stated, "my dad was adopted, so there's no way we are related."

He laughed. "It's okay, I wasn't worried. I was handed down the name and the bloodline. So we are in good shape, nevertheless. No incest here!"

"I'm glad we confirmed that! Are you close to your dad?"

Abraham looked straight ahead as far as his eyes would take him down the darkened street. His smile quickly faded. He paused for a moment as his brow crinkled. "He wasn't…umm…"

Liv picked up on the uneasiness, "In good standing?"

"No, not really…we've never really been…"

Her hand touched the back of his head. His blood pressure dropped. Her fingers stroked the back of his neck, decimating the stress. He closed his eyes and his vitals descended back to normal.

"What about you? Are you close with your parents?"

"My mom, she is always getting on my case. She gets on my nerves. She always has to be in control. My dad and I are closer. He is laidback, but it's my mom who wears the pants. They fight once in a while, but I can tell they are not in love anymore."

"I'm sorry…I didn't mean to bring out negative thoughts."

Liv bowed her head, it was her smile that now faded. The momentum shifted as she took her hand off his neck and placed both hands in her lap. He grabbed her hand back and kissed it.

"When I get married, I'm going to make sure I am in love and not just so someone can take care of me. God should come first in any relationship. That is very important to me and the man I will marry will put God first. That's why I think I'm fascinated by you because you put God first no matter what."

"God *is* the focal point in our lives. If I ever got married, it will be God, me, and my wife…together."

"Is that how your parents are?"

"People marry for the wrong reasons and divorce for the wrong reasons. I believe in the vows that you make to the other person and being in it for the long haul. Until death do us part, right?"

"*Us?*" She could not hide her huge grin.

"You know what I mean! Don't get a big head."

Liv laughed and swung her arm, hitting him on the chest. "Shut up! You know you wanna marry me!"

"Maybe, I would…*if* I was the marrying kind!" He wasn't quite sure if he really was the type to be married. After all, Liv had considerably changed things since the party. He wanted to tell her how sexy her eyes were, but he held back. He wasn't the type to give such compliments early on, but rather feel out his counterpart and he wanted to further understand what made her tick. It was the psychologist in him that was determined to preserve the psychological edge in any circumstance. Nevertheless, he was busting at the seams.

The warm feelings God blessed human beings to experience were all present when he connected with her. On every level, their union formed a triumvirate thus far, with God overlooking His spiritual creations, two beings complementing one another beyond the earthly plane.

Her personality made her that much more beautiful, and her sweetness revealed a side that he could not get enough of. Like magnets in perfect harmony, their attraction was unparalleled. The sunroof opened up, exposing all the stars above. Midnight was fast approaching, and sitting in the car in front of her house had become a ritual. The autumn weather was nice and cool, which made them want to enjoy each other's presence more. Being hot-blooded, he preferred cool and breezy nights and she preferred the same. Cold weather was her favorite and the temperature was to her liking.

"I'm thinking it could be a traditional Mexican wedding? *If* you were the marrying kind, I mean. You are Mexican, right?"

"Ummm...I'm human."

"You know what I mean, silly."

"I wasn't born in Mexico and neither were my parents. I have a ton of Indian blood. I can't grow a beard, much less facial hair. Does that help any?"

"I like the way Latina sounds. It sounds sexy."

"A Latin wedding, that sounds nice or maybe a Hawaiian one. Wait, what I am talking about! I'm in no condition to get married!"

"Well, *if* you were, you'd have a lot to offer, Mr. Abraham. By the way, you look yummy in your BMW. It looks good on you."

"Thank you. It was a gift to me, from me, for finally beginning my life with a new career."

"That's a great gift, but why a BMW?"

"You're not going to believe this story, but one day, back when I used to work at the Spurs Shop downtown, I see a silver M3 roll up and park out in front. I was in my last year of college and a few months out from graduating, so I counted the days until I was out of there. So here's this car out front and I'm thinking, *Who the heck is this in this awesome-looking sports car*, right? Well, out comes Tony Parker. He had been coming by like once a week, at least, and this was the first time I see the M3, and at that point, I said to myself, 'The day I make it, I'm going to get one of those,' and that's the day I decided it would be a gift to myself."

"Wow! That's amazing! And here you are! You made it, Mr. Abraham. I don't understand why you don't have a girlfriend."

"It's been tried before," he said with a wide-eyed expression.

"I bet all the little girls in your class are in love with you! Hey, how's that little girl, Justice? Is she doing better?"

"She's doing really well, a total transformation. Her teachers were asking me what I've been doing to help her behave, but it's really just attention that she needs."

"This is going to sound crazy, but do you know how I see you?"

"No, I don't. Do I want to know?" He questioned curiously.

"It's funny because I see you in the S or Superman way and in the Mr. Abraham/Clark way too. You save lives, not in the physical way but the mental and spiritual way…and your alter ego helps Pre-K kids during the day. I bet the kids love you!"

"And I love them. You're very observant. I see you caught a lot of subtleties, like the S."

"I noticed a lot of your friends at Palo Alto call you that."

"I must say, I do love your thought process with alter egos and saving lives." He giggled. "You're in superhero training and you don't even know it!"

"I can be your Lois! You can go ahead and love that thought as well," she said slyly.

She sat sideways facing directly toward him with one leg folded on the passenger seat. He was relaxed and his body language showed it. She reached over and placed her right hand on his face. His left cheek felt her energy flow through him. The connection was too powerful for him to resist. He had been overtaken by it.

The process of getting to know each other was an adventure. Physical contact was in no way a breach of personal space, as both parties welcomed it. When she touched him, whether it was caressing his skin, a heartfelt embrace, or just a simple hand massage, it felt like heaven.

"Abraham, thank you for helping me. I was the damsel in distress and you saved me. You were right about my ex-boyfriend. It was like you knew he was going to disappoint me, but you let me go anyway, knowing that I had to go through it. It was like a heads-up from God. Once again, you were there without actually being there.

You're my mentor, my instructor…that's what I will call you the Instructor. What do you think?"

"You just like adding all these nicknames, don't you? But I like it…instructing in the ways of life!" He laughed.

"Your words are powerful," she said in awe.

"The power of words can change a life," he countered.

"Like mine?"

"I can only hope that I helped change yours for the better, even if it wasn't much. You see…psychology is my ally. People always ask me, 'Why psychology? You'll never make money with a degree in psychology,' but I don't believe that. The world runs on psychology. It is the motivation of individuals to become better than what they currently are…to *evolve*."

"Just like you are always evolving? You speak with such passion."

"It's what I believe, and I feel, sometimes people need to hear that. Words are like wildfire. They can consume everything in its path and they are burned into the psyche. When the fire spreads, it leaves a blazing trail straight into the mind, thus, providing a new way of thinking. The question is…which words you choose to light up, good ones or bad ones. It is the essence of human nature."

"And you're all about the fire, right?" She laughed.

"It's my weapon of choice. A fire rises." He grinned.

"The best part about your little operation is that it remains a secret to the world."

"As it should be."

"All this sets you apart from your peers. Working undercover, nobody knows who you really are." She noticed the subtleties that others easily overlooked.

"And they don't need to. When it's for the Lord, they don't need to know who helps out, just that they've been helped."

He stared up at the stars through the moon roof, "God, thank you for this amazing woman," he whispered, "I want to tell her the truth about me, but I don't know if I can." His silent prayer had her ogling in his peripheral.

"You said your three things already, but I waited for you to say it…there is another secret. I've seen it. I've felt it…but it's one that you're not going to tell me."

"You might not understand," he spoke softly.

"How many people know about it?"

"A handful maybe." He took a moment to ponder the question. "Maybe less."

"It's okay, I understand. I do."

"I can't tell you yet, but…"

"It's okay, Abraham, I understand. I just know. You have something, something special." She felt the power of God flowing from him and she bathed in it. "It's from God, isn't it?"

His eyes began to water. He didn't say another word. The anomalous characteristics he possessed were by no means easy to explain. Inadequacy set in when an individual questioned his extraordinary abilities. "For some people, they are visible and evident enough…" he yearned to gather the words to help her understand, "…that these same people always question what they witness."

"That's why you're always under attack?"

He shied away from anyone that noticed these talents and avoided anyone who pried or pressed the issue. "There are those that are scared of it, those that are threatened and those that hate what they don't understand."

"I'm not afraid. You're not a threat to the world, and I don't hate you for the special person that you are. I love you for it," she said genuinely.

"You know me without knowing me." A tear rolled down his cheek. Her presence soothed his soul. "I feel as though I can be normal around you…like I can let my secrets be known."

"Isn't that what God intended you to have them for? For the world to see your gifts?"

"Not everybody, Liv."

"Are people jealous?"

"They can be."

"They envy you, Abraham, I can see it. Your brother does, it's obvious."

"Donnie? He's my brother. He has my back no matter what."

"And he's also jealous of you. I can tell. People can be envious and want what they cannot have. I see the way girls look at you and guys. You are loved, just as much as you are hated, and it's not even your fault. I bet you've had friends betray you and plenty of psycho girlfriends." She picked up on the intricacies and the burdens without difficulty.

"That's why it's not for showcase." Stunned at her empathic skills, he gathered himself. "Can I ask you something?"

"Anything," she said soothingly.

"If we were to ever end up together, would you be willing to go through all that? If someone was in distress and needed my help, would you understand? If someone went psycho? If I, we, were betrayed? If I were loved and hated?"

"Yes, I would."

"It's going to be hard. Maybe I belong to the world. Sometimes, I think that's why God sent me…to use my abilities to help make things better. I never thought I could really belong to anybody."

The words were harder than she could bear. Tears filled her eyes, but she spoke the agonizing truth. "Honestly, I would love to be yours. I *do* understand the way your life is because of the things that you do. The way you try to divide yourself, and because I understand, I'll know how to deal with it. You can leave me to help others and the rest of the world for that matter, and I'll know why."

He paid close attention to her words. Her genuine speeches were admirable and her heart pumped care and concern.

"I pray to God to protect you, knowing that there is someone out there, like you, saving those who need to be saved in the most sacred ways. I'm a believer, just like when you saved me. I thank God for you," she paused. "I'm sorry. I got ahead of myself."

"It's okay, really. I appreciate the honesty. I'm recording it in my memory banks right now."

Her laugh concluded her seriousness as they had transported to a time yet to come.

"Why would you record that?" she asked curiously.

"So I can never forget those sweet words."

The palm of her hand cupped his cheek. He placed his hand on top of hers and slid hers up and down his cheek from his temple to his chin. "It fits perfect. Your hand fits perfectly on my face."

He gazed at her. Their eyes began telling each other stories, and like a good book, they couldn't put each other down, for every page, every word, every chapter kept them intrigued.

"It feels like it was meant to be this way. You know what else fits perfectly? I noticed it earlier when I hugged you. My face fits directly on the side of your neck. You know, like a puzzle piece that fits directly in another, that's what it felt like."

"Maybe God planned it like Adam and Eve," he added

"How so?"

"When he created me, he probably kept a rib of mine and then made you, but dispatched you to earth six years after me so we could find each other."

"Like soul mates."

"Yes, like that," he agreed, and unbeknownst to him, he was becoming a believer. The wavelength was uncanny, and with each conversation, they began to delve deeper into their own metaphysical plane.

"I never thought about the term 'soul mate' until now. There is a story by Plato, you may have heard it, where it says that people once had four legs, four arms, and two faces. So one day, they were split in half and, from that point on, had to spend their lives looking for each other…looking for their soul mate."

She listened intently. "Abraham, you know what?" Her face glowed and her eyes locked on to his. The universe called to her and all the stars that hung overhead whispered into her at that moment. "We fit."

The statement echoed in his soul. Simple and to the point, these two words embodied their gravitational pull to each other. "We fit."

She was his equal, and as her feelings poured out, he realized that this merging of souls had arisen on the day he found her.

"It was meant to be," he whispered. "You see all those stars up there? God made all those things out there and down here, but He didn't forget to create the bond of a soul mate. He didn't forget to make you and me. Perhaps you *are* the Lois to my Superman."

"Beautiful words."

"I do have one more secret I can share. I'm a writer. Maybe you can read some of my work some time."

"I would love that! I wonder what Mr. Abraham would write about. Hmmm."

"I'll keep you in suspense until the next time, but you did get one more secret. Not the one you wanted, but you got a bonus, nevertheless!" he said optimistically.

"You can tell me anything," she reassured him.

"I'm glad that I found you…or should I say, clicked on you."

Her wavy dark brown hair covered the side of her face as he admired her profile. He could feel himself beginning to love every inch of the woman that God allowed him to find. The slight curve of her nose was a characteristic she hated, but one that he adored.

"You say you belong to the world, but I can change that, if you give me a chance to show you," she said, as the tone in her voice proved that her plea was genuine.

He believed in her. He touched her soft cheeks and stroked her chin with his thumb. "Okay. If what you say is true, then that remains to be seen, and from what I can tell, the chances of that happening are great."

With one press of a button, the moon roof slowly slid shut. The early morning mist left condensation on the glass that now separated them from the stars above. Liv lifted her arm and left her handprint on the glass. The impression became visible as the faint street light gave it life.

"Is it okay if I leave my handprint there?"

"Sure. I'll never clean it, so at night when I open the moon roof and look up at the glass, I'll always see your handprint."

Liv took that response as a joke and laughed. "Yeah right! As soon as you get home you're going to clean it off."

"I won't. I'm going to leave it up. I promise."

"I guess that remains to be seen, huh?"

And now it was Abraham who laughed at her joke. Pound for pound, she held her own no matter the circumstance.

The wee hours of the morning had them exiting the vehicle. She looked up at him with her 4'11" frame and placed her arms around him. He enveloped her with his arms and experienced an electric charge that he was fast getting used to. As their night was coming to an end, they embraced and held on to each other for what seemed like forever. Saying bye for the evening was never easy, and every time they would try and leave each other, another ten, fifteen, or twenty minutes would pass by.

Just as the night sky did, they fell silent and stood as one on the sidewalk, and as they held on, she slid her face into his neck and she fit perfectly.

XXI
WATER

Donnie ran as fast as he could and slowly began to decelerate. Sprinting at full speed, his outbursts of energy were not for training, but for releasing frustration. Stress prolonged him for some time now, and it begged for release. "Come on, faster," he mumbled. This time, he preferred the eruption to be constructive, rather than destructive, unlike many times before.

The demons in his heart instigated their assault. "I don't want to go back," he murmured to himself, "leave me in peace." The engagement for the evening was important to him, and he didn't want to let his brother down.

In the meantime, he frantically tried to quiet his mind. *Why hasn't she called?* he thought. He began to sprint one last leg. "Faster! Faster!" he whispered to himself, "let it all out." Lucy consumed his thoughts. "Don't lose focus," he cried out.

Controlling his anger had been challenging, and he was treading water, desperately seeking to avoid drowning in pity.

"Yo, Donnie!" He heard a familiar voice yell in the distance. Abraham waved from the side of the natatorium. "I'm taking off right now, but I'll see you in a few hours?"

"I'll be home by then," he assured Abraham.

"You better! It's Celebration S! Don't forget to dress up!"

"Will do!" Donnie shouted back. He focused once again on the concrete track. "I can't let him down," he whispered.

With a few minutes to spare, Donnie sat at the kitchen table. Grandma Josie heated up rice and beans on the stove. "Mijo, you want to eat before you leave?"

"Yeah, I'm a little hungry."

"You haven't been eating…you look thinner."

Worried that she would continue to pry, he answered nonchalantly. "It's only three pounds. I've been working out a lot."

"Girl trouble, isn't it? Lucy's a good girl. Take care of her, mijo."

Donnie piddled around with the spoon on the table, pretending to ignore Grandma Josie. *How could I tell her about Lucy?* He thought.

Grandma Josie had been responsible for most of his transformation and transition. The metamorphosis he had undergone kept him alive and he was grateful for her guidance.

"Is there anything else troubling you?" she asked, handing him a plate of rice and beans.

"No," he said, refusing to look into her eyes.

"Your friends? School?"

"Not really," he replied, picking at his food. "Grandma, who were my real parents? What were they like?"

"¿Mijo, porque me preguntas? *Why do you ask?*"

"I always wondered about them…did they not want me? I mean, how come I never knew them?"

Grandma Josie stirred the pot of frijoles without missing a beat, but her emotions inside were aware that it was time. She turned the knob on the stove, making sure the frijoles would not burn and grabbed a rag from the countertop to clean her hands. She wiped them thoroughly and placed the rag neatly where it had been moments before. She stalled as much as she could and finally sat at the kitchen table where Donnie waited patiently for her answer.

"Mijo, why do you want to know so badly? You came out to be a fine young man. You are in college, you have a beautiful girlfriend, and your friends are good people that care about you. Why live in the past?"

He sighed heavily. *If she only knew,* he thought. "Grandma, I just want to know why…it's been bothering me for some time now. Please tell me. I know you have your secrets."

Grandma Josie took a few seconds to gather herself. "Where to begin," she spoke softly. "Your father…" She looked up at the ceiling searching for the words to describe what once was. "Your father was a smart man…very intelligent. He lived here in San Antonio. He was very good with his hands, a hard worker…very good at creating and fixing things, especially planes. He wanted to go into the military and be a fighter pilot. But things changed when he met your mother."

"What do you mean 'changed'?" he asked curiously.

"Well," she continued, "Instead of going into the military, he wanted to buy a plane and fly around the country. Your parents met in high school and that's when he decided he would take her with him on his cross-country adventures. He learned how to fly at Stinson, that old little airport on the southside, and he became pretty good."

"What did she look like? My mom, I mean."

"She was beautiful!" Grandma Josie went on without missing a beat. "He was reckless and spontaneous and she was sweet, good-natured. They were opposites, for sure." Grandma Josie smiled, as she reminisced on a love story she was privileged to witness. "She wore dresses all the time," she continued, "She had curly dark brown hair that went a little past her shoulder, from what I remember, and she hardly wore makeup." Grandma traveled back in time, as she gazed out the kitchen window. "When your father finished up flying lessons at Stinson, that's when things changed again. His instructor offered him a job to fly all over the country, that's when I lost track of him."

"You never heard from him or my mom again!?"

"Oh, I did. Every few years, I would get a letter or a phone call, but that was it."

"Is that how you found me?"

"Yes, mijo. Your father sent me a letter many years later. He told me where to find you," she said with much reluctance.

"So they gave me up?" Donnie asked somberly. "They gave me up." Disappointed at her response, he took a moment to let it sink in. "They gave me up," he said, once more, this time whispering to himself.

Grandma Josie looked on helpless. She dreaded the day he would ask that question, and now, he heard it for himself.

"Mijo, you're a great young man. The Bazans did a good job raising you..." Grandma Josie attempted to console him, but there was nothing she could say to soften the blow.

"No, they didn't." He shook his head in disgust.

"Don't say that, Donnie. They did the best they could. Nobody is perfect, and they gave you all the love and support they could possibly give."

"Grandma, I don't get it...why didn't you get me here sooner? I could've done more with my life here in San Antonio."

Making sense of this news was no use. The answers he desperately searched for were now answers he wished he'd never heard. It only raised more questions and, with that, more confusion. His thoughts betrayed him now that he knew the truth. His feelings began to guide him down a path he vowed never to return to.

Grandma Josie studied him. His eyes twitched and his brow crinkled, fluctuating in and out of confusion.

"I called the Bazans as soon as I found out you were alive. That's when we agreed to bring you to San Antonio. They told me what you had done, and we decided that you needed a fresh start."

"My father is still out there somewhere?"

"I don't know. This is the longest I've gone without hearing from him."

"I don't understand! How come I didn't know them? Please tell me. I know you know the truth," Donnie shouted. His emotions spewed out of control. "I'm sorry, Grandma...I didn't mean to yell at you. I don't want to be lied to anymore...I'm ready to hear the truth."

"Okay, mijo," she exhaled, ready to deliver the news he desperately longed for, "I figure you're old enough to hear it now. Your mother died after giving birth to you."

"She died?" His heart broke upon hearing his worst fear come to light. His eyes began to tear up and his hope vanished in an instant. *I never had a chance to meet her,* he thought. "What was her name?"

"Helena." Grandma Josie welled up with tears in her eyes as well.

"My father is still alive, though, right? If he is, there is still hope for me," he asked Grandma Josie, looking for confirmation. Rather, he spoke frantically trying to convince himself that he was not beyond saving. Disappointed and confused, he proceeded to ask his next question. "Grandma…what was my father's name?"

Grandma Josie hesitated to answer. She looked out the window again, as if she had forgotten the name of her son. The conversation had gone too far for her to turn back now, so she carried on, "I named him Jesus," she said, shaking her head, "He hated his name."

"Just like I hate mine," Donnie added. "Why didn't I come live with you after I was born?"

Grandma Josie chose her words carefully. "Your father told me you died at birth too."

Donnie fell silent. "Why did he lie to you? Did he not want me? Why didn't he want me?" On the outside he kept his reserve, but his inner core brewed fierce emotions.

"Donnie, I know it doesn't make sense and maybe your father had good reason to lie, maybe it was to protect you, I don't know. He didn't tell me the truth about you until you were a teenager. Up until then, I didn't know you were alive, otherwise, I would've brought you home sooner."

Donnie listened to her words keenly. *It's not her fault,* he thought. "Grandma, you are the only blood I have left. I've been denied answers my whole life. I made a whole bunch of mess, caused destruction…I was deprived of answers over there in LA. But I found them here. I found you here."

"Mijo, you are loved so much. The Bazans love you and took care of you. I love you. That's all that matters."

His aggression dialed down considerably in San Antonio. Wreaking havoc only brought pain. "Grandma…" Donnie hesitated in asking his next question. She knew well what his follow-up would be after disclosing the truth he desperately wanted to hear. "My father *is* alive, isn't he?"

Grandma Josie stared into his eyes, giving a silent sigh. Much to her relief, a knock came at the door.

Donnie sprang from the table. "It's Abraham. I gotta go, now. I love you."

"Mijo, be careful!" Concern beamed from her eyes as the car pulled away. As soon as the car was out of sight, she grimaced in pain. Soon, she wouldn't be able to hide it from him. She desperately hoped and prayed that her work was not in vain. "Don't be like your father…"

"A celebration for Mr. Abraham!" Donnie yelled out the window. "Man, this car is nice! It has some power, definitely not like the Hondas. Movin' on up! I haven't even been in it since you got it! What's it been? Almost a month now?"

"Something like that." Abraham let out a deceiving laugh.

"I bet Liv has been in it way more times than I have!"

"Man, don't start! You know I don't like when you get all girly on me!"

"Nice moon roof!" Donnie slid the cover aside, exposing the glass above. "It's all dirty…the least you could do is keep it clean." He wiped the substance off the window with his hand and sleeve.

"No! Don't clean it!" Abraham shouted with urgency.

"Why? It's dirty."

Abraham gasped with discouragement. "Nothing…never mind." Her handprint, he promised her he would leave it untouched. *It could be worse,* he thought.

"What exactly are we celebrating?"

"Life! We are celebrating life, brother. I need my right hand man in attendance, you know what I mean?"

"Of course, like always. You know, I gotta be honest, I'm kinda jealous," Donnie confessed.

"Jealous?"

"You made it out of this hellhole in inner city, and I feel like I'm drowning."

"All right, talk to me," Abraham prodded immediately. "Lucy?"

"I dropped my classes, Lucy and I are done, probably for good… and I just found out my family abandoned me, my real family *and* my foster family. It hasn't been a five-star day, or week, for that matter."

With little time to waste, Abraham concentrated on the facts. "Okay, let's start with the positive. First off, you're alive." He glanced over at Donnie. "It could be a whole lot worse. Second, it will pass. You're not gonna be stuck in a rut forever. You're gonna bounce back, I have no doubt. You know how I know this? Because you always do!"

Donnie nodded in agreement. Abraham had a way with words, and Donnie was a believer in the power of eloquence.

Abraham continued, "And lastly, you have a good support system…your grandma, me, your Palo Alto family…you're gonna be all right."

Donnie soaked in the rebuttal. His silence was neither confirmation nor resistance to the truthful testimony. Abraham let the words sink in and the counselor in him was rather used to the awkward silence, so he let it pass until Donnie was ready to speak.

"You're right, you're absolutely right. I knew I could count on you. There is no sense in getting depressed over events I can't control, right?" Donnie felt reassured.

"And here's our stop." Abraham said, relieved that the therapeutic speech worked, "You snapped out of your funk right on cue! I wasn't sure if I could pull it off in such a short amount of time!"

"You work wonders, bro! Once again, your words did not disappoint, Abraham and his magical words. Wait a minute," Donnie paused, gathering his thoughts as they exited the car, "Is Liv gonna be here?"

"Of course, she is! Why?"

"You know what that means? I'm flying solo!"

"There's enough of me to go around," Abraham said jokingly. "Don't start getting all little girl on me."

Abraham and Donnie entered the Volcano as it lit up the night.

"Hey, did you invite everyone from Palo Alto?"

"Almost, why?"

"Did you invite her?" Donnie raised his finger and pointed at the girl walking into the club.

"May?"

"Good luck tonight, brother. You're gonna need it," Donnie cautioned.

"I guess tonight all the water signs come out to play." Abraham showed no signs of deviating from the plan at hand. "I'm not worried. I'm cool with everybody. She's more than welcome to join us."

"All right, it's your funeral." Donnie teased.

* * * * *

Liv detected his energy as he entered the fiery inferno. "Baby!" Liv shouted. "You're here! You look nice," she said, smothering him with hugs and kisses.

He engulfed her and soaked up her love. "You look ravishing! Let me see your heels."

Liv raised her leg, making an L-shape, and then wrapped it around his leg and attached herself happily.

"Black and silver! Sexy! I love 'em! Those muscular calves get me every time!"

"Oh, do they, Mr. Abraham?" she said slyly as she glided her arms around his waist.

"Yup!" He leaked out his answer just before her lips smooched on his.

She grabbed his hand, leading him to the guests in attendance. "Some of your friends are here. You can tell them hi and then I wanna see you on the dance floor immediately!"

"As you wish!"

Donnie stayed back, waiting for May to enter. He posted up at the bar closest to the door. "Donnie!" May greeted him.

"May, it's been too long. You look great! How's Minnesota?"

"Eh, it's all right. I get to see snow all the time. Other than that, I wish I were here at home."

"Hey, you can't beat a free ride, though!" Donnie reminded her.

"And that's why I stay up there!" she said sarcastically with a smile. Her focus and her sights turned to the man who was once hers. "Abraham? I heard he's a teacher now. Is he here?"

"He's on the dance floor," Donnie said confidently.

"With?" she asked as her brow crinkled.

"Liv."

She scanned the dance floor curiously and noticed a girl wrapped around him. "Is that his new girlfriend?"

"Yes…" Donnie answered, noticing the hope fade from her eyes. "Why do you ask?"

May glanced from the dance floor down to the floor. Her mouth dropped slowly as she exhaled. "What happened to Avril?"

"It didn't quite work out, but she doesn't believe that."

"Of course, she doesn't. Avril is crazy!" She concurred with Donnie, all the while gazing at the couple dancing and laughing. "He looks happy. I'm happy for him…he deserves the best."

"What about me?" Donnie desperately attempted to disrupt her train of thought on the man she stared at.

"Oh…you deserve the best too," she responded in an effort to avoid being rude. Her attention returned to the couple who gave sweet kisses to one another.

"No, I mean, what about me? Have you ever considered how good I'd be for you? You never gave me a chance. Why?"

Her face twisted with a grimace. "I just…I don't see you that way, Donnie. You're a good person and a good friend…that's all."

"I'm not…I'm not any of those things…" he paused, "I'm better…than him."

"You have Lucy and she is great, right?"

"Lucy and I are done. Now that it's over between her and I, maybe we can give it a try. I have always had a crush on you. What do you think? Abraham has moved on…and so should you!"

His urgency only infuriated her further. "I don't want to try with anyone. I'm good where I'm at. He is your brother! Don't you guys have a code: never date your brother's ex?"

"Not today!"

"Like I said, I'm good where I'm at."

"When you're ready, we can try. I'd be so good to you," he pleaded.

"No, Donnie, it'll never happen!"

"You're making a big mistake! I would move up there with you in Minnesota, I would do the things he never did!"

"Donnie, there's a reason for that…" She shook her head as her eyes closed, recalling the memories of what could have been. "And you and I are just friends. Even if I wanted to date you, I wouldn't because you're his brother. I can't believe you would do that to him! Tell Lucy I said hi."

May scurried off, leaving disgust in her wake. Donnie held his position at the bar. Fury resided within him. He eyeballed his brother from afar, and his thoughts suddenly betrayed him.

"I hate him," he mumbled. "No…he is your brother and he loves you," he said secretly to himself. "Focus, Donnie!" He pleaded with the darkness. "Don't let hate get in. Don't give in!" His decrement was taking shape, and it begged for a return to its prime.

XXII
MAY FLOWERS

March 2001

Cartoons were her favorite. Pepe Le Pew relentlessly pursued a pussycat in an attempt to woo her.

"Beby," she said sweetly, "do you think he really loves her?"

"I don't know. Maybe, it's fun and games for him or perhaps the thrill," Abraham knew where the conversation headed, as her curiosities peeked at their current situation.

"The cat is in love with him and now he doesn't want her." She laid her eyes on Abraham. "It's a simple cartoon, but it's probably true, right?"

"What do you mean? True?" he questioned.

"Relationships…they're usually one-sided. Is that how it is with you and me? You wanted me, and now that I'm in love with you, you don't want me anymore?" she asked as gently as her sweet voice would allow.

"Whoa, hold on there, who pursued who? If I recall correctly, wasn't it you that asked me out and kissed me first?" He laughed, recollecting their first real outing together.

Although Abraham made an effort to secretly change the subject, May pursued, nevertheless. "Beby, so is it true?" she asked innocently.

Pepe Le Pew faced a dilemma and Abraham felt his pain.

"Is what true?" he responded, pretending to be focused on the cartoon. He could feel the heat, and he heard her ask her next question before it was even airborne.

"You don't want me anymore?"

He could read the suspicion on her face. Her curiosity, combined with the broadcast at hand, led her to this line of questioning.

"Why do you say that?"

"Like the cartoon, he caught her and now he doesn't want her anymore. Is that true?"

Abraham stalled by asking questions. He hesitated before answering a question he was unsure or uncertain about, especially when it came to relationships.

"No," he answered her half-heartedly. Boredom began to set in. She loved him so much and the pressure of reciprocation mounted.

"Are you sure?" she asked.

"Yeah," he responded convincingly in order to avoid a fight or ending up losing her prematurely. Uncertainty flooded his mind. Being neck deep in a serious relationship was a first for him.

May grew up without a father. Her decisions at times required guidance and he seemed to fill that void. His father-figure presence created a stability that she had never known before. Her love suffocated him at times, but the counselor in him understood the psychology of it.

Nearly six months into the relationship and it remained non-exclusive.

"Abraham, how come you don't…" she searched for the words carefully, fearing that she would scare him away, "why don't you wanna be my boyfriend?"

"I don't know, I just…I don't like being labeled, I guess. I don't like titles. It's like being someone's property. I don't like the idea, if that makes sense."

Disappointed, she wrapped her arms around him, hoping that he would come closer to being what she had been wanting all this time.

"I love you."

"Do you?" he questioned suspiciously.

"Yes," she answered convincingly.

"Why?"

"You're perfect. Even your flaws are perfect," she said, as she admired his profile.

"Don't call me that."

"Why not? Abraham, I don't understand…"

"Because…I'm not."

"But to me…" she eyeballed him with love, "you are."

"Don't put me on a pedestal," he sighed heavily, "That's not where I belong."

"Why not?"

"Because you're not always going to see me like that, I make mistakes. And when I fall off…it's going to hurt," he aimed to reason with her.

"Why are you so scared?" She struggled to make sense of his words. She wanted so desperately to find what made him tick.

"What do you mean?" His tactics were failing him this time around. He did his best to shake her off, but each time, she got braver and farther in her questioning.

"Why are you scared to commit? It's like…you're afraid to get close."

She held him tighter. He sat on the edge of the bed, dejected. Both his arms dangled by his side and his head looked down as if he was a little boy being scolded. Frustrated by her questions, he couldn't avoid the truth. Holding her off for so long only brought on more questions that he severely disliked.

"I…I don't know what to tell you…"

"It's okay, you can tell me." She wrapped her legs around him, trying to comfort and soothe him. "What happened to you?"

"When I was little…" he breathed heavily, "when I was four… something happened to me."

"Something bad?" she asked cautiously, as this was the farthest he had gone into detail.

"Something traumatic…"

"Is that why you don't want to get too close?"

"Yes."

She returned to hugging him. Not once did he look over to her. His eyes remained on the stains of the gray-colored carpet in her tiny room. She wanted more, more emotions from him, more information and she wanted to dig it out of him, but she knew better than to prod.

"You can tell me whenever you're ready. I'm not going anywhere. I love you."

He sat still as can be. As far as he was concerned, the conversation was over. She looked in his eyes, at his hair, at his small child-like ears, his chubby cheeks, and his puffy lips.

Nothing.

Her obvious examination did not bring on a response. Her whole body engulfed his, as she sat sideways, arms and legs draped around him. She kissed him on the cheek…and waited. No response.

"I'm yours…" she said softly, "even if you don't claim me."

XXIII
PREDATOR

"You still got this book?" Donnie said with amazement.

"Yeah, you know I love mythology," Abraham responded with a laugh.

"Which kind? Greek? Roman? Egyptian?"

"All kinds! You know this, brother!"

"This is the class you registered for just for kicks, right? It was a class you didn't even need and still took it with your brother from another mother." Donnie recalled.

"I'm surprised you remembered…somebody had to hold your hand through the process," Abraham teased.

Donnie flipped through the pages. "Look at this lion…it's pretty sick. He's got a lion body, a goat head sticking out of his back, and a snake for a tail…is that what you are? A Leo…mutated or something."

"Nah, I'm just a regular lion. That right there…is something else entirely, definitely not a Leo."

"Interesting stuff," Donnie said, as he perused through the pages.

"Why do you think I kept the book? Anyway, so what's going on?" Abraham threw on a shirt and grabbed his belongings placing them in his shorts.

Donnie laid the book down, releasing a deep breath. "I'll brief you on the roof."

"We're going to the roof? It's that bad, huh?" Abraham looked to Donnie for a response, but his face showed signs that the lights were on, but no one was home. "Let me just get my shoes on."

Abraham turned his back to Donnie. Quickly recognizing he had a couple seconds, Donnie stuffed a folded paper into some shorts lying on the sofa. "Just in case," Donnie whispered, and he patted the pocket for a final farewell to this place he called his second home.

The two walked down the street to the old Seed Company building. "I haven't been here in a few years. This is...I mean, *was* part of the training route. You remember when we used to climb up to the top?" Abraham paused for a moment to let Donnie reminisce the old antics.

"You're too quiet. It's serious, isn't it?" Abraham let his instincts kick in.

"It is," Donnie said somberly, "I haven't felt myself the past couple of days. I feel like...I'm losing control."

"What do you mean?"

"I can feel it coming back. It's brewing inside me, and I don't want it to."

"What is?"

"When I came to San Antonio, I made a promise to my grandma. I promised I would never speak of what happened in Los Angeles...to never do the things I did there, over here...and now, I'm having a hard time holding it together."

"I'm here for you, bro...no matter what...whatever you need."

"I need to tell you something. It's been eating me up inside. I can't hold it in anymore."

"It's all right...take your time."

They went to the side of the building to the fire escape, kicking up dirt in their wake. The grass was still. The moon gave them some light as they climbed to the roof. Abraham led the way. He sensed that Donnie was in severe distress. They sat side by side with their feet dangling three stories high.

Donnie began. "I've never told anybody this, at least here, in San Antonio. I trust you."

"Of course..." Abraham reassured him, "this stays between you and me."

"A long time ago, there were seven of us. We started out doing normal kid stuff...stealing and just running around in the streets. I was fourteen. After that, it became addicting. It started escalating and then we started robbing people." Donnie stared at the streetlight down below. His recollections had not faded in the least. "The thrills were unlike anything I'd felt before. I felt powerful. I did horrible things, terrible things. Coming to San Antonio changed everything. I don't know what I'd do without my grandma. I owe her everything."

"That was a long time ago," Abraham recalled the stories Donnie once told. "All that doesn't matter anymore."

"Abraham...I did things I can never take back. Deep down, I know that I'm not right. I'm just not a good person."

"I don't believe that, Donnie. People make mistakes, but life goes on. We're only human...it's okay. You remember what I told you, it doesn't matter how hard you fall, all that matters is how you respond and you've responded well, brother. And let me tell you something else, you *are* a good person."

"Abraham, you don't understand. I'm not...*good.*"

"You *are*! You are what you believe, and if you believe you're not good, then that's what you'll be! The past is the past, and that's where it belongs. I don't wanna hear that kinda talk!"

"There's something else...and it's something that never goes away. Sometimes the past doesn't always stay in the past," Donnie said in a low voice, oblivious to the pep talks being shot his way. His feelings phased in and out of rage. Stillness seeped in, balancing the frequent stabs of fury, and it was then, that a calm revelation escaped through his teeth.

"I killed people."

Stunned, Abraham quickly denied his confession. "No, I don't believe that!" He couldn't comprehend Donnie taking a life.

"I robbed, broke into homes, vandalized businesses, stole cars, and harassed innocent people among other things…and I killed. And every time, it got easier. Do you know how easy it is to take a life? It's not hard at all."

Speechless, Abraham sat in silence. What words could he possibly conjure to respond to that? This version of Donnie was one that he was clearly not familiar with.

"Thank you, Abraham. You are the only real friend…true friend that I have ever had. Thanks for being there for me. You and my grandma are the only people to ever give me hope. I just needed someone to hear me out. I couldn't hold it in anymore. I'm trying to evolve as you say, trying to make myself better…and…it's hard. I don't want to go back to that…I don't want to live like that anymore…I *want* to be a good person."

"You *have* changed into a good person. You don't need to go back to that," Abraham pleaded.

"My struggle was never with the world…it was with myself." Donnie sat still. A teardrop escaped from his eye. He and the Darkness had been good friends way back then, and now, it called to him once more.

"Donnie, that life is gone, everything and everyone."

"I'm the only one left. Some are dead now. Some are in prison, and I was the only one that the police never caught or identified. I guess I got lucky." Tears streamed down his cheeks. He wiped his nose and continued, "I would go to my place, my sanctuary…up there by the Hollywood sign, just sitting…looking down at the city of angels, I felt like an angel, even after all the sin I had committed. That was the only place that no one could touch me and no one ever had a clue where I went."

The conversation ventured into a realm that Abraham was not prepared for. His counseling skills went out the window, and it was on a level so personal that only his faith was able to summon up tactics to help his friend.

Donnie confessed further, "I felt like two people. One of them saw the light, what a normal life would be like…and the other….

is like home. It's all I know. I was born with this sickness to cause hurt…to crave destruction."

Donnie felt the presence of an old friend. It snuck in like a thief in the night and was getting comfortable in a familiar place that it once resided. Donnie was giving his best efforts to render it askew, but it made no difference and he sensed it was only a matter of time before he succumbed to it.

No, no, I can beat you! I did it once before and I will do it again! Donnie continued to fight with urgency, and if Abraham was his only hope, then he needed him now more than ever.

"You know what I believe?" Abraham countered, "That people were created with a heck of a lot more good than evil. You could say it might have to do with your environment…Los Angeles…San Antonio…but it in the end, it has a lot to do with who you are. Look at the person you are now. The one that sits here, right in front of me, he is *good*. I know you believe that! Two different people, yes, but you have *chosen* to be good!" Abraham delivered a reasonable refutation and his optimism to bring Donnie out of the confusion remained unclear.

"I didn't choose to be all the other things! I didn't!"

"What other things? You are who you are," Abraham said with sincerity, "and you are my friend…you're my brother."

"Then why was I born a cancer? I don't mean the crab, I mean like the disease. Why did my parents give me this name that we shouldn't dare speak of? I know damn well where it comes from! My grandma won't tell me she's dying and she won't tell me what *really* happened to my parents. It's some big secret that I mustn't know about. You tell me, brother? Can you explain that? Maybe…I don't know, maybe I am sick. What if I'm not meant to be good? What if…I don't have a choice?" Donnie drifted off even further into the blackness.

"But you *do* have a choice! We all do!" Abraham struggled to reason with him.

"My destiny has already been chosen, I'm just fighting what I really am."

"No, you're choosing to be what you really aren't. It's choice versus destiny. Your destiny may be decided, but it's the path we choose to follow that makes us who we are. God is testing you to help you break free! It's up to you. Bitter or better…"

"I don't wanna take this bullshit test!" Emotions discharged furiously. The Darkness capitalized at the outburst. *No, you're not gonna win today! I can beat you!* Donnie orchestrated his calming techniques, the ones that Grandma Josie taught him to keep his nerves under control when they were threatened with anger. "All I know is that I did a lot of bad things and I hope that God has forgiven me," his voice leveled out to a tranquil tone.

"Don't forget to forgive yourself. Let it go…" Abraham did his best to match the intensity of the trials they faced in the moment at hand and his empathic abilities helped to sway the sickness off course temporarily.

"Survival means sacrifice and I can't tell the difference anymore…I can't tell if I'm winning or losing." Donnie sniffled. Redness took over his nose as his light complexion faded. Without wavering, teardrops rolled down his cheeks. A tune played softly. The Nokia phone in his pocket rang.

"Hello?" he answered softly. "Yes, this is Donnie."

The woman on the other end of the line did not hesitate to deliver unfavorable news.

"What happened?" he asked.

Relentless, the Darkness neither slowed nor wavered. It pierced and prodded, searching for a way to wreak destruction once again through the fleshly vessel it once inhabited.

"Okay, I'll be right there…" Donnie said, as he hung up the phone clearly disturbed.

Abraham put his arm around his friend, hoping to transfer positive energy to lead confusion and stress astray. He immediately sensed his pain, his struggle, and his current trial. It was internal, deep in the core, and the conflict never ceased.

"I gotta go…she's not doing good…" Donnie said, wiping his tears away.

"Don't worry, brother," Abraham reassured him, "I'm gonna stick till the end."

Donnie swiftly vacated the rooftop, and he disappeared into the night.

The Mustang roared as it sped off down below. Abraham tracked the car until it was out of sight. He took a moment to gather himself. The emotional transference disrupted his natural frequency, and he patiently rerouted his reserves to bring his higher state of consciousness back online.

He remained on the rooftop of the old Seed Company building, keeping watch on the neighborhood below. *How are we gonna get out of this one?* he thought. They faced many trials together, but this one was drastically different. Abraham began his process of survival the only way he knew how, through prayer.

"God, please guide Donnie…show him the way…he is hurting, confused, and lost. He needs You more than ever. Please allow me to be the instrument to bring him back to You. In Jesus name, I pray. Amen."

XXIV
CRACKS IN THE ARMOR

"Grandma! What happened?" Donnie ran in hysterically. He and hospitals were not friends. He despised them like a dog would a cat. Love sprouted in his heart in recent years, but no love grew for the cold place he sat in with Grandma.

She groaned softly in her half-conscious state.

"Sir?" The nurse entered quietly as he was oblivious to his surroundings. "Are you her grandson?"

"Yes, I am," he replied, never taking his eyes off Grandma. Grandma lay still, helpless.

"I'm glad you're here. My name is Amy and I've been with her since she arrived. Does she have any medical conditions? Any medication she is allergic to?"

He glanced at her wristband. Eyeballing the date of her birth, he memorized it with one look.

Josephine Garcia 2-29-32

Leap year, she can't be in serious condition, she is only seventeen years old, he thought. Constantly looking for loopholes or a way to evade danger, he had always come through, but death, he could not escape.

"No…" he said, holding Grandma Josie's hand. "I don't believe so."

Grandma Josie reached for him, placing both hands around his. "You need to know something. Your parents…" Grandma breathed little by little, struggling to get out the words that she so desperately needed to. "Your parents were alive when you came to me. They loved you. Your mother…she didn't know you survived. She thought you died at birth…she made plans to see you…" Grandma fought to breathe now. Donnie let her speak as much as she could. He listened intently to every word. His greatest fear was coming to light. He was losing her, and as her life hung in the balance, his sanity did as well.

"She came from Boston…I spoke to her before she made her way. I didn't know…it would be the last time…I'm…sorry…I, I couldn't tell you because I knew…it would break your heart…it broke mine." Weaker and weaker she grew, but still she mumbled on, getting her words out as promptly as she could.

"Her plane fell and…so many others went down, too, that day."

With tears gushing out, he held on to her hand. His other fist clenched; holding his forehead, he cried hard in silence. The pain grew exponentially, and there were no signs of it subsiding.

"And…my dad? Is he alive?" Donnie squeezed out the words before it was too late.

"He wasn't…he wasn't a good man. He did a lot of bad…in the world." Grandma was fading. Her light was getting dimmer as the minutes passed.

With a tremble in his voice, he pleaded with her. "Grandma, just tell me. I need to know."

She made a promise to herself, never to tell him the truth, but that promise, she couldn't keep anymore. It was time for him to know, for better or for worse. "He died the same day, mijo…the other plane went down. There were four that didn't make it."

That fateful day, Donnie remembered it like it was yesterday, and so did the rest of country, for that matter.

"A lot of people died that day?"

She nodded, ever so slowly.

"When the towers fell?" he asked for confirmation, but he already knew the answer. "He stopped them?"

"No..." she hesitated, grasping for air, "he helped them...I am not proud of him and what he became...I am proud of you...you have a lot of him...in you...all the mistakes I made with him...I wanted to make right with you...mijo...your mama loved you... and your father did too. I know he did...because he gave you up..."

"If...if he loved me...as you say...then why would he? Why would he...give me up?"

"He gave you to a loving family...a good home...something he could never give you, mijo. A better life, he wanted for you. This, he told me...he couldn't change...what he was."

Donnie had reached a place he had never been before. Pain ran deep, and the more information he heard, the more his soul was spewing out of control.

"I didn't want to tell you...but you have to know...the truth..." She struggled to gather herself. "Mijo, don't be like your father..." Her voice trailed off. Her eyes fluttered and her gray hair lay tucked behind her head, resting in the pillow.

Donnie panicked, realizing they had little time left together. He squeezed her hand tightly, as if to give her more life through his, more time to stay with him. Stability gave way, and he was busting at the seams. Emotions, like a tidal wave, overtook him, and he was traveling to a place he had never been and, in turn, to a place he didn't want to be. Stunned, he held her hand with the both of his.

"Grandma, I don't know what to do! What do I do without you?" Donnie cried out helplessly.

"You have...my...book...use it."

"Your Bible?"

"Yes..." She struggled for a breath. "It's...yours...now."

"Grandma, please don't leave me...I need you!"

"Mijo, just...love..."

He waited for her to finish. He waited and waited...

A breath emerged from her body after a few seconds, and a few seconds after that, one more sputtered out into the open air, in a room now lifeless and deprived.

"Grandma? Grandma!"

He shook her arm. Tears poured out. His blurry vision didn't distract him from the moment at hand. His hands didn't let go of hers. "Grandma, wake up!"

It was his last chance. A last chance to bring her back into consciousness, and with each passing second, the chances of her never returning increased dramatically.

Grandma was gone.

His soul began decaying. The long journey to feel love and empathy, happiness and joy, all the years of building up to what this great city brought to him, was erased in seconds. Love left him. Happiness scoured away. Hope withered. And as she passed, his soul died with her.

He could feel himself returning to what he once was. *Don't be like your dad,* he thought. Grandma asked that of him, with her final words, and he was incapable of making her final orders come to light.

No, Grandma, I can't do this, he thought. His inner light ceased, as his moral values began the rotting process. Darkness took hold at once, and even with his reserves working overtime, his soul seeped into blackness.

XXV
SHOCKWAVE

Liv sat crisscross style on the floor, enamored with his enlivened story of scheming. "I'm working on a surprise. It's a good one, too! I must go on a top secret mission! I'll let you know all the—"

Abraham froze. His smile of excitement dissipated. His expression was stone-faced and filled with worry.

"What's wrong?" Liv panicked. She jumped toward him, guiding him to her bed. "Here, sit down."

He stared blankly, concentrating on the wall in front of him. His brow crinkled and his mouth gradually dropped.

"Baby, what's wrong? You're scaring me."

A bombardment of nervous anxiety fell over him. He tugged on his ear, struggling to dispatch the uneasiness that came over him. "I don't know…something's wrong."

"Are you feeling sick?"

"Something's happened…" He moved his shoulders up and down, trying to shake off the overwhelming disturbance. "Someone close to me, they're in distress."

"Who is it?"

"I can't pinpoint it, but something is definitely out of place… gimme a second to catch my breath."

Liv picked up his arm and placed it around her neck. She kissed his cheek and rubbed his chest in a circular motion. "Calm down, baby."

He let out a deep breath. "Thank you. I don't know what I'd do without you." He half-smiled, hiding the queasiness in his stomach.

"Just relax," she said calmly.

His head sprang up from meditation. "It's Donnie. I think he's in trouble."

"Are you gonna go to him?"

"Yeah. I think I know where he is." He slowly stood up from her bed as she massaged his hand.

"I'll be here waiting." Liv said with a heartfelt smile.

Abraham revved up the M3. He allowed his feelings to facilitate the computations of Donnie's whereabouts. His instincts never lied nor were they rarely wrong.

He let his heart guide him.

The drive over to May's house seemed like a lifetime. She lived a couple of miles away and the apprehension began to overtake him. As he turned on her street, he was ready to see it with his own eyes.

He called Donnie's phone. No response.

His knee began to shake uncontrollably as he pulled closer to the residence. Breathing heavily, he saw the vehicle on the street. The Mustang was parked stealthily by the curb, and the deceptive forces that brought him here kept him for a minute longer.

That's why he didn't answer, Abraham thought.

He maneuvered for another pass. Driving past the front yard, the anxiety began to decline. "At least he's safe," he muttered.

Cruising to the stoplight, his phone rang. *That was fast,* he thought. "Hey, are you all right?"

"Yeah, uh, yeah." Donnie was able to squeeze out a few words.

"Talk to me. I know when you're lying. How bad is it?" Abraham waited patiently for a response.

"I'm all right, I'm just fixing to go to sleep. I'll brief you in the morning."

"Are you at home?" Abraham questioned, sensing his deceitfulness.

"Yeah."

"Look, you don't have to lie to me. Just let me know that you're okay."

"You don't deserve her, you never did. She deserves better, someone like me."

Abraham recognized the transformation taking shape. "All right, Donnie, are we really gonna do this or what? You've lied to me twice now. You don't fool me. Going after May isn't going to make things better. Just be straight up with the truth! Otherwise, I can't help you!" Abraham listened intently for a response, but dead air was all he received. "Don't make me do this." Abraham closed his eyes. He dropped into silence and set his search in motion.

"Stay out of my head!" Donnie yelled through the cell phone, clenching his fist. He squeezed his eyes shut to prevent any unauthorized entry.

"I gave you two chances to be straight up with me. I'm family, I shouldn't have to do this!" Abraham struggled to maintain his emotional outbursts.

"Look, I'm sorry, I just can't deal with this right now," Donnie said, dejected.

Abraham backed off and canceled the mental breach. "Okay, I'll let you be. I just need to know one thing. Are you at May's? Just be honest," Abraham instinctively gave him one last chance for the truth.

"No."

The third lie was enough. *He's up to something and it's bad,* he thought. Abraham continued the interrogation fishing for clues, "Your grandma is not doing good, is she?"

"I said I'll brief you in the morning!" Donnie said in a raised voice.

"Brief me tomorrow." Abraham dropped his pursuit to uncover the truth for the time being. *What the hell just happened?* he thought. "I've never had to this before…he's family," he said quietly.

Abraham set course back to the only woman who could emotionally repair him, the only woman who could pull off such a feat for that matter. Amidst the realization of the path Donnie was headed, he knew that he was going to need Liv if he was to have any chance of a breakthrough.

Liv walked out to the street in her pajamas. The light pink color doused with Supergirl emblems provided some relief along with her smile, as he pulled up to her house.

"Nice touch," he said, referring to her nighttime selection. He gingerly crawled out of the vehicle like a battered boxer.

"Do you feel better? Is he okay?"

"No."

She wrapped her arms around him. "You look like you need a hug."

His arms swarmed her as his body and mind decompressed. "You always seem to know what I need."

"Don't worry, baby. It'll be okay."

He released a heavy gasp. He never thought the day would come when he had to use tactics on the one person he never needed to. He had to tell Liv the truth. She was too quick to recognize when things were out of balance. He sensed a storm on the horizon. He gripped her tighter than ever before and calmly confessed. "No, it's not. Something worse is brewing."

XXVI
FALLOUT

"You wanted to see me?" Abraham questioned her motives.

"Abraham, I need to talk to you. He is going nuts! I don't know what is going on with him and you, but he's not acting right. He's out of control…" Tears swelled up and her voice shook. May was not one to be shaken easily, and her urgent request to see Abraham was not her usual.

"What's going on?"

"His grandma died last night."

"What? He didn't even tell me. I knew something was wrong, but he refused to talk to me."

"He got mad and then he…" May let a few tears escape as she desperately tried to gather herself. "He tried to punch me."

"What! What happened?"

"He tried asking me out and I said no. You and him are like family, and I couldn't do that to you. He insisted and I refused. He came over last night. He said he needed a friend and I guess he thought it was his chance to coerce me into being his…"

The ding of an incoming text caught his attention, "This is him, I know it." Abraham opened the message and read it carefully. With eyebrows raised, he handed her the phone. "Read it," he instructed her.

"I think May is mad at me. She wanted to go out and I rejected her, so there, I didn't lie."

"What an asshole! I'm so disgusted! What is wrong with him?" A few more tears ran down her cheek.

"I don't understand why he didn't come to me. I could've helped him," Abraham paused, "It doesn't make sense. Why would he do this?"

"He said you were always with Liv now and that you had changed."

"That's not true! I've always been there for him. He knew that." He turned to face the street and paced toward the car. "I could've helped him," he mumbled.

"Abraham!" May screamed. "He's calling me!" In the palm of her hand, her phone vibrated vigorously. She answered harshly, "What do you want?"

"I just want to know if you're still mad?" Donnie asked calmly.

"You're lucky I didn't call the cops!" May looked over at Abraham. "I'm gonna put him on speaker," she whispered to him.

Abraham crept back to the front steps of the house. He listened to the lies Donnie spewed out.

"It's my fault. I'm not in a good place right now. Lucy broke up with me, my grandma died yesterday, and Abraham abandoned me. You're all I have left."

May snarled. Her eyes fumed with anger as she shook her head back and forth.

"If you want to keep your friends, I suggest you start telling them the truth."

"It's done, I have no friends! The real truth is you could've been happy with me. He has everything. I don't get it, he doesn't deserve it…or you. You're making a big mistake."

"No, I'm avoiding one," May argued against his plea, "We are just friends, nothing more. I take that back, I don't want to be your friend at all! You don't know how to treat your friends, much less keep them!"

Donnie heaved his phone at the wall, and it exploded to pieces. May fueled a fury he hadn't felt in years, and he welcomed it like an old friend. He focused on his next move, and like a deadly flowing magma, he inched closer to burning everyone around him.

He picked up the phone and dialed from the land line in an empty house he no longer called home.

"Hello..." the mystery girl answered.

"I can give you directions and I promise you, you will find him."

* * * * *

May seethed with anger. Her whole body shook, enraged at the daring attempt he made to reconcile. "I can't believe what he's become. He's sick."

Abraham placed a hand on her arm. "Let it go. He won't bother you anymore." Distraught at his behavior, he consoled her and processed this turn of events. "I did nothing wrong to him."

"He's jealous of you...he hates that he can't be like you."

"That's exactly what Liv said...I don't understand. He had all the potential in the world to be something great. This is not him."

"Abraham, maybe this *is* him."

She reached out to give him a hug. "I'm sorry. He is not the person we once knew. He's not your family anymore." She held him tighter. It was the closest she had been to him in a long time. *Only if he could be mine again,* she thought. Without missing a beat, she spoke of what she witnessed a few nights before and of the girl who had his heart.

"Liv must be a great girl," she said with sorrow.

"She is."

"When I heard you and Avril were done, I thought there might be a chance again."

"A chance?" he questioned, fishing for details.

"To be with you...I don't think neither of us was done with each other yet."

With a heavy sigh, he thought about his next words carefully. He desired for reconciliation with her, but that was before Liv. Liv had changed things dramatically for him, and now, it was he that couldn't return to a relationship that once carried so many possibilities.

Her five foot three frame glimmered with hope. Patient for his response, she stroked the back of his head, as she once did years ago.

"You're right. I wasn't done, but now…I'm not there anymore. I'm sorry."

"You looked happy the other night with her. She means a lot to you, I can tell," she said as she digested the agonizing truth.

Abraham looked her in the eye with a mouthful of certainty. "She does."

"Abraham, do you think…" she delayed, uncertain in asking the question, "there will ever be an 'us' again?"

He struggled to keep his composure. A year ago, those words would've made him shout atop the Tower of Americas that she was his, but now, they didn't mean nearly as much. He knew in his heart that he wanted Liv. He was at a loss for words. He rallied the best response to explain the truth. "May, I need to tell you—"

A screech of tires blared in the neighborhood as they skid on the street. "You motherfucker! I found you! You're not done with me yet! He told me you'd be at this whore's house!"

Shock overpowered the both of them. *What the hell is she doing here? How did she find us?* he thought.

Avril got out of the car quickly, leaving it in the middle of the street. That was the least of her worries as she marched to the sidewalk.

May pulled him by the hand. "Come on, let's go inside."

"You're a fucking liar and a cheater! I hate you!" Avril continued her onslaught of expletives.

"Avril, you're a freaking psycho! Leave me alone, already! It's over!" Abraham yelled.

"Does she know about your other whore, Liv? You're a fucking asshole! Donnie was right about you! You ain't shit! He told me where to find you! Some friends, you have!" Avril heaved insults in with no remorse.

Abraham stopped one step shy of entering the house. Emotions loomed heavy as he contemplated to unleash them on Avril. "Just like old times," he whispered. He turned around to face her, and at that moment, he felt a tug on his arm.

"Abraham, don't. She's not worth it. Just let her, she'll go away after a while," May urged him to reconsider. His anger began to swell, but she was right. He turned to May and stepped inside the house.

"Come back here, you asshole!" Avril's rants continued as neighbors peeked out to see the ruckus. Her efforts didn't waiver as they heard her yells from inside the house.

May redirected her concentration on Abraham. She surveyed his baby face and his soft cheeks. His eyes were fierce and powerful, and she always wondered what lay behind them. His inner thoughts she could never read, but not once did she doubt that his decisions were for the best.

"Abraham, you need to be careful. You can't trust anyone that is a mutual friend to him. He'll exploit you any chance he gets." She looked upon him with concern.

"That's why I have to prepare," he uttered, deep in thought.

"For what?"

"For battle…" he said, sighing heavily, "I know him well, and he's getting ready. I don't want to leave anything to chance."

"Wait until Avril leaves and then I'll go with you," May said eagerly, ready to stand by his side once more, even if it was just for support.

"No, you have to stay here. It's just like you said, he'll use anyone I know against me and I don't want to risk you getting hurt," he reminded her as he lunged forward, going down to one knee.

"Prayer?" she asked, reminiscing on his faith-based background.

He cupped his hands together and meditatively closed his eyes, seeking the energy to revitalize and protect him from the dangers of the world. He brought her attention back to the reason she asked him to come. "Darkness never takes a day off."

XXVII
BREAKING BREAD

Sitting across from one another, the two men glared at each other. The aroma in the restaurant was overwhelming. Once a festive place for them, none of the intricacies mattered anymore.

"Hi, Rosita, we'll have our usual," Abraham said, never breaking concentration on the staring contest.

Rosita took the order, glancing over at Donnie. She looked back to Abraham. "Todo está bien, Abrahan? *Is everything okay, Abraham?*"

"Yes, Rosita. Gracias. *Thank you.*"

Rosita smiled and walked over to the kitchen, allowing the two men converse. In a voice of desperate need, Donnie spoke first, "Man, why don't you talk to me anymore? I hate this shit. I have no one to talk to."

Abraham stayed quiet for a moment. Donnie sulked in his chair; his hands remained in his pockets with a distressed crinkled brow.

"The last time we were here…our lives were heading in different directions. It didn't matter where we were going because we stuck together. Now, that is the least of my worries. I forgive you. What you did was wrong, but I can forgive."

The sorrow in Donnie's eyes caused Abraham to doubt his decision.

"Abraham, I'm sorry, I let emotions get the best of me."

"Emotions come with a price…"

"I know," Donnie said softly, "You know, if it were anybody else, I usually wouldn't give a fuck about any of my actions."

"It doesn't have to be that way…you should always apologize when you are wrong, and it shouldn't matter who you have wronged…" Abraham said, unwavering, "as long as you apologize and are better for it."

"I'm not perfect. I'm not like you, always right," Donnie sneered sarcastically.

"After all this time, you truly don't know what I'm about. I'm not mad at you…after all we've been through…and you want to betray me like this…" Abraham paused, searching for a loophole to justify his actions, but the damage was done and there was no such validation he could give. "I forgive you, but you're just another person to me now."

Donnie acknowledged the statement with silence. His reluctance to accept another loss spawned the last remaining goodness in him to appeal. "Well, if it is going to be this way then, I am truly sorry for what I did. I lost my grandma and I wasn't thinking straight. I've been spiraling out of control. My whole life has been a lie," he said in a calm manner. He sputtered out the final remnants of light left in him. Darkness struck fiercely at his heart.

Abraham looked on him with sadness. "I can't help you anymore. There are bigger things going on in my life than me and you right now. I'm sorry, Donnie."

"Don't call me that. I'm not going by Donnie anymore. You can call me by my real name now. Go ahead, say it!"

Abraham shook his head slowly. "I'm not."

"You never had a problem wanting to say it before. Go ahead, you can tell everyone now. It's what I am…a sickness, a disease, a cancer. This, this is who I really am. You don't know me. You never did!" Donnie allowed the rage to swell. It engulfed him, and he let the darkness consume his every nerve.

"No, that ain't who you are."

"I'm tired of hiding who I really am! This *is* my true self. Abbadon! Say it out loud. Come on!"

Abraham refused to speak.

"Don't punk out now! Say it!" Donnie provoked him, frantically seeking a way to get a rise out of him.

"I can't. I disagree." Abraham witnessed the transformation taking shape. On his end, hope held strong, as the darkness flooded the compartments in the fleshly capsule that belonged to Donnie. His brother was giving up, and no earthly action could counter it. "You are lost, Donnie."

Failure to evoke emotion, Donnie retreated to a calm state. "I'm actually better than I've ever been. This is what needed to happen, and if you're not with me then, am I to say that you're against me?"

"As long as you don't cross me again, then we'll be good. But make no mistake, if we are at opposite ends again, I'll be ready for you."

"You don't know me! You don't know what I'm capable of!" Donnie threatened.

"Likewise…but the question is, how far are you willing to go?"

"Oh, I think you know the answer to that. You are one of only a few people that know my history. Consider it a privilege and a warning of what you might become."

"There is a huge difference though, Donnie. All those people whose lives you took were helpless, unsuspecting, and not ready for what was coming. They didn't have a chance. I'll be ready."

"We shall see." Donnie was determined to make his intentions known. "But make no mistake, I do what I do, and if you get in my way, I will not hesitate to bring you down by any means necessary."

Their eyes locked, fiercely entangled once again in a staring match. Abraham leaned over and spoke defiantly, "Never bluff unless you're prepared to back it up."

"You of all people know, I'm not bluffing."

"When I came here today, I thought that there was something to salvage from the good man I once knew. But I see now that there's nothing left to salvage. I wish it were different…" Abraham began to let go. The transformation took them both by surprise, and now the point of no return was upon them. Donnie's eyes took on an unfamiliar guise consumed with hate. "I can't save somebody that doesn't want to be saved. I leave it in God's hands."

"Fuck this!" Donnie banged on the table and stood up, kicking the chair out from under him. The patrons in the restaurant froze at the thunderous bellow.

The plates Rosita carried plummeted to the floor. A loud crash echoed in the restaurant as food splattered every which way and ceramic exploded into dozens of pieces.

"I'll get you this time." Abraham raised his finger, pointing to the food and mess spread out on the floor.

"I'll get you the next." Donnie pointed his finger at Abraham in a threatening manner, as he walked out of the restaurant peacefully.

The process of recovery was immediately set in motion. Severing every known connection to Donnie irrevocably meant discarding a part of his own life as well.

"Donnie is gone," he whispered.

Life is full of twists and turns, remember that! Abraham coached himself as he'd always done.

Recover!

He endured verbal punches that foreshadowed a showdown yet to come.

Prepare for battle... Internally, he commenced the mental training. If Avril had taken him to the limit, then this meant a whole new level of spiritual warfare he'd never known. Donnie was well equipped to unleash far much worse.

No! He reasoned, *God will fight for me...*

The person in his midst was not one he knew. Abraham bowed his head in prayer, "Let it go...he doesn't exist anymore. The ghost from his past has taken his place. His name is Abbadon now. Don't let darkness overtake him. If there is any light left in him, let it shine through. I trust, You will find a way. In Jesus name we pray. Amen."

Darkness, however, clamored with victory.

XXVIII
FROM THE BOTTOMLESS PIT

June 1978

    He studied the home extensively. The family that occupied it had longed for a surprise that only God could deliver, and He chose this night to answer their prayers. The individual, shrouded in darkness, devised a plan to give his progeny a chance. He had no choice but to relinquish, perhaps, his only hope at a normal life and give a worthy family this precious gift. Delivering his blood to complete strangers would alleviate stress. This would be the last time he would lay eyes on the only beautiful thing he could ever create. The light began to chip away at the blackness that surrounded his heart. He felt its strength demanding to break through, and he despised its presence. This was the only way to escape its relentless attempts.

    He placed the package on the front step and placed the note inside. It expressed his only request for what he would never see again. He rang the doorbell and walked away from a life that would've been great, but it just wasn't meant to be. He had work to do. The light that pleaded to purge the ice from his heart faded away, as he did, into the black of night.

Josef and Maria were about to sit down for dinner when they heard a ring at the door. They looked at each other surprised and wondered who the mystery caller could be. Josef crinkled his brow, causing his eyeglasses to shift slightly. He pretended not to notice the hazel flow of discomfort that streamed from Maria's eyes. He sprang up from his chair and in a firm voice said to Maria, "I'll see who it is, honey." He hoped that his assertiveness would do the trick of diminishing her worries.

Josef walked over to the door, praying it wasn't a hoodlum asking for money. The Bazans didn't exactly live in the best neighborhood. The new subdivision sat borderline to the mean streets of the crime-ridden Compton. With new houses going up by the day, hooligans feasted their eyes on new hunting grounds.

He wanted to open the door hesitantly, but he did not want his wife to sense the fear brewing inside. With a firm grip, he reacted forcefully awaiting a mugger on the other side. Josef prepared himself to look into the eyes of the would-be assailant. Much to his surprise, no one stood in front of him. Puzzled and relieved, he immediately thought some jokester sat hidden in the bushes, laughing at their latest prank. He stepped forward and, unbeknownst to him, accidentally kicked a package with a blue blanket draped over it. Josef knelt over and uncovered the unexpected gift. Shock ran through his body as he fell silent.

"Maria!" Josef shouted with disbelief.

Maria jumped up frightened and rushed to the door. With tears in his eyes, Josef spoke, "Maria, He did it, He answered our prayers!"

Josef moved aside so she could see the miracle on the doorstep.

"Oh my! It can't be." Tears streamed down her cheek. Her depression ceased the moment she laid eyes on the prize before her. "A beautiful baby boy!"

"God brought this gift into our lives and the proof sits at our doorstep. I can't believe it..." Josef reached in the carrier and found an envelope tucked next to the baby boy.

"There must be somebody out there," she insisted. "Perhaps, somebody left him by accident."

As he opened the letter, he looked up at Maria. "I don't think so, Maria. He was left here purposely..."

With much reluctance, he read the letter out loud.

"He needs a good family to raise him. I chose the both of you to do me this honor. I cannot give him the life he deserves, and the Lord knows that he needs it tenfold, and so I give him to you. There is only one thing I ask of you and that is to keep the name that I have chosen for him. Please respect my wishes. His name is Abbadon."

"Abbadon?" Josef pondered the name, "Abbadon." He folded the letter and placed it back into the envelope. "I know that name," he whispered to himself. "I know where it comes from. Who, in their right mind, would name their child that?"

"Josef, I don't think that's an appropriate—"

"I don't know if we should keep him," Josef cut off Maria before she could finish her sentence, "An abandoned baby? Maybe he's not meant for us. We should call it in and report it."

"No!" Maria shouted. "We can't do that! We can't just let him go!" She bargained for the infant's life in desperation, "He *is* meant for us! You read the letter, whoever left him wants *us* to raise him! It's a Godsend...Josef, please don't turn him in," she pleaded. "This is our chance...to have a child of our own."

His nerves calmed for the moment. She spoke with such conviction that he stopped dead in his tracks on his way to the phone in the living room. "Honey...I'm just trying to do the right thing."

"This *is* the right thing!"

"Is it? I don't know...this is crazy. And what if we aren't supposed to do this? I mean, who are we to take care of this baby? An abandoned baby at that!" His mind flooded with doubt.

"Who are we not to take on this blessing?" She attempted to put his doubt in perspective. Unbuckling the baby boy, she wrapped his light blue blanket around him and held him close.

Josef rarely disagreed with his wife. He trusted her. He loved her, and it was her love that brought him to believe in a higher power. Together, they made a good team and he relied on her willpower to see them through the toughest of challenges. He consoled her when fear overpowered will, and it was his emotional strength and intellect that kept their foundation solid.

"Are you sure…that we can do this? Can we really raise a baby… that's not ours? That we found on a doorstep?" Worried, he contemplated the obstacles to come.

"Josef, look at me…" She grabbed his arm as she held the baby boy. "We can do this!"

His reluctance began to sway. "Okay…I put my faith in you."

"Don't put your faith in me," she reminded him, "put it in God. This gift in my hands is from Him. Don't lose faith now." Her face drooped almost to a frown. "I need you."

He dealt a heavy sigh upon hearing her words. "You do a great job at making me think twice. It's hard for me to turn down your persuasive powers," he said with a grin. "I guess I don't have a choice," he chuckled.

"Our vows, how quickly you forget. I'm with you to the end, remember?"

He nodded and looked into her beautiful hazel eyes. "I'm with you to the end."

"Then this is our family now," she spoke with confidence, eager to begin the journey, "And the name, I don't—"

"Maria, it's just a name. It will have nothing to do with how we raise him."

"He's just an innocent baby…we can't keep that name for him. It's not right…" she said in a voice of reason.

"Have faith, like you said. Trust me. You convinced me to keep him." He gaped into her hazel eyes, searching for her understanding. "Please honor this request."

"Even if it goes against everything we believe?" she questioned.

"It doesn't. This will be an opportunity to show the world that miracles do happen. And just because he has this name, there is still a great chance for good. Besides, this is a blessing. It is the least we can do. I'm with you to the end, remember?"

Maria giggled. "Now you're the negotiator, huh? Can you believe this? We have a baby!"

Josef hugged the both of them. He glided his hand through her hair and kissed her on the forehead. "God is good."

XXIX
M POWER

At this point, Ron remained a man without a face. "Abraham, I'm telling you…come on up to Dallas…you won't regret it. I got her sitting out here all nice and pretty."

Soon, Abraham would have a face to go along with the voice on the other end of the phone.

"All right, I'll tell you what. Let me call you back in a couple of hours, and I'll let you know if I'm going to make my way up there. And if I do, it will be tonight. Sound good?"

Seeing the prize up close was a tantalizing thought. His mouth watered at the idea of adding another to his collection, and more importantly, it was a collector's item that he would share with the woman who owned his heart.

"That sounds great, Abraham. I can pick you up at the airport… just let me know what time," Ron spoke with genuine excitement.

"Okay, I'll call you in approximately two hours. Oh and by the way, I'll be bringing my wife. She has no clue. It's a surprise for her."

"Bring her! She's going to love it."

"Talk to you shortly, Ron."

♌

Abraham moved in on the counter surreptitiously. "Mam, I'm so embarrassed to say this, but you are so incredibly gorgeous. Do you have a boyfriend?"

"Baby! You came to see me!" Liv exclaimed.

"I thought I'd surprise you."

"You did! I love surprises!" she said, batting her eyes with a huge smile.

"And I love giving them! I treasure that look on your face every time I show up unexpectedly. You look great in that barista outfit."

"Oh, please. I look horrible," Liv gasped. "It's fun working here in the middle of the store, though. Lots of strange people stroll by."

"It's the southside, remember?" Abraham reminded her of the clientele residing in the surrounding neighborhoods. Growing up on this side of town had its trials, as well as its traditions. "This H-E-B is nice! I need to do my grocery shopping here more often."

"Yes, you do!" She demanded, "Because I'm here now and you can come see me and then shop, in that order. Got it?"

He snickered, admiring her aggressiveness. "I'm sure all the guys ask if you have a boyfriend. Don't lie…" he said jokingly.

"Well, what should I tell them? Do I?" Liv batted her eyes flirtatiously at him.

"I don't know. *Do you?*"

"You're so silly."

"You probably tell them no, don't you?" he said jokingly.

"Do you want me to say yes?" she said, with hope flowing from her voice.

"Actually, I do. I want you to say yes…to joining me on a business trip. Will you accompany me?"

"Hi, Abraham!" A woman popped out from the back. She was an older woman in her forties and manager at the coffee shop.

"Hi, Denise!" Abraham greeted her.

She had grown used to his visits and slipped him a caramel macchiato. "Not that you need it," she said with a chuckle, "You're always so full of energy."

"Thank you!" he said, smiling, "And this is why I come over here…I feel like royalty!"

"No flowers today?" she asked, surprised.

"Nope. I got somethin' better!"

"Really? Liv is a lucky lady," she said, glancing at Liv.

Liv innocently blushed. "I am."

He focused his attention back on Liv, "So, lucky lady…"

"I get off in an hour. Will you wait for me?" she replied, unsuspecting of the spontaneity that awaited.

"Of course, I'll wait for you!"

"What kind of trip is it today, Mr. Abraham?" She recognized his intentions of whisking her away on one of his escapades.

"The kind of trip that requires a plane…" He enjoyed captivating her with his choice of words as her light brown eyes lit up.

"Right now?"

"Yes, as soon as you get off work."

"I thought you meant a trip to the other side of town! Where will we be going?"

"Dallas," he said with confidence.

"Abraham, are you serious? Why? You're joking right?"

"I can't tell you why, but I need to know if you will go with me. Right here, right now, we leave with just the clothes on our back. We can catch a plane as soon as you get out of work." Abraham pulled his cell phone out of his pocket, ready to make the call on her command.

"Oh my gosh! I need to go home and change first. I don't want to go in my work clothes!"

"So is it a yes?"

"Yes, baby!"

Abraham hopped on the phone and swiftly made the transaction. Within five minutes, two seats were secured bound for Dallas. "Liv, our plane leaves in two hours, so once you clock out, we have no time to waste."

Astonished at his fantastical whims, she smiled from ear to ear, shaking her head. "You are crazy, you know that?"

"I've been told. You're rollin' with Abraham Moreno now!"

"You sure know how to sweep me off my feet," she said blushing. She appreciated his methods of living in the moment, standing by his side soaking up the impulsiveness of life. "Did all your other girlfriends reap these kinds of benefits?"

"Just you, honey bunny! That's the truth."

♋

"Baby, I can't believe we're doing this. Are you sure it's okay? I mean, me tagging along on your business trip?" she said in awe, switching her gaze from him to the airplane window and back.

"Of course, I need you on this one," he said slyly. "Oh, by the way, I kinda told the guy we're meeting that you were, uh, that you were kinda…" He sighed with a sharp smile. "My wife."

"Seriously?" She beamed bashfully. "Well, it's believable. We both have the same last name."

"There you go! So would you do me the honor of being my wife this evening?" he asked politely.

"Absolutely!"

"This role-playing is gonna be fun! We have about twenty minutes before we land, so I'm gonna go ahead and prepare for the role." Abraham put on his serious face. "Let me get in character."

"You're such a dork, I swear!"

"But you love it!"

"That, I do. I love you, Mr. Moreno," she said with passion, as she had done countless times before.

"Whoa, easy now!"

"What? I'm getting into character!"

Laughing hysterically together, they admired each other, and even as the plane descended from the heavens, they remained high up in the clouds.

♌ ♋

He did his best to conceal his excitement. He peeked over at Liv. She had no clue yet of the events unfolding before her. Ron had been gracious enough to pick them up from the airport as they were minutes away from the surprise.

"It's finally good to meet you, Abraham!" Ron greeted them as he stepped outside the car.

"It's good to finally meet you too, Ron! Thanks for picking us up at the airport. I really appreciate it." Abraham glanced at Liv, giving her an encouraging smile.

"I know you're up to something," she said quietly.

He sensed the anxiety streaming in her body language. "You okay, baby?"

"Yeeeeesss," she responded in an attempt to control her nervousness.

Abraham hopped in the front seat and Liv occupied the back. "She gets a little shy sometimes. I asked her to accompany me on this business trip. I hope you don't mind, Ron."

"Not a problem at all. I'm glad you could make it out here with your husband, Liv. He's quite a character."

Liv laughed. "Oh, I know! Believe me!"

Abraham chuckled at the exchange. She had no idea what was up his sleeve. "So, Ron, how long have you been in business?"

"A few years now, we have a small location about ten minutes from the airport. That's where we have the product of interest for you to view, and let me tell you, it's nice!"

"If it's as sharp as you say it is then, I'll have no problem signing off on it. Oh, and as long as my wife approves, it's a done deal!"

"All right, you won't be disappointed!" Ron turned back to glance at Liv. "Liv, you're gonna love it!"

Ron pulled into the parking lot and presented the gem that brought all of them together. He staged it beautifully to sit in front upon entering, as it sparkled beautifully in the moonlight.

They exited the vehicle and walked over to the prize.

"Do you know why we are here?" Ron asked Liv as all eyes were on her.

"No," she said calmly, with her eyes moving side to side.

"We are here for you. *This* is going to be yours." He outstretched his hand, slowly swiveling his body and arm around in unison, until it was in direct alignment with a shiny black car. The stunning sedan boasted chrome wheels and the limo tint covered the car, suitable for a covert operation. "Let me go get the key, so we can take it out for a spin."

Abraham reached for Liv and put his arm around her. "Baby, do you like it? This is why we came on this business trip," he placed his hand gently on her cheek, "to buy you a car."

Her light brown eyes radiated happiness. She was helpless to conceal her smile throughout the evening, which now stretched from ear to ear. "I love you," she whispered.

He held up her chin, gently kissing her on the lips. "Are you still in character, wifey?"

She smiled, wrapping her arms around his waist, pulling him closer. "That was for real. But if you're still role-playing, that's fine. I don't mind."

"Honey, if I were really role-playing, we wouldn't be here. Now, let's go test drive this sucker. Let's see what she's got! You wanna go first?"

"No way! It's a racing car! That thing has too much power for me!"

"M Power! I think it's fitting, unified in the M."

"Marriage?"

He nodded. "I was thinking more like Moreno."

Ron approached the vehicle with the key in hand. "Are y'all ready?"

"Ron, you know I've been ready!" Abraham called out.

He escorted Liv to the passenger seat and tucked her in the vehicle. She eyeballed him making his way to the driver side door. "Baby! I can't believe this. You're actually going to get me a car?"

"Why not?" he said excitedly as he sat in the driver's seat. "Let's test the power of the M. I can't wait! I've been waiting for a long time for this!"

With a simple twist of the ignition, the engine roared to life. He pressed the gas to the floor. The car growled with exaggeration.

"You're like a kid with a brand-new toy, I swear!"

"Liv, what do you think?" Ron asked.

"I think my husband is full of surprises…" She glowed, never taking her eyes of Abraham.

"He really loves you," Ron put his two cents in as he spoke the obvious.

Abraham shifted the console into drive. He roared the M3 onto the main street, leaving dust in his wake. Adventure had always enthralled him, and as they sped off, he stared into her eyes, driving faster and faster amidst the bright city lights of Dallas.

XXX
TITLE BOUT I

"Waiter!" Abraham waved down the server for the evening. He briefed him on the elaborate plan and hoped his theatrics would be unveiled on cue. After spending countless hours preparing, his romantic scheme was now coming to life. "When I give the nod, bring out this envelope," he said, giving his last set of directions.

Liv returned from the ladies' room, full of smiles. He had the advantage of knowing her dinner rituals. She sat for two seconds and excused herself for a pre-meal hand washing.

"You look amazing!"

"Thank you, baby! I thought I'd color coordinate since I know you like that." Her eye shadow for the evening was a lovely purple that complemented her button-down blouse of the same color. The eyeliner revealed the true beauty of her eyes. The light brown color of them flaunted her sexiness, as one look would place him in the palm of her hand. The intricacies exploited his animal instincts. Her exotic features made his blood hot, and resistance to her womanly advances were futile. He loved her dearly without declaration, but his body language told the whole story.

She wiggled in her seat, making herself comfortable. "It's a beautiful day. I love the Riverwalk. It's so romantic, don't you think?"

"That's why I picked it. Since we both love downtown, it was a natural choice."

Casa Rio was a fan favorite of tourists and natives alike. The colorful umbrellas, aligned next to the river, added spectacular color to the radiant scenery.

He stole her hand, caressing it on the table. "This is a day you're never gonna forget. I promise you. After all, it is a day of love."

"Every day is a day of love for Mr. Abraham, isn't it? That's what you teach your Pre-K kids too, right?" She sighed, "Loving everybody but me!"

"Things change," he said confidently, "That being said, you have been the greatest thing to come into my life. I don't know what the heck I was doing before this…before I clicked on you. You were a needle in a haystack…" He grinned, his charm on full throttle. "I love you."

She felt tears forming. She waved her hands in front of her eyes to prevent mascara from running onto her cheeks. Spilling her emotions was common for her, but it was a trait he admired.

"It just feels right." He smiled, finally relieved to tell her the truth. "Like the heavens brought us to each other, to find one other… it was meant to be."

"I love you," she said, struggling to compose herself. "It's about time. You know how long I waited for you to say that?"

He laughed hysterically. "I've never been this deep in uncharted waters, so bear with me."

"Scared?"

"Scared, nervous, excited, joyous, happy, passionate…a little bit of everything."

Abraham nodded discreetly to the waiter. Unaware of the gesture, she pulled out a mirror to check if another application of eyeliner was necessary.

"Don't worry," he said, as she peeked from behind the mirror, "you look great."

"Ma'am, I believe this is for you," the waiter said, as he presented the envelope, startling her.

"Oh…" she said, surprised, "thank you."

She looked to Abraham, surprised and giddy. He shrugged his shoulders, pretending to have no clue, but the half-smile gave him up immediately.

She smirked and stared at him. *He's up to his old tricks,* she thought. She felt up the envelope. "It's bulky. What did you stuff in here?"

"Since this is our first Valentines together, I wanted to make sure it was a special one. Open it up!"

Tearing through the envelope, her smile never ceased. She pulled out documents and brochures. Her eyes widened as her jaw dropped to the floor.

"No way!" she shouted. Her hand covered her mouth as she struggled to find the words. "Are you serious, Abraham!? Oh my gosh, I can't believe this! Hawaii!"

"My love knows no bounds," he said triumphantly.

Abraham cruised down the street and noticed a vehicle parked in the middle of the road. The style and the color scheme he recognized, but hadn't seen in some time.

"Is it him?" Liv asked nervously.

"Yeah…" With much apprehension, Abraham responded, "Something's up…"

The silver M3 roared into the driveway behind the black M3 that was parked peacefully. He walked over to the Mustang and its driver who waited patiently for him.

"What are you doing here?" Abraham said sternly.

"I came to see how you were doing," Abbadon said suspiciously.

"I'm good. What do you want?" Abraham intended to keep the conversation brief. His feelings alerted him that a visit from his former friend was for a more sinister purpose. "What do you want?" Abraham asked once more infuriated.

"An apology," Abbadon said with a smirk of deviance, his face filled with confidence knowing that buttons were being pushed.

"You're crazy if you think I'm gonna fuckin' apologize to you. After everything you did to me. You owe me an apology."

Abbadon's plan was beginning taking shape. His hope of Abraham reacting outraged was coming to fruition. He wanted his rival to hurt the same way he did, emotionally and physically.

He focused his energy and tactics at the man who hurt him, and more importantly, he felt the need for overwhelming revenge. The darkness, after all, was his friend. He had been involved with it many times before and welcomed it, rather than turn it away. He allowed the darkness to pulsate through his veins.

Exiled from these feelings, he now remembered what it felt like to be alive again. Siding with the shadows that longed to return, his allegiance was full blown as he proceeded to attack his new enemy. "You know I have to admit, I was hurt at first when you weren't my friend anymore, but I got over it fast. You taught me to recover quickly, so I did."

"And you taught me to be ruthless, so I'm ready," Abraham interjected.

"Are you? Make a move and see what happens," he said, challenging him in a mocking manner. He stepped out of the car, seeking further provocation.

Upon fully exiting, Abraham grabbed his shirt with both hands and looked directly in his eyes, "Or what, motherfucker?"

"Abraham, you can't handle me, you'll get your ass beat. If that's what you want, then go for it, let's see what you got."

"Abraham, don't!" A voice yelled from the passenger door of the M3. "Don't do it! Let him go!" Liv ran from the car. She pleaded with Abraham, acknowledging the transformation taking place. "Baby, please don't do this! Don't be like him!"

Abbadon's smile began to widen. "You're at the breaking point..." he muttered, "go ahead, come on over, it's fun, here."

The temptation of releasing his anger was brewing inside, and Abbadon could sense it like a shark in bloody water.

He let go of Abbadon's shirt. His brown eyes, full of innocence and love just hours before, turned cold. Abbadon, calm and cool, stood his ground face-to-face.

"Fuck you!" Abraham seethed with anger.

Abbadon opened the door to his car and, as he was about to enter, turned to face Abraham once more. "Hey, your sister Michelle, she lives in Athens, right?"

"What?" Abraham was caught off guard by the question.

"Yeah, building 3, an apartment on ground level? I'm pretty sure that's it. Anyhow, have a good day now," Abbadon said in a relaxed tone. He closed the door and revved the engine preparing for takeoff.

Abraham ran to the car door emphatically. "You don't know where she's at! Even if you did, I will be there. You touch her and you're fucking dead!"

"How can you be there if I already am?"

"What are you talking about?"

"Sometimes, you need a little help from your friends. My eyes and ears are outside her apartment as we speak." He sighed heavily. "You know, it's sad what a person is willing to do for the right amount of money. Everybody has a price, even you."

"Who's over there? Who did you send?"

"You forgot to say please."

"Who, motherfucker? Who?"

"Actually, you know him well. He was a good friend of yours…" He revved the engine forcefully. "Didn't you dub him The Gun?"

"You sent him?"

"What'cha gonna do now?" Abbadon's voice turned cold. "I told you not to fuck with me! All I have to do is say the word. By the way, she has a nice loft." As soon as the words left his mouth, he sped off, creating a cloud of smoke from the burning rubber.

Abraham ran to the M3 in a rage. "He's not gonna get away, this time," he said as the engine roared to life, "I can catch him." The car reversed furiously, the back tires peeled out as he sped off wasting no time.

"Abraham, don't!" Liv quickly sprang to tears. She ran to the street, desperately trying to reason with him, but he was gone.

Abbadon took a series of turns. He picked up speed on South Flores, ignoring the traffic lights and stop signs. He glanced in his rearview to see the sleek M3 gaining on him. Abraham pursued him vigorously, matching the violations and weaving in and out of traffic.

Closing in fast on the muscle car, he dialed Michelle's number while maneuvering through traffic. Her phone rang endlessly until finally it picked up. *"Hi, you've reached Michelle. Please leave a message."*

"Shit, pick up!" Panic struck him. He continued on, his nerves overflowing with rage and adrenaline. He dialed a second time in desperation.

In the distance, the crossing gates lowered as a locomotive boomed down the track. In an effort to avoid the preemptive collision, Abbadon accelerated, flipping the nitrous oxide switch; the Mustang catapulted through the wooden gates.

"He fucking went for it! Here we go!" Cringing at the sight, Abraham pressed hard on the pedal, flying past Briscoe Elementary Academy. The road elevated slightly where the tracks intersected, creating a concrete ramp. The Mustang touched down with minimal damage, scratching the undercarriage creating an explosion of ephemeral sparks.

If I lose him, I lose Michelle, he thought. The M3 hit the concrete ramp at one hundred and twenty miles per hour. The car lifted off, and as it rose in the air, the train pummeled through, missing the BMW by a couple feet.

The M3 crashed to the street sliding uncontrollably drifting to its left as sparks and debris accompanied it. Losing momentum from the unstable landing, Abraham pounded the pedal, once again, refusing to lose sight of the Mustang and saving Michelle.

"This guy doesn't give up," Abbadon plowed on, making a hard right onto Cevallos Street. Traffic screeched to a noisy halt as the Mustang glided sideways. The silver BMW followed suit, weaving through the standstill of traffic that froze at the sight of the pursuit. The M3 roared in his rear view. He punched in a few digits on his cell phone, and the screen came to life. It read, "Calling The Gun."

After two failed attempts to reach her, he persisted with a third attempt.

"Hello?" Michelle finally answered.

Her sincere tone crushed him. "Michelle, where are you?"

"Just getting home, why?"

"Listen to me, there's somebody over there waiting for you. Don't go inside the house!"

"Abraham, what are you talking about!? I'm already in the apartment complex, why? What's wrong?"

"Michelle, call the police right now, don't get out of the car, call the police! They're gonna try to hurt you, just call the police and call me back. Quick!"

"What are you talking about? You're not making any sense! What do you mean somebody is waiting?"

"Michelle! Just trust me!"

Abbadon gave detailed instructions to his reunited colleague. Tommy Gun listened carefully on the other end of the phone.

"I just want you to scare her. Don't hurt her, just scare her. We need to make our presence known in Ohio. We need to send Abraham a warning. How can he stop us if we're all over the place, right?"

"Is it working out as planned?" Gun questioned.

"It's going smoothly…I'll call you back when he's down," Abbadon said calmly.

"All right, I'll give her a good scare and then head back."

"This is where we take his heart," With confidence, he shifted gears in the Mustang, inching closer to the showdown he envisioned.

* * * * *

Pedestrians scrambled aside as the Mustang and M3 wailed past. La Tuna picked up business in the late afternoon and the spectacle at hand caught the attention of the happy hour crowd. Drifting onto Probandt Street, Abraham's phone rang and he answered hysterically, "Michelle! Are you in the truck?"

"Yeah. What—"

"Just listen to me, okay? Look around for anybody suspicious and wait for the police!" he warned.

"Abraham, I'm scared."

"I know, just trust me…stay on the line with me."

"What's going on? Are you in trouble?" she asked frightened.

"I'm gonna kill him, Michelle! All these motherfuckers, I'm gonna kill. They're not gonna get away!" He spoke with vigor. The darkness grasped onto him as rage helped with the infiltration.

"Abraham, calm down, you're scaring me," her voice trembled.

He sensed her fear. The tone in her voice rendered him helpless. The anger multiplied, and in order to resist his heart from breaking, he allowed it to manifest. In this desperate attempt, he realized the odds were severely stacked against him. "Look around…a big guy, he's about six five…you can't miss him. He could be anywhere."

"I don't see anybody," Michelle replied, as she scanned the area.

* * * * *

Whizzing through traffic lights, Abbadon backtracked to the inner city neighborhood. With his plan taking shape nicely, he improvised the final phase with dastardly diligence. "All right, old buddy, let's see if you're ready."

Concentrating on dodging vehicles, Abraham pursued intently. Multitasking, he pressed the speaker phone button rather than fumbling around with the cell phone.

"Michelle, what's going on? Talk to me!"

"Abraham, nobody is here…I think a police car is coming."

"Okay, wait until they get there and—"

"Abraham! Somebody's coming out of the bushes!"

"What does he look like?"

"I don't know. I can't see him yet. It looks like camouflage."

"That's him!" he shouted.

"Abraham, he's running toward me. Abraham, help me!" Terrified, Michelle yelled for her life.

Tommy Gun rushed the truck at full speed. The police car crept closer, and with nowhere to hide, he had no choice but to get to Michelle quick. He tried to force open the door with no luck.

"Aaaaahhhhhhhhhh...he's trying to get in! Abra—" Michelle was gone. Before she could say another word, the phone went dead.

"Michelle! Michelle!" Abraham cried out in a rage. "You motherfucker!"

Abbadon took a hard left onto Theo Avenue, luring his bait into the trap. He crossed the bridge and swerved unto the opposite side of Concepcion Park. Punching on the brakes across the street from the park, the dirt and rocks billowed up, creating a cloud of dust. He climbed out of the car and waited for his challenger to arrive.

Abraham, braking wildly behind the muscle car, produced a second cloud of dust dispersing in the air. Testosterone ran amuck, as Abraham exploded out of the M3, looking to dismantle his new enemy.

"I'm gonna kill you, motherfucker!" Abraham laid into him like a freight train, punching him repeatedly, knocking Abbadon back several feet from where he stood. A right hand to the face, a left to the stomach, and an uppercut sent Abbadon crashing against the Mustang. He grabbed Abbadon's shirt furiously and threw him to the ground.

Abbadon smiled. Despite the force of blows being laid into him, his plan worked perfectly, pitting his former friend against the fatal fury of rage.

"I'm gonna fucking kill you!" Abraham tore into him with incredible force, oblivious to his surroundings.

A thunderous blow belted Abbadon on the jaw. Unsuspecting of the brutal offensive, he hit the deck hard. *He's stronger than I anticipated,* he thought. Hoping to slow him down, he grabbed a handful of dirt, flinging it to Abraham. The dirt entered his eyes, halting the assault momentarily.

"I've taken your best punches!" Abbadon managed to let out an unsettling laugh.

Adding further to his rage, Abraham gave a swift kick to the groin that surprised his overzealous opponent. Abbadon buckled to his knees. Abraham sent a knee to his face, laying Abbadon on his back. Jumping on the downed warrior, he pinned him, delivering multiple blows.

The winds carried the unmistakable wrath as the activities of Concepcion Park were brought to a standstill. Yells filled with anger blazed through the afternoon air.

Throwing punch after punch, Abraham plowed through his opponent. The spectators looked on, stunned at the frenzy. Abbadon bled from his mouth, but that didn't stop his chilling provocation.

"Is that all you got, Abraham? I'm disappointed."

"Fuck you!" Abraham crossed over to the dark forces he swore never to return to. He now appeared as dark as the adversary in front of him. Back at the house, Liv warned him, but her cries were in vain.

Abbadon maneuvered, slinking his way out from the offensive outburst. He blocked Abraham's attacks, and he patiently waited for an opening to put his nemesis into submission.

The fight brought them dangerously close to the cliff of the river. Unclear of his position, Abraham planted his left foot down for leverage to bring about a left fist. His footing gave way, leaving his leg dangling down the steep side of the ledge. The rock he slipped on plunged down into the river below. He fell to the ground, grasping the rocks desperately trying to avoid the same fate.

The patience of Abbadon paid off. Abraham struggled to crawl back to safety, but it was too late. The opportunity presented itself, and with the advantage at hand, Abbadon ran over to him, gaining speed and forcefully swinging his right leg, exerting all his power into the face of his foe. The incredible force sent Abraham crashing down to the river bed. Rolling down to his defeat, he felt jagged edges dig into his body, poking him like needles. The weeds provided no relief and were useless in slowing his descent. What seemed like hours to reach the river was only a few seconds, as he lay banged and bruised helplessly on his back.

Coming to a full stop, he felt the water crash against his body. He detected blood flowing out into the stream. A sensation of pain ran through his body. The rocks provided a worthy beating that left him motionless. Severely dazed, he struggled to keep conscious.

How did this happen. I had him!

Despite his unfortunate condition, he sensed the inevitable was upon him. Abbadon won. In a matter of seconds, the battle reached its conclusion, one that he was sure of winning. What seemed to be a victorious day took a turn for the worst. His thoughts raced, contemplating the death that waited as he lay defeated.

Liv is waiting for me…they got Michelle now…I can feel the water rising around me.

He wondered if anyone had been alerted to his plunge.

The police are on their way, they will find me…

Abbadon made his way safely down the steep riverside. He was sure to find bones broken once he climbed down for a closer look. He had a chance to finish the fight his way. He crept around Abraham, splashing water purposely onto him, parading around his helplessness. Abraham moved slightly and his eyes were nearly closing. The powerhouse that sent thundering blows to Abbadon had been dwindled down to washed-up wreckage.

"You fell right into my trap. I'm surprised it worked so well, honestly."

Abraham felt the vibration of the water flow into his ear canal. He hated anything that came near the vicinity of his ears, especially the left one. His defective ear didn't matter now, but the vivid memories of the pain it caused, resonated tenfold. The most awful sensation was that of water entering his ear canal.

"And now this fight is mine! You know what's funny? I know you hate water. It's your kryptonite, right? Look at the strong and caring, Abraham! Just as I explained to you earlier…beaten! You never had a chance. Your little girlfriend can't help you, and you can't help Michelle now."

Abraham strained to move as the words Abbadon spoke made his blood boil. Abbadon circled his downed prey, taunting him. He lifted his right leg and delivered a forceful blow to his chest, leaving his heavy boot to hold his incapacitated adversary down. "Since water is your weakness…we will test it. In a few seconds, it won't hurt anymore."

Abbadon grabbed him by the shirt and lifted his upper body out of the water. Abraham was helpless to respond as Abbadon turned his body over into the water. Too weak to escape, Abraham suspected his last stand was now taking place.

Abbadon gripped a handful of wavy hair and plunged Abraham's face in the water. Scrambling for air, there was nothing he could do. The damage had been too severe.

The water scared him. It always had. And now he was going to die by the element that he feared the most.

God, please, I don't want to leave. I'm not ready. Liv is waiting for me…

He pleaded.

Liv, I need you.

He began fading.

He remembered her smile. Her scent, right around her cheekbone, emitted her intoxicating body chemistry. He could see her now, hovering on top of him, caressing his face. Her voice whispering sweet words, "I love you…"

He wanted to hear her say it one more time.

Abbadon was stealing his life and cheating him of being with her.

"Baby…I love you…"

His body went into shock once the water entered his lungs. Fifteen seconds was all it took to make the writhing subside. Darkness wrapped itself around him and carried him away.

He lay at the bank of the river. His body rippled with the tide, lifeless.

XXXI
REVELATIONS

"Mr. Moreno! Mr. Moreno!"

Abraham heard a voice call out to him. His dreams and the real world were blended into one, not knowing which was which.

"He's coming around," said an unfamiliar voice. He broke into consciousness a little groggy like he had awakened from a year sleep.

Whispers floated about. He made out three people, blurry and unidentified, one on the move and two at a standstill. His eyelids cracked open slightly. They were heavier than a pair of punching bags. Slowly blinking, he gained momentum in returning to the real world, leaving the dream world in his wake. Blinking harder and rapidly, he struggled to regain his eyesight. He had always been 20/20 and never had it been so difficult to focus his vision, no matter how far or near. *I must have taken quite a beating,* he thought. The two voices went from a whisper to clear articulation. Their soothing voices comforted him immediately and in them was the sound of worry and love as he could feel all of it at once. Blurry still, he could feel his vitals restoring to full power.

Gloria and Liv stood bedside, waiting patiently for him to fully awaken.

"Hey, dude." Gloria spoke first as he could hear the worries in her voice. Her typical "hey dude" line was one of relief, but also of a great scare as well. Looking upon him with a half-smile, she looked at ease. Liv, however, was on the verge of tears; her eyes were so watery it looked as if she could cry the San Antonio River two times over. Never shy about showing her emotions, she found no use of hiding them either. Her posture was noticeably filled with worry. She studied his eyes. Not only could he sense her fear, but her eyes told the story as well. Her hand touched his, and it made all the difference as the pain subsided instantaneously. He felt her inner workings; the outcome was so close to devastation, Abbadon had done considerable damage. She couldn't speak. The anxiety and lump in her throat made for a stream of strenuous waterworks. The doctors told her if he didn't wake soon, the complications could be more serious than anticipated. Too weak to venture in fully, he wished to know a bit more, so he took a peek.

"Ma'am, are you his wife?" the doctor asked.

"Yes, I mean, no," she replied. "How is he? Is he…is he going to be all right?"

Signs of life were low, she could sense it. It was the water. *Damn water,* she thought. His weakness, certainly, and his fear, undeniably.

"We are monitoring his vital signs at this moment, and since he came in unconscious, there is a serious risk involved. We have been giving him oxygen, and we are waiting to see if his blood tests return to normal. We are observing him for acute respiratory distress syndrome which can occur after a near drowning. What this is exactly is multi-organ failure due to the trauma. Lung problems can also occur, so we will hold him overnight for that as well."

She was not capable of holding her reserve. The difficulties of being a cancer were highly identifiable at this point. Emotions ran rampant, and her end of the dialogue ceased between her and the doctor. The doctor, not easily fazed, waited for a moment for Liv to catch her breath. Even without high heels, she towered over Liv by nearly a foot. She felt empathetic; however, her profession molded her to be strong like an oak.

"Mrs.…Ms. Moreno," Dr. Montgomery corrected herself, "since he does not need mechanical support to breath, we are hopeful."

"Is he…is he going to…will he recover?" she asked in a shaky voice.

"It's too early to tell, Ms. Moreno," Dr. Montgomery paused. Her eyes filled with sorrow. She had given terrible news countless times, but this time was different. Liv was different. Her emotions gushed onto the medical floor, and the doctor was in the midst of being consumed by them.

"I'm not going to lie to you…he arrived comatose and the outcome may be that he has some permanent neurological damage or if things go terribly south…he could…die."

Liv began to cry uncontrollably. It was an ugly cry. Her sobs could be heard throughout the halls. Dr. Montgomery put a hand on her shoulder, but it didn't matter. There was no consoling her and each second hurt more than the last. She had found her soul mate and now he was being taken from her, as his life hung in the balance. *It's not fair,* she thought. She mumbled a few words to which the doctor could not make out.

"God, please don't let him leave me, please don't take him."

"Ms. Moreno…I don't mean to offend you in any way, but it's okay to have…hope."

Liv raised her head and took a peek at the doctor, her hysteria ceased momentarily. He had spoken through her. She knew it was him working the only way he could. *He always says that,* she thought.

Hope…

* * * * *

Venturing in and out of someone's thoughts took a substantial effort, and it was a power he couldn't afford to muster in his weakened condition. *She's in bad shape,* he thought.

A fourth person entered the room, hurriedly. Detective Balderama was fast becoming a friend, even after the disappointment of Abraham not going to the academy. It seemed like such a distant memory now, as Detective Balderama stood bedside opposite of the ladies in his life.

The doctor was rummaging around the room, placing medical equipment on the tray that he had no use for the past couple of days.

She was a nice-looking Caucasian woman in her early thirties. She smiled and spoke with a Southern twang. It was the same doctor Liv had spoken to upon arrival. Their bond was now three days old, but had aged considerably to what one would think was now three years.

"It's time to wake up, Abraham. You've been out for a while, guy."

Abraham glanced at her name tag. It read Dr. Montgomery, MD. His thoughts began to scramble faster than the speed of light, and before a normal thought process could occur, Detective Balderama spoke in a firm tone. "Moreno, how are you feeling?"

"Like crap," Abraham mumbled.

"Well, you took quite a pounding from what I hear, and it looks like you're going to recover."

"How long was I out?" Abraham spoke with a worried tone.

He glanced over at Gloria, and by her facial expression, he knew it wasn't good. Her reluctance spoke volumes.

"Two days," she said somberly.

The detective quickly took over the conversation. "Moreno, can you describe the identity of the person that attacked you?"

"Yeah, it was Abbadon, Abbadon Bazan, 5'10", 180 pounds."

"Are you sure?"

"Yes, I'm positive. You can ask Liv she was—" Abraham sprang up from his bed in horror, his memories coming to light. "Michelle! Mom, where's Michelle? Is she all right?" He recollected the main reason he pursued Abbadon through the inner city. The rage, the anger, and all that had gotten the best of him. Fury plagued him the last couple of years, and this current defeat nearly cost him everything.

"She's fine, she's okay, Abraham, everything is okay. She's safe," Gloria said gently as she placed a hand on his shoulder.

"What happened? Is Gun still over there?"

The adrenaline spruced up his vitals too quickly. Liv squeezed in on Gloria's right and placed a hand on his chest to calm him.

"Moreno, no need to worry, I spoke with the Athens police department a couple days ago and Thomas Holloway has been arrested and is now in their custody." Detective Balderama reassured him before vitals came crashing down via cardiac arrest. "He is going to be in Ohio for a while, so relax…he's not going anywhere. Back to the matter at hand, Abbadon Bazan, was it?"

"Yes." Abraham said, refocusing his thoughts on the man that betrayed him.

"I usually don't respond to disturbances," Detective Balderama confessed. "An officer, a good friend of mine, called and let me know that…you were down. I took the liberty to get the samples of skin under your nails. Are you sure it was him?"

"It was him," Liv interrupted as she looked over to the detective. She nodded with an affirmative as she turned away. The memory of witnessing his lifeless body remained fresh in her thoughts.

"The reason I ask is because the evidence that we collected from your nails was inconclusive. It did not match any of the assailants we have on record."

"What do you mean it didn't match?" Abraham interjected.

"Moreno, the skin sample we found under your nails belongs to the person that attacked you, but we do not have a match in any of our records. As of yesterday, we searched for this mystery man's DNA, even on CODIS and found nothing. I have a hunch there is more to this, that's why I agreed to take the lead on this one," he said with sincere concern. "Are you sure there wasn't anybody else who attacked you along with him?"

"I'm positive, it was only him. I'm *positive*. There has to be some kind of record on him," he said with conviction. "He's had a run in with the cops before…in LA."

"All right, Moreno, I'll continue to work on this. If you have any questions, call me."

"So he's on the loose and no record of the destruction he's caused…"

"Moreno, I'm doing everything I can, just concentrate on getting better. We'll be in touch, and don't worry," he said reassuringly, "we'll get him."

Abraham lay back on the hospital bed and stared at the ceiling. He had been awake for no more than ten minutes and it was a long day already.

"Abe, I'll be back later. Liv and I are going to go eat lunch." Gloria placed her hand on his forearm. She wasn't much for affection, and that was the best form of it she could muster.

Liv, on the other hand, did not hold back. "I'll come by tomorrow, baby." She leaned in to embrace him. Her light brown eyes were surrounded by redness. "I love you."

She slowly slid away, not wanting to let go of him so easily, and he grabbed on to her hand, gently holding on for as long as he could.

✝

A few hours later, Gloria returned. The smile she wore glowed throughout the shadowy room. "Hey, I thought this might keep your mind busy." She wasn't one to give out surprises on a whim and definitely never giddy to give gifts either.

"What is it?"

"Open it." She simply smiled in anticipation of his reaction.

The gift had blue wrapping paper labeled Man of Steel all over it and silver S shield logos. He studied its dimensions, two inches thick, and weight, a few pounds, about three if he had to guess. *A book,* he thought. She wasn't trying to disguise the item in any way, no parlor tricks. Any such thing would not suit her style.

He unwrapped it. A present this late in the evening unquestionably meant that his hospital stay spooked her terribly.

"Seven fifteen," he glanced to his wrist, pretending to check an invisible watch. "It's way past your bedtime," he said with amusement.

"Eight o'clock is my bedtime, so I have forty-five minutes. Hurry up and open and it, dude."

He proceeded to unwrap it taking his time. "I'm gonna go as slow as possible opening it. I'm honored that you actually wanna spend time with me. I may have to die more often." He busted out in laughter.

Gloria went from a smile to a look of puzzlement. "Died? Abe, who said you died?" Worry suddenly filled her core, once again. *Had someone told him or was he on to something?* she thought.

"Mom, you know me. There's no fooling me. You know I can feel it."

"Yes, that's what I was afraid of." She approached closer bedside. He instantly knew her serious look of an oncoming speech. Her tone turned firm. "Abe, I want you to relax and concentrate on getting better. Don't worry about going back to work or anything, okay?"

"Mom...why do you say that? I feel better already." He actually spoke the truth to her. Since awakening, his restoration improved dramatically.

"Abraham! You have to recover and get better. You might feel better, but your body needs time to heal. Your...your mental state needs healing too. Come on, Abe, you know what I mean. I know you're not...right...right now. A mom always knows. So don't rush it. I can sense things too, ya know!"

"I'll see what I can do," Abraham mumbled. Her words and reasoning did carry truths he was not ready to face yet. On the outside, he was close to running on all eight. The inner workings, however, were another story. The psychological damage was evident in his body language. Now, wasting no time, he ripped the paper off the gift.

She was right, he thought. Time would be his friend on this one, and maybe not even then, was a guarantee he would heal fully. The surprise now carried much more meaning than it had a few seconds prior.

Maybe this will help me heal, he thought.

The back cover showed itself and the description was unmistakable. "This is it!" he clamored.

His eyes lit up. The magical book that eluded him for so long touched his fingertips. The title read *Superman/Doomsday*.

"Isn't that the one you wanted?"

"You found it! I can't believe you remembered!" he said in amazement. "I've been looking for this book for a long time. Superman and the greatest villain he has ever faced in every single showdown to date! Thanks, Mom! You did good," he said, grinning as he admired the book.

Abraham hadn't smiled in days, much less laughed, and Gloria, the mother who never showed emotion, had an unorthodox way of cheering him up.

Once Gloria left, Abraham wasted no time examining the graphic novel he yearned to get his hands on. He flipped through the pages like a giddy little boy, fascinated that all the stories were gathered into one compilation.

He scanned every picture rapidly. "The origin of Doomsday…" he whispered to himself.

For him, it was equivalent to uncovering treasure at the bottom of the ocean. The backstory of the behemoth that killed Superman was no longer a tantalizing question mark.

The Doomsday creature had been genetically engineered to be a killing machine, a monster who could withstand anything thrown at him. The creature had evolved beyond death. His only purpose entailed total destruction. Like Superman, he was Kryptonian; however, his DNA and features were a mutated version, and it was an abomination that sparked fear in Superman.

The science aspect intrigued him, and with each page, he became emotionally invested.

"Interesting…" he whispered, "wait a minute…" he paused, reflecting on what he just read, "the DNA…" The mystery commenced to unravel before him, the missing piece to the puzzle that plagued him the last twelve hours.

Dusk had fallen in the midst of his gaze out the twelfth-floor window. The pink and orange rays lit up the skyline, penetrating the chrysalis of a room that held him captive.

"Is it possible?" he said aloud. In the dim room, he contemplated the next move.

XXXII
REGENERATION

The DNA… he thought, *It has to be…it's the only explanation…*

He needed to get out of the hospital in order to investigate this revelation. Just as he began pulling the tubes out of his arm, Dr. Montgomery entered abruptly. He quickly pretended to adjust them with embarrassment rather than remove.

"Mr. Moreno, I have good news," she said cheerfully, "You are being released!"

"That *is* great news! I've been ready to get out of here."

"Mr. Moreno, I have to tell you…your recovery has been an amazing one. I mean, it certainly is a miracle that you fully recovered. Vital signs have returned to normal without any lung or neural complications. The Man upstairs must really be on your side."

☦

Grandma Marcella swept the kitchen floor as she anxiously awaited her grandson. She loved him more than anything, and it showed by her nonstop worrying of his well-being. She was old-fashioned and stronger than the population currently half her age. She truly came from a generation that was from another time. Born in

1930, she carried her morals and values into the twenty-first century where they no longer existed in the populace around her.

"Grandma, I'm home!"

"*Mijo! ¿Como te sientes?* Love! How do you feel?"

"I'm okay, Grandma, did you miss me?"

"*Sí, cómo no. Estuve bien mortificada. Ya comiste?* Yes, how could I not. I was very worried. Have you eaten?"

"No. I'm not hungry."

"*Mijo, necessitas comer! Hice carne, quieres un taquito?* Love, you need to eat! I made some meat, do you want a taco?"

"No, Grandma, I'm okay."

"*¿Quieres que te cura?* Do you want me to cure you?"

"Yes."

"*Voy a curarte de asustó.* I'm going to cure you from the fear."

The last of her kind, she was also the last remaining generation of the *curanderas*. Gloria and Aunt Margie could pull it off when they needed to, but Grandma Marcella was the genuine article. She knew the remedies that existed in a time when doctors prescribed medicines as a last resort. Her rituals, passed down from generation to generation, were rarely practiced in the world.

"*Voy a sacar un huevito pa quitartele frío.* I'm going to get a little egg out so it's not too cold."

"Grandma, you know I don't care if it's cold."

He had told her a million times that a cold egg on his skin didn't bother him. Hesitant, she grabbed a towel anyway and, for the two seconds it took to walk over to him, cradled it as if it would magically take away the coldness.

She began the curandera ritual with what sounded like gibberish. She spoke in a whisper. Her words were hard to make out, but he knew the prayers in her native language, Spanish. How could he not, he had been part of this custom for twenty-three years. In times of great distress, the egg is what served as a form of defense for the one she would easily give her life for. She brushed the egg over his arms, chest, and legs as if he was more fragile than a newborn chick.

The session made him feel at ease as it always had. Immediately after, she would crack open the egg and let it sit in a glass of water to settle. He lay still on the couch in a meditative state when he heard the front door swing open.

"Baby, you're home!"

Liv entered, happy to see her love again. She sat beside his still body, leaned over, and gave him a welcome home kiss.

"Hey, darling," he said sluggishly.

"Aren't you happy to see me?" she retorted.

"Of course I am, baby!"

Abraham leaned upward to feel her soft lips on his. She looked at him with a serious smirk. His reluctance gave him away, and she knew him too well to brush it off.

"What's wrong?"

"I need your help."

"Help with what? Talk to me." Worried, she braced herself for the worst.

She helped Abraham sit upright. He felt sore, but at least he was alive.

"Research," he said with a grin.

Just as he was about to discuss his intentions, Grandma swooped in with the glass of water that held the egg in its custody.

"*Está feo el huevo! The egg is ugly!*"

The egg had transformed. The yolk lay at the bottom of the glass with numerous white strands extending from its body much like a spider. According to Grandma, the results depicted a worst case of *maldad* or bad stuff that came from within him. She called it *envidia* or *asustó*.

"*Mijo, no te vas a ir a ninguna parte, necessitas descansar. Love, you're not going any place today, you need to rest.*"

"Okay, Grandma, Liv is going to help me with something anyway."

"*Bueno.* Good."

☦

Research immediately began on the laptop that brought him luck in finding Liv. She had been an unexpected blessing, and with the technological good luck charm, he counted on lightning to strike twice. Searching for confirmation to back up his theory, he needed to brush up on his scientific vernacular. On the heels of an investigation, he was confident to exploit the missing link.

"I've catalogued through all my memories. Every serious conversation Abbadon and I had and in his confessions, he said that he never got caught by the police, but everybody else in his crew did." Abraham paced back and forth in his room, concentrating on retrieving information from memory. "He also said that the police *may* have had a sample of his DNA, but it wasn't his because it didn't match. So I know that his DNA is the key somehow."

"What about fingerprints? Wouldn't the police have gotten fingerprints from him?"

"No, from what I recall, he was never processed or so he claimed, and his tactics were…are very meticulous. He strategizes and plans…his endgame…has always been…exploiting enemies."

"What about blood? A hair strand? Saliva?"

"The police had obtained a DNA sample, but they did not tell him what kind. He didn't believe that they did, but he said that if they had one, it might've been a blood sample. He didn't go into further detail, and I never asked about his past. I should have though, considering the situation we're in now." Abraham rambled on. He loved bouncing ideas off Liv. Her thoughts were valuable to him, and her detective skills were sprouting by the second. "Nevertheless, Abbadon is smart. He could've sprayed ammonia over the blood at the scene. He is clever and cunning."

"Abraham, I'm going to ask you something, and I want you to tell me the truth."

He looked away and abruptly sat in his chair, wanting to avoid the serious truth, but his actions gave him away instantly. When something important came up in conversation that she needed to know, he knew the exact wording and tone she used to get answers from him.

"Has he ever killed anyone?"

He fell silent. He couldn't lie to her. His eyes concentrated on the computer screen in front of him as if the question had never been asked. She became shaky and her voice trembled.

"Abraham?"

He sighed heavily. "Yes, he has."

Her eyes began to tear. He knew where this was going, and as much as he wanted to avoid the emotions she was going to spill, it was too late.

"He could have killed you then? He meant to kill you, Abraham, you could've died that day."

Tears rolled down her cheeks. It was the first time she faced death. Her feelings never hid secrets, and she always claimed that it was the cancer crab characteristics surfacing.

"Baby, I'm still here. He didn't take me down. He knew where and how to hit me…but I'm still here," he said reassuringly.

He rose from the chair and sat next to her on the bed, placing his arm around her. Her face remained hidden in her hands as she began to cry uncontrollably with the sudden embrace. She loved him, and he could feel the connection between them as he held her.

Individually, they existed, but it was their emotional and spiritual connection that allowed them to feel the same emotions as one entity.

"He told me once that he loved you. How could that be true if he meant to kill you? He's a liar. You don't do that to the people you love."

"Liv, he may have at one time, but you have to understand that he never felt love in his life. His foster parents gave up on him and sent him here, and when he finally felt loved, he didn't know how to handle that. He told me once that he believed he was sick, so I ask you, is it destiny or choice that makes us who we are? Sometimes, I think maybe he was right. Maybe he didn't have a chance."

"That's no excuse! We can always choose who we want to be."

"Can we? What about me? Look at what I have. I didn't ask for this. Why did God send me with these…these things! That, I'll never know."

"But, Abraham, you do have a choice. We always have a choice! He sent you for a reason, don't you see? You can use what you have for great things or for destruction. We all have a choice."

"I don't know, anymore…" his voice trailed off, "I want to still believe that. I failed…" He sensed rational feelings surfacing. "I failed my friend."

"No, you didn't. He failed all by himself. He chose to do what he did…I don't want to lose you." Her tears eased up as he wiped them away gently. He softly stroked her hair out of her face and kissed her on the forehead, planting his lips delicately.

Glancing over at the monitor, he detected a book left open next to the laptop.

Liv, puzzled at first, knew that he had picked up on something. She knew well that his insight and intuition were hardly ever wrong and the detective in him was close to solving the mystery.

He picked up the book, never taking his eyes off the page. "He opened this book the last time we were in here…Greek mythology…" Quickly, he jumped back on the laptop computer, and within seconds, he had his answer, "I know what he has."

He typed away furiously. He had no substantial evidence, but he knew in his heart and based on various clues, this is what he had been searching for.

"I remember reading about it and researching this irregularity. I was fascinated by it and I forgot its name until now." Abraham glared at Liv victoriously.

He pointed to the screen which described the anomalous genetic strand that his former associate possessed.

"This is it, right here."

Liv listened intently. She marveled at his abilities as a detective, and she trusted his hunches.

"But, Abraham, how can you be sure?"

"Liv, I can feel it. This is it. This is the key we've been looking for! I have to tell the detective."

"And what if he doesn't believe you?"

"Trust me, he will."

XXXIII
CHIMERA

"Moreno, are you nuts? How did you even come up with this?" Detective Balderama dismissed the fantastical claim.

The reply was not one Abraham expected, much less, what he was ready to hear. Liv was a good listener and the luxury of having someone hear wild claims, he had gotten used to.

"Detective, I know it sounds crazy, but I really feel this is the explanation for all of these discrepancies."

"You're telling me you're making accusations on a whim? You're making claims based on a hunch?"

"Look, I came down here because I thought you'd believe me… so just hear me out. Please."

"All right, Moreno…you have two minutes. Go."

"Okay, first off, Abbadon confessed to me the crimes he committed in LA. In those confessions, he never got caught, but the rest of his gang did. Out of the seven members, he was the only one that came off clean. Now, you can call this luck and that's what I originally thought, but then, I remembered what you said to me at the hospital. This leads me to clue number two. You mentioned the DNA sample could not be identified. Back in LA, the police could not indict him even though allegedly, he claimed they recovered a

DNA sample of his. Take this into consideration, the DNA is the key here, and when I investigated further, I found this."

Abraham handed the detective a printout with detailed information on it, in hopes of swaying his judgment.

"Detective, Abbadon has chimera."

"What the hell is this? A mythological creature?"

"Yes and no. I mean—"

"Okay, Moreno, time's up! I don't have time for this!"

"Wait! His DNA is a combination of mismatched parts. He has two sets of DNA!"

"Is this for real or something you made up?" the detective spoke in an irritated tone.

"No, I didn't make any of this up. See for yourself. It exists in less than 1 percent of the entire population and some people don't even know they have it. It's likely he doesn't even know he has it either. It's something he would've told me."

"And he tells you everything!?"

"Yes, he does…he did…at one time…and that is why I believe this to be true. I've gone through all his confessions, his claims, his sins, and everything else that he confided in me. Trust me, I wouldn't be here if I thought it wasn't worth a look. I've done the research, Detective, and nobody else knows him better than I do!"

Detective Balderama reluctantly perused the information. "And how the hell do you know he has this? Did you take a blood sample of his and have it tested?"

"No, I can't say that I have but…I can feel it. It's the only explanation that makes sense, and I guarantee you, if you get him in your custody, we can find out for sure. We just need a blood sample, a hair strand, and saliva to test and you'll have your answer. That's all we need, and if I'm wrong, then we let him go and that's that…but if I'm right, then we can link up with LAPD and match up our samples with theirs and bring this guy down. Detective, what's the worst that can happen?"

Detective Balderama gave a sigh of uncertainty, but Abraham did have a point, he thought.

"I'm sorry, Moreno. I can't invest the time nor the manpower to conduct a full-scale investigation based on a hunch or your personal theories. You're not a cop, so stop pretending to be one. Let us handle it from here. All right?"

Abraham shook his head in disappointment. Detective Balderama stood his ground. It was eerily reminiscent of the sergeant standing his ground a few months back. He couldn't catch a break in this building. Catching a criminal easily took precedence over a failed career, and he didn't want to give up on pleading his case this time. The detective had a point and what could he say to counter that unfortunate fact.

"You're right, I'm not a cop and I'll never be one. I just thought I could help. I apologize for wasting your time."

"Look, Moreno, I'm sure you would've made a great detective. My team and I have been doing this for years. This case is in good hands, trust me."

Dejected, Abraham acknowledged the sour truth. "Copy that." He gazed at an empty cubicle next to the small one they occupied.

The detective noticed the discouragement as Abraham's face turned to stone.

"Do you know why I called you randomly during the processing detail?"

"No," Abraham said somberly. None of that mattered anymore.

"I did it because you were one of the best. You may not have been as tall or strong as the others, but there is something in you that I noticed," the detective paused, "you had heart. And that doesn't come along too often. So it didn't go your way, no big deal. Whatever career you take on, I trust you'll be good at it."

As the detective gathered his belongings, his cell phone rang. Abraham glanced at Detective Balderama.

"I'll see my way out." Abraham nodded as the detective answered.

"This is Detective Balderama."

He walked out of the room filled with cubicles galore. Numerous times he had been in and out of this building, once upon a time when the dream was still alive. The atmosphere felt different. It was more business than excitement, more of a past time of a great experience rather than the healing wound he thought it would be. The detective didn't listen like he thought he would, but it made no difference. He and Abbadon would cross paths again, the only question was when. Detective Balderama was right. He didn't need Abraham.

I'm not a real detective, he thought. The exit door neared, and he was certain this would be the last time he would step foot in this building.

"Moreno! Moreno!" Detective Balderama shouted down the hallway. A sense of urgency rang in his voice.

Abraham turned immediately to face the detective. He walked swiftly, his crinkled brow brewing with distress.

"I just got off the phone with one of my detectives. I said I would keep tabs on him…it's not good. Do you know a Lucy?"

"Lucy? Yeah, I do, actually. I don't know her well, but if it's the same Lucy we are talking about…she is Abbadon's girlfriend."

"I'm afraid so. She called about an hour ago. He's done some damage here, and according to her, he's not done. Perhaps you're right. I'm going to bring him in."

Abraham expressed a sarcastic laugh. At this point, he knew the detective well enough to give him grief.

"That's funny how that works, huh?"

"Yes, unfortunate and funny. We have no time to waste. We have to bring him in before it's too late."

"What do you mean, 'too late'?"

"Lucy said he is on his way out of town to God knows where. With any luck, Officer Ramirez can track him down within the hour."

"It's good you stayed late, huh? It's a sign, Detective. Now is the time to put him away for good," Abraham said confidently.

"All right, Moreno…we'll give it a shot! But if you're wrong… you'll never have a chance at joining the force again!"

"That's all right, I'm considered permanently unsuitable, remember? Besides, if I'm right…you get all the credit, Detective!"

"Let me make a few calls and get this rolling. I call you tomorrow, let you know the status and brief you on the details."

"Thanks, keep me posted."

It was the first time, in a long time, that Abraham had a positive outlook on things to come. Psychologically, he genuinely felt at ease. He wasn't alone. He had backup from his police brothers and sisters. Underneath the positive, vibrant exterior, lingered the undeniable truth. A truth he would never admit, much less say out loud in public. He couldn't take on Abbadon alone. Nearly losing his life was something that he refused to take a chance on, again. He lost the first title bout horribly and, much to his dismay, did not want to see the results of a second.

XXXIV
SECOND CHANCES

"I love you so much." Liv seized every opportunity to express her feelings, and even at that, words were not enough. Still shell-shocked, memories haunted her dreams. Nearly losing Abraham left her traumatized, and each time she held him, it was torture letting him go.

She lay with him on his tiny twin bed, and somehow they nestled in comfortably. He cradled her with his right arm. She rested her head in the crevice between his shoulder and chest. Her right leg rested on top of both of his as they physically became one.

"I love how you love me. Unconditionally…and without judgment. Fighting…I mean, losing…almost dying…made me realize just how much. I don't want to go another day without you by my side."

Abraham explored this new wave of emotion. He never delved this deep into a passionate predisposition. In light of recent events, he refused to counter the spellbinding sensation he felt with her. Skeptical of the soul mate theory, each passing second since the day he met her, he was becoming a believer.

Three nights passed since his release from the hospital, and each night, she spent it with him, tucked away in his cozy quarters. Her healing powers worked at restoring him, and it was her presence alone that mustered up miracles.

"I'm just going to hug you forever, Mr. Abraham. I bet your kids miss you at school. I know I would if I was four years old," she said with a laugh.

"They do! Ms. Melendrez said to take as much time as I needed. The kids made pictures for me, she said."

"I bet Justice misses you a lot!"

"She's having a hard time. She's cried every day since I've been gone. Ms. Melendrez said Justice thought I died, so they told her to make a picture for me every day that I'm gone."

"Poor baby. You should go visit her. Let her know you're okay."

"That's a good idea. I can pick up all the cards the kids made for me. Ms. Destiny is holding them for me until I get back."

"She likes you! A girl can always tell when another girl likes a guy. You probably have a crush on her, just by the way you talk about her."

"She's cute, I'm not gonna lie. But someone else has my heart. Some girl I met a while back. She has an exotic look to her, long curly hair, sexy as hell! You might know her, she lives in your neighborhood. Beautiful girl, light brown eyes, honey complexion, about 4'11", give or take. You might know her…"

"I might…"

"Well, she's got my heart."

"She's a lucky girl."

"The best! I'm never gonna let her go." Abraham held her tighter.

"Abraham, why do *you* love me?"

He kissed her gently on her forehead, "You have succeeded where everyone else has failed."

"Is that why you hug me even tighter now?"

"I guess it's what death does to you. Being near it makes you appreciate the little things more."

Liv smiled peacefully, gravitating toward his lips. She kissed him softly and glided her nose up and down his cheek like a little kitten. Her healing methods worked every time, and it was then that he dozed off into a peaceful sleep.

XXXVI
REVENGE

Abbadon walked slowly up to the front door. Rage welled up inside, but he saved it for the right moment. He padded the back of his jeans, making sure that the 9-millimeter handgun was safely tucked away and out of sight. Josef and Maria had a surprise waiting outside their doorstep much like they did nearly twenty-five years ago.

The doorbell rang as he waited in anticipation. He remembered the abandonment. Now, he had evidence of their lies and this offense he could not simply dismiss. He traveled back to Los Angeles to return to the home he despised. In retrospect, it was also a return to his former self.

Maria opened the door. Her mouth dropped. Words escaped her as total shock rose to the surface of her being. Her eyes widened and it was too late to hide her nonverbal cues. His presence at the doorstep signified the point of no return.

"Abbadon…I…what a surprise? How are you?"

Abbadon smelled fear. Already, the advantage was his as he nonchalantly stepped through the door. He entered with ease and began running on instinct.

"I thought I'd stop by and pay a visit. I was in town and wanted to see how you and Josef were doing?"

Draped in a silky black and red dress, it was evident Maria dressed up for a night on the town. Josef and Maria showed no indication of their age. Both looked as if they just stepped into their 40s. Maria barely had any gray on her head, and Josef's only sign of aging was a receding hairline.

"We are good. How are you? It's been a long time…good to see you. We meant to call you for your birthday…"

"And Josef? Where's the old man at?"

Abbadon spoke in a mocking manner as he sensed lies emerge from her mouth. Desperately, Maria struggled to stay calm, but her nervousness had overtaken her. She walked into the kitchen, preparing a glass for Abbadon.

"Oh, he is taking a shower. Would you like something to drink?"

Abbadon ignored the question but instead proceeded with questioning of his own. "I take it you were on your way out? A night out on the town?"

"Yes, actually. Your father…um Josef, I mean, is taking me to see…"

"He is not my father…my father abandoned me, but you and Josef did the same, so I guess it makes no difference, don't you think?"

Abbadon took her lapse of wording and capitalized on the error.

"Honey, have you seen my black shoes?" Josef shouted out. He was unaware of the guest awaiting his presence in the living room. Abbadon paced back and forth in front of the fireplace as he noticed all his pictures had been removed. It was as if he never existed in this household, and it caused anger to spew out of his pores. He had been forgotten, abandoned, and betrayed many times over, that this outrage added fuel to the destructive fire that he yearned to unleash on the Bazans.

"Abbadon…" Josef had a stunned look on his face. "What are you doing here?"

"Josef! Good to see you. Aren't you happy to see me?"

Confused, Josef attempted to gather himself as he adjusted his glasses.

"Um…yeah. Of course! How have you been?"

Josef walked over to Abbadon as Maria sank back into the kitchen. He outstretched his hand, but Abbadon rejected it. Instead, he stretched out his arms and gave Josef a hug. With a half-smile, Josef had been taken by surprise and did not have a clue as to how to react.

Abbadon, on the other hand, perplexed his opponent. His tactics were running on autopilot. His strategies for war were now strictly instinctual.

"I missed you both and…" Abbadon desperately wanted to pull out his handgun and end his association with the Bazans, but he decided to move in slowly. "I wanted to discuss some business."

He paced back and forth, from the fireplace to the couch, calmly and stealthily.

"You both lied to me…about my parents…and now, I know the truth. I was denied my chance to be with them while they lived."

"Donnie, we didn't know they—"

"Quiet," Abbadon demanded in a firm manner. "You've always known my true name. It doesn't matter now. Your deceitfulness… will be your undoing."

The Bazans were in trouble as a predator walked in their midst.

XXXVII
FAITH

Climbing the steps up the concrete platform brought the soreness back to life. Like an old man grimacing in pain, he walked into the school. Upon entering, the door on the left and the windows next to it remained the same after all these years. The green tile floor looked to be the original tile he walked on for the first time nearly twenty years before.

"Hi, can I help you?" a lady greeted him before he made it any further into the building. She emerged from the door he immediately passed. She did not wear a smile. Her black slacks and gold button-down shirt made her appearance darker, much like her black hair. She was not familiar and her tenure was less than ten years at the school, otherwise, he would've remembered her.

"I'm just visiting. I was a student here years ago."

"Really? How long ago? You look so young!" She smiled finally, and as she approached him, they stood eye-to-eye. Her heels made it so, and they were a good three inches at that.

"Eleven years. I attended kinder through eighth, here…class of 1993."

"Wow! That was a few years back! So what brings you here?"

"Just taking a trip down memory lane…is it all right if I look around?"

"Sure. Take your time."

* * * * *

He had known St. Leo's since the day he was born. The kindergarten hall was just off to the left. Slowly, he crept over to the entrance of the kindergarten wing. In amazement, he recognized the tree painted on the wall, but instead of leaves, colorful handprints took their place. Thirty-four little hands graced the wall long ago, and a blue handprint to the right of the tree got his attention. He placed his hand over it. His hand overtook the blue one forged on the wall. So small, he thought, and yet he remembered the day he laid his hand down to imprint. On the bark of the tree, written in white, it read:

Kindergarten
Class of 1985

Exiting the school, he made his way across the street to his intended location. He hesitantly approached the church. For him, it was home. His return was not for nostalgia. It was for answers. The search for them plagued him to the point of misguided purpose.

The church was empty. Countless times he came to pray alone and to cry alone. It felt more intimate to have the church to himself. It was just him and the Lord, one on one.

He recollected the many milestones along his spiritual journey. Baptism, first communion, confirmation, and one day, hopefully in the far distant future, he would have his final service here.

He walked toward the altar, stopping at the fifth row to his right. He kneeled, made the sign of the cross, and sat at the end of the pew. He closed his eyes and commenced the meditation process.

Returning home never failed him before and he hoped this time was no different.

I need you. I've struggled to maintain balance, and I can't go on like this. Guide me, show me the way, and keep me grounded. It is only in my weakness that you make me strong. Amen.

* * * * *

"Hello there," a voice echoed from the altar, "a familiar face returns."

Abraham remained still. His half-hearted smirk displayed a deluge of distress. "Father Richard, it's been a long time."

The priest made his way down from the altar. Stealthily, he closed in on Abraham bringing his cheeriness with him. After all these years, his attire stayed the same, all black with the exception of the white square by the lump of his throat. He slid into the fourth pew and positioned himself comfortably to view Abraham. "What brings you back?"

Abraham looked up to the cross that Jesus hung from. He shook his head. "I needed to come home. Restoration, you know?"

"Fortunately, I do. Your history here is admirable and your loyalty, unshakable. I'm glad to see that you come in from time to time. Many lose their way and never return. Or some do and just need a reminder to continue on. It's not faith you're lacking. Guidance is what you're seeking, isn't it?"

"It is," Abraham nodded, "I need a whole lot of it, right now."

"When was the last time you confessed?"

"Reconciliation? When I was eleven or twelve, maybe."

Father Richard studied him. The energy levels were off considerably. His disengagement was evident. "Anger...temptation...uncertainty...they surround you."

"I feel...like I haven't been myself. I feel numb. There was a fire inside, and now, it's going cold...no meaning anymore."

"Are you sure it is not fear that drives you?"

"Fear?"

"It's not hard to see that your faith has been shaken. The light flickers, but it's not what it used to be."

"For the first time..." he struggled to get the words out, "I'm..." his eyes watered and he fought to keep himself steady.

"What is it that you are afraid of?"

"Something that I have never faced before...I was challenged and I failed...miserably. And something changed after..."

"You mustn't look at a failure as a loss. It is an attempt at getting better…a learning process, if you will."

"I know what I have to do," he mumbled.

"In order to overcome your fears…you must face them. It will be scary, frightening, and maybe even traumatic, but even though you walk through the darkest valley, fear no evil, for God is with you."

Dejected, Abraham sighed with exhaustion. His injuries were long healed on the physical level, but his psyche was beaten down.

"You faced death twice last year. I heard about the first one and the second one, I saw on the news. It was brutal. Were you afraid then?"

"No."

"Why not?"

"I just wasn't."

"You weren't alone, right?"

"My friend and his son were hurt. There was blood everywhere…and Jeff was crying."

"And you?"

"I didn't get hurt."

"You didn't have a scratch on you, did you?"

"No."

"God works in mysterious ways. He will throw you trials, but nothing more than you can handle. His ways are higher than ours and we may never know what the reasoning is at the time, but it is always for the greater good," he smiled and raised his hands in praise, "to make a difference."

"My reasons for making a difference have been skewed lately…" He lowered his head.

"I believe there are two kinds of people…those who are born and those who are sent. Everybody has a purpose…and the ones that are born go through life and do enough to get by. They opt to not use their gifts to the fullest for whatever reason or make no effort to find it." He paused and took a deep breath. "The people that are sent have a purpose, a mission. They use every bit of talent that they have, and if they succeed in their mission, then they are the ones that make a difference in the world. The question is…which one are you? I look at you and have seen you grow up. I know which one you are, but do *you*?"

Abraham shook his head up and down confirming he understood.

Father Richard acknowledged in agreement. "I have a strong feeling you know which one you are. In all my years of being a priest, one thing is for sure. Not everybody receives a baptism by water, but everyone goes through a baptism of fire."

"And a fire…rises," Abraham added, and as he did, the flicker ignited.

"Abraham, just believe in yourself like you always have and you'll be all right. Just do what you always do…this trial of yours is just another stop."

"I'll try."

"Once you overcome your fear, your faith will lead you. You see, your fear has clouded your mind. You need to look beyond your fear, and when you do that, you will find your faith."

XXXVIII
NIGHT IN OLD SAN ANTONIO

"Baby, I'm glad you came out with me." Liv desperately tried to get him out into the real world, and her latest attempt proved successful. "You're a NIOSA veteran out here, so you can show me the ropes. Whaddya say?"

"Sure," he said, a bit more energetic than he had been in days past.

She pulled into a parking lot directly across the street from La Villita. He slipped her a ten-dollar bill to cover the fee, smiling contently from the passenger seat. She gave him a loving smile in return.

Walking through the parking lot, she attempted small talk. "I didn't know this was a church. I always overlooked it during fiesta."

"St. John's…since 1857," he said slyly.

"You're quite the historian, Abraham," she said giggling.

"Well, not only that, I've also been parking here for the last five years myself during NIOSA. You tend to pick up a couple things here and there," he laughed.

The streets surrounding La Villita were shut down and enclosed with privacy fences all around. It was a city within a city in the heart of downtown. Together, they stepped into the little village.

"You get the tickets, and I'll get in line for a burger. I'm hungry," he said, touching his stomach.

"About time you have an appetite," she said, relieved. *Maybe a night out will bring him back to normal,* she thought. "Okay, baby, I'll meet you at the booth."

"A few booths over in Clown Alley." He pointed down the enclosed street where people walked freely, playing games and eating at booths on both sides of the street.

As he stood in line, he could the smell the aroma of the meat on the grill. He hadn't craved a burger in some time, and he couldn't resist chewing on the meat like a predator claiming victory over prey. *I need to get back to my old self, craving a burger is a good sign,* he thought.

Liv eyeballed him from the ticket booth. He felt her penetrate his soul. Her light blue tank top and plaid shorts caught the attention of college boys around her. She paid no attention to the mischief of drunken guys gawking. Her concentration on him never faltered and her love for him could not be shaken.

She's beautiful, and she's all mine, he thought. "I need to be better…for her. Snap out of it, Abraham, you're better than this," he mumbled to himself.

He smiled and waved to her, indicating he was on his way back. *I can do this, it's all in my head,* he reasoned.

Before he could fix his concentration back on the burger booth, a shoulder pummeled through him, knocking him aside. Patrons partied hard, and it was not uncommon for many of them to be diminished to a drunken stupor.

"My bad, homie," the young man said drunkenly.

"No worries," Abraham gestured to him.

"Come on, baby, it's too crowded here. Let's go to the windmill," Liv said as she swooped in to save him from the drunken onslaught of partygoers.

Navigating through the crowd was nearly impossible. La Villita crammed in thousands like a can of sardines. Even with police officers spread throughout, maximum capacity had no meaning.

They passed booth after booth of food and booze, being bumped and groped along the way.

"Excuse me."

"Watch out!"

"So sorry, pardon me."

The party overwhelmed the senses. Abraham matched frequencies with each and every person that passed them. Liv led the way to the windmill, periodically checking on him by turning to wink or rub her thumb on the back of his hand. She held on to him tight, never wanting to lose him again.

Shouts and yells, ranting and raving and various types of social debauchery took place in the area of the windmill. Faces flew by, some recognizable, while others, not so much.

"Everybody comes out of the woodwork during NIOSA," he said to her. "People you wanna see and people you don't wanna see."

"Does it really matter anymore? You have me now." She winked with a smile.

His nerves calmed for the moment. While grazing random strangers, the sensation varied from love and hate to joy and sadness. The energies surrounded him, and at present, there was no escape.

A large Hispanic man loitered by the beer booth in Windmill Station. He was bald, overweight, had a light beard, and wore conspicuous sunglasses. Looking rather out of place, Abraham accidently bumped him. The inadvertent contact disrupted the energy flow that he labored to level out. Jealousy and envy emitted from the heavyset man. Without recoil, hallucinations leaped from the excess emissions.

"You're afraid!"

"You don't like water, remember?"

"You're gonna lose!"

"You can't beat him!"

Abraham veered off to the margarita booth in an effort to recover.

"Baby, what's wrong?"

"I'm sorry...I...it's too much." He wiped his face with his hand, removing the sweat from his brow. "I'm all right, a little overloaded, but I'm good. I could use a drink, though," he chuckled.

"You asshole! You're with this bitch now!" A woman screamed amidst the crowd. "I knew it! You're fucked up!" The woman hollered in her drunken state.

Avril charged through the crowd like a bull aiming for a red target. She set her sights on capturing Abraham to unleash her resentment.

Plowing through the masses set the populace off balance. A wave of bodies crashed into Liv and Abraham, knocking them aside.

"Abraham!" Liv cried out. Her hand separated from his.

"Liv!" he hollered for her, but she disappeared in the myriad of people.

"Where are you, you son of a bitch!?" Avril continued her hunt, with only her voice threatening the airwaves.

He was pushed onto a path outside Windmill Station. "Liv!" He searched for her, turning left to right, front to back.

The darkness had come. It came looking for him, wanting to join with him like a parasite searching for a host.

Before it could sink its teeth into him, a body crashed onto him. Hurriedly, Liv seized him, pulling him away from the scene and leading him out to the street. In a panic, they raced down East Nueva and onto Alamo Street like they were being pursued. Together, they held up under the archway of HemisFair Park. Visibly frustrated, she wanted answers.

"What is it? What's going on?" Her voice trembled. "It's been two months and you're getting worse." Tears began to well up. A culmination of aggravation and concern flowed from her body.

Not once did he look her way, but he could feel her energy spreading toward him. She grabbed his hand gently and held on to it. He was quiet and on the verge of shutting down. She pursued no further and quickly revamped her tactics. She didn't want to lose him, not the man she loved, to dark forces that were beating down his door. Rather, she chose love. *Love was always the key,* she thought, and her healing powers complemented his. *Okay, Liv, go back to the beginning,* she coached herself.

"Walk with me," she said soothingly. She prompted him, and he complied, refusing to make eye contact.

Unlike their hurried pace a moment before, she made it a point to walk together slowly without a care in the world. *It'll buy me time to cool off and for him to open up,* she thought.

The path of the red brick road had historic houses on either side, and he studied them as if it was the reason they strolled down that way.

"Are you okay?" she asked kindly.

"Yeah," he said in a low voice.

They passed the three-story hollow clock tower and the Institute of Texan Cultures to their left. The red brick road led them to the Tower of Americas, and she stood confidently, overlooking the city-wide party. Just outside the entrance of the Tower, several water pools and artificial waterfalls stretched across to their right and as they marched along, Liv soaked up the waters' natural properties through her sense of smell. It rejuvenated her to the calm state she thrived in. Stopping thirty meters from the base of the Tower, she finally turned to him. She peeked at him innocently and gave him a hug, wrapping herself onto him. Her touch spoke in a comforting tone. He sensed her emotions. *I'm sorry, I just want you to be okay.*

Resting his head on top of hers, his cheek lay in her hair and her energy revived him to his normal frequency. They held on to each other in the middle of the path while partygoers passed around them. She poked her head over his shoulder and noticed a bench jutting out from the steep side of the hill, opposite of the water display. "Let's go up there," she motioned.

She led the way, and he followed behind her for support, protecting her from falling backward.

"This is a cute little bench! Oh, it's made of ceramic and I love the colors!" She placed her hand on it, admiring the blue and white color scheme.

They plopped down on the bench together.

"It seats two comfortably," she added, "or should I say, it seats *us* comfortably."

He smiled, letting out a breath of contentment.

She pointed to the sun at their three o'clock and placed her arm to rest on his back. "Look, baby. Your favorite time of day."

He swiveled his neck over to the sun setting, and as he did, the last rays of pink and orange restored his aching soul to full power. His nerves calmed and the safe elevation of the bench kept threats at bay. He had the advantage of higher ground.

With her arm gently rubbing his back, she slid it closer to her and placed her hand on the back of his neck, caressing his hair.

"I don't want us to be like this," she spoke softly, "to always be on the run or looking over our shoulders."

"It's me he wants to hurt."

"You? Abraham, it's anything and anyone who loves you, who associates with you. Look what happened to your sister. Abraham, we're in this together. You think you took that beating all alone? No, I took it with you," she paused, catching her breath, "I almost lost you and…it's not fair. I had you for a few hours…you finally were in love with me and he almost robbed me of that, robbed *us* of that. You haven't been the same. Don't get me wrong, I am grateful to God that you are here with me, but I don't have you fully like I did that day and I hate him for that," she regrouped, recognizing emotion was overtaking her. "I'm sorry…that's selfish of me."

"No, I'm sorry. You're right…I haven't been the man you first met."

"Abraham, listen to me. It's okay to be afraid…it's *okay*."

Gazing at his white and black Nikes, he drifted off into his thoughts. *I have to tell her,* he rationalized. The request from the detective had been eating at him all day. Needing to talk it through with Liv, he released the burden of his task onto her ears. "The detective wants me to ride with his task force. They leave in twenty-four hours…"

She froze, her breathing ceased for the moment, and her eyes widened at the sudden confession. "When were you gonna tell me? When you were gone? Abraham! Where are you going?"

"I haven't decided if I'm going to go. I just don't know, Liv. I don't know what to do."

"Why does he want you to go? I…I don't understand…why you?"

"He knows I can find him. He says that I, better than anybody, knows his tactics, his methods of operation, and the places he hides out."

"And where is that?" She did her best to calm down.

"Los Angeles."

"How does the detective know that Abbadon is in LA?"

Abraham hated to give her more bad news, but the way things were going lately, he had to relay the information to her before she heard it from someone else.

"Lucy called the police and reported Abbadon. The detective got word of it, and she confessed what he had done and his intentions…Abbadon raped her."

"Oh my god." A huge sigh of disbelief and shock came across her face. The news had taken a toll on her emotionally, and she appeared drained as her beautiful light brown eyes were now red and swollen. She gathered herself and redirected her course of action. *God, lead me to say the right words to him. Help me to be his rock. Help me to be his light in darkness.*

"Are you my soul mate, Abraham?"

With a puzzled look, he turned to her. "Of course, I am. Why… why do you ask that?"

"What do soul mates do for each other?"

"They complete each other."

"And they challenge each other. The can see into each other's soul and can bring out great things that nobody else can. Wouldn't you agree?"

"Yes, I do."

"They can bring out great spectacles that we never knew we were capable of. I believe in you…what do you always say, 'It doesn't matter how hard you fall…and all that matters is how you respond.' He almost robbed you of everything, he beat you, remember? The terrible things he did to you…your life he nearly stole…along with all the precious things people take for granted. So I ask you, how would Abraham respond?"

"For the first time, I'm afraid…I'm afraid, that if I go over there, I'm gonna lose and that means…" his voice trembled, "…that I'm not coming back."

Her light brown eyes teared up heavily. It was a truth she didn't want to face either. The reality of the situation settled in her and she gained her resolve. "Baby…I don't want you to go, but the detective is right. I know you can stop him. You can save lives by finding him."

"I can't beat him."

She desperately refocused her faith. "God gave you gifts to help people, I know you're scared, but you can make a difference. Isn't that what you are all about?"

"I help people…I don't catch criminals…"

"And what about Jackie? You brought her to justice, didn't you? How is that different?"

"She wasn't a murderer! This *is* different!"

"Saving the world is hard, but we have God on our side, don't we?" She switched up her tactics to those of faith.

"We do," he whispered. "People will know what I have…and it makes them uncomfortable…"

"Since when do we hide our faith in God?"

"It's not my faith I'm hiding…it's what I can do…"

"Abraham, people will always be scared by what they don't understand. But this is bigger than you…and me."

"Liv, even if I do find him, what then? I do this and we take that chance of…"

"No, don't even think like that! When you come home, I'll be waiting for you…and you *will* come home."

He admired her strength and beauty. She was an emotional wreck, but somehow, she held the both of them together.

"Do you remember when we sat in your car outside my house? I told you that I would be there with you, to stick it out, even if that meant you had to go off far away. I would pray for you to return to me, no matter what. You said to me, 'That remains to be seen.' *Now* is the time when we are being tested, *you* are being tested. I'm afraid too, but, I'm gonna stand with you. I have to have faith, *we* have to have faith that we'll get through. Without faith, then all that we stand for…will be for nothing. You can't live like this, always looking over your shoulder. You have to go through it."

He stared at the dirt, his eyes trailing down to the foothill.

"A baptism of fire," he whispered. *Father Richard was right,* he thought.

"I don't like it either…but only you can find him. I'll be here waiting for you, just come back to me safely." Her eyes watered once again. Her strength grew exponentially from all they had been through together. "I know you've been having a hard time and you've been knocked off course…" She reached in her pocket and pulled out a small silver piece. "I got something for you. You're gonna face challenges that will scare you, test you and…" she paused, teetering to avoid the lump in her throat, "try to kill you…and when you're in doubt or afraid or you think you can't go on, open it up and read it."

She rubbed the bottom of the cylindrical piece, showcasing a pin that held the message inside. She placed the keychain in his hand. On the side of it, he noticed two symbols, one above the other.

"Alpha and Omega," he whispered.

The pin was miniscule, and he attempted to slide it out and remove the message.

"No," she said sternly, putting her hand over his, "when you need it."

He nodded. "You're right," he said quietly, "I have to find him."

"And you will."

"It's funny…my gut told me this would happen. I guess it's the storyteller in me…Abraham and Abbadon…Genesis and Revelations. Perhaps, it was meant to be this way…"

"Abraham, promise me you won't face him alone and that you'll call for help. Promise me!"

"Okay…I promise."

"Let your faith be bigger than your fear. Remember what you stand for…" she said quietly to him. "And remember…what you're fighting for."

XXXIX
TITLE BOUT II

Abraham couldn't afford to drag his feet any slower as the detective waited for him to arrive. They were leaving tonight, and he was already regretting his decision to join the team.

"Moreno! Glad you could join us. I just briefed the team, and we are moving out tonight, that's why I asked you to meet me here at the airport. This investigation has been upgraded to a manhunt. Our orders are to apprehend the suspect dead or alive. You were right. I'm sorry," the detective apologized with sincerity in his voice. He patted Abraham on the back. "I should've listened to you. Lucy had an old cap of his. We found a hair follicle and tested it. It matched the DNA sample found here in LA to one of the worst crimes in the city's recent history. The situation has gotten a lot worse." He sighed heavily, pausing to relay the news. "We found coordinates in Abbadon's house."

"Coordinates?" Abraham questioned.

"Yes…and they pinpoint the exact location of the White House. We're not sure what that means, but the FBI does not take threats lightly and they're not taking any chances, so they've asked us to move out immediately. They've upgraded this case to a priority concern. We'll meet up with the FBI and LAPD as soon as we land in Los Angeles."

"Detective, he wouldn't...it's a decoy," Abraham tried reasoning.

"Moreno, it doesn't matter. We don't leave things like this to chance, especially after 9/11. We need to capture him immediately to find out what his intentions are and if he has any associates aiding him. I need your help. *We* need your help."

Abraham shook his head. His wide-eyed look was evident of a man on high alert. "I can't believe this."

"I know he was your friend. If we have any chance of getting to him quickly, it lies with you," Detective Balderama spoke with empathy.

The team hopped on the jet, and Abraham took his seat in the front of the plane. *What the hell I am doing here,* he thought, but it was too late. The plane had been cleared for takeoff.

The plane touched down in three hours flat. Nervousness and noxious emotions ran freely, but Abraham concentrated on his resolve.

"All right, team, listen up! This is our guy on the tube!" Detective Balderama pointed to the monitor on the plane. The local news broadcast a special report which had the anchorman in a most serious tone. "The suspect is considered to be armed and dangerous. If you see this man, please do not attempt to apprehend him instead call the police. His whereabouts are unknown at this time."

Instinctively, Abraham felt the wave of chaos continue. "Death is here," he whispered. *His only motivation is to do as much damage before he's caught,* he thought.

"Yes, I understand. We have a lead on the suspect, and we need to reach the scene immediately." Detective Balderama hung up his cell phone and glanced over at the man who was the ace up his sleeve.

The experience was intoxicating. Anxiety raced through his body. It was a real manhunt, one that he dreamed of being a part of, but not exactly how he pictured it. The moment at hand would have been more meaningful, if it wasn't his friend they were after.

The task force exited the plane via the stairway and onto the tarmac. The detective waved him down, calling Abraham over to the squad car.

"Sanchez!" Detective Balderama yelled to one of the officers. "Take the team to the van and follow us out."

Sanchez saluted with an affirmative.

"Moreno, you're riding with me. This is Officer Lowe of the LAPD."

"How ya doin'?" Abraham greeted the officer.

"How are you tonight, young fella?"

"Good," Abraham said as calm as possible. The adrenaline rushed through his body too quick for him to act normal.

"Is this your new recruit, Detective?"

"Yes, it is. He's fresh off," Detective Balderama spoke a half-truth.

Do they think I'm a real officer? he thought. He didn't want to ask. Surely, it would look like he didn't belong if he dared to inquire.

Officer Lowe was an older African-American man in his early forties. He had the look of a seasoned fighter who had seen war plenty of times on his watch. "We'll rendezvous with the LAPD task force and the FBI when we arrive at the Hollywood Hills. I hope your tracker is right on about our suspect. He's killed two people tonight so far."

Is he talking about me? Am I the tracker? Is that what the detective said to the officers? Abraham questioned in his thoughts.

"Are you all right?" Detective Balderama spoke calmly. His tone showed no sign of nervousness at all.

"Yeah, I'm okay," Abraham responded.

The detective noticed the anxiety pour off him like sweat. He wanted to reassure the newest member of his team, "Don't worry, Moreno, it'll be over soon. Just stick close to me and you'll be all right. I just need you to lead us up there."

The detective was confident in Abraham's abilities, the ordinary and perhaps the extraordinary as well. Either that or he lied incredibly well. In any case, his persuasion succeeded and the respect and confidence the detective had in him was enough for Abraham to feel invincible. He was beginning to believe he could overcome his fear, and with plenty of backup, he would survive and return to Liv in no time.

Arriving at the base of the hill, the LAPD and SAPD met face-to-face for the first time, and both parties briefed each other.

"Detective Balderama, the DNA sample you sent matched up with a suspect involved in various robberies and numerous murders. This looks to be our guy, if he's up there," said Detective Sandusky of the LAPD. "On top of the two murders he committed tonight."

Abraham fell quiet as the team proceeded to the most likely location that their target might be. In the company of trained professionals, he did his best to keep his poise.

"All right, Moreno, you're up!" Detective Balderama called on him.

Abraham didn't acknowledge as he played out possible outcomes in his mind. He tried to hold it together as to not make a fool of himself in front of the rest of the team.

God, please get me through this. Guide me, show me the way. Give me the strength, courage, and guidance to get through this night.

He prayed, hoping for a miracle.

The two teams huddled before embarking on the trail. He tried desperately not to let the officers see his knees buckling. His reserve allowed him to walk confidently over to the detective.

"If I'm right, he is up there waiting for us," Abraham spoke with as much confidence he could spew out.

A large man, standing six foot three, intervened. His vest and tactical gear hid the muscular physique underneath, but it was obvious his lean stature was one he didn't take for granted. "Detective Balderama, the quickest way up is through the Hollyridge Trail. Teams have been dispatched to the other trails around the base of the hill. Nobody is coming or going without us knowing. I would suggest hiking it from here. If he's up there, we can catch him by surprise on foot."

Detective Sandusky did his homework. He instructed his men to strap on the night-vision goggles.

Detective Balderama looked up to view the sign that Los Angeles was famous for. "All right, let's go. Be careful walking this terrain and let's watch each other's six. He could be anywhere and catch us by surprise. Goggles on."

The team walked cautiously as the LAPD unit followed suit. The team stealthily crept up the trail leading to the Hollywood Hills.

Abraham hiked up rather shakily. He began his operating procedures with his senses working like clockwork. His concentration flooded and spilled over the hillside.

"He's near," Abraham mumbled to Detective Balderama, "I can feel him."

Detective Balderama scanned the area. He had his men divert in two directions. The terrain of the Hollywood Hills was potentially dangerous, especially at night, so he took every precaution necessary.

$$\Omega$$

I'm not alone this time, he thought. Abbadon had company from law enforcement agencies from two different states, the FBI and a friend that he was now at odds with.

Overwhelmed, he remained still. *I have to be creative to escape this one,* he rationalized. So many times, he had dodged bullets by avoiding capture or certain death. This time, a strong feeling surfaced as he faced the truth. One of the outcomes, he successfully avoided all these years, was now in jeopardy of becoming a harsh reality.

$$\alpha$$

Abraham lingered behind the officers, feeling out the area. They were about ten yards ahead of him when he suddenly stopped dead in his tracks. The man that nearly killed him lurked near.

He pulled out the silver keychain, carefully removing the pin. Out came a tiny scroll, and he unraveled it meticulously despite his hands shaking uncontrollably. The time had come, and before reading it, he made the sign of the cross. *Bless this man, dear Lord, that you have sent to me as a gift in my life, for he does Your work. Amen.*

He folded it back together and placed it back in its casing. Upon installing the pin, he held it tight and kissed it.

"I love you," he whispered and placed it back in his pocket.

Along the path, a fence safeguarded the sign and prevented tourists from falling over the steep edge of the hill. Nearing the fence, he studied it closely. *He's been here,* he thought.

Abraham scaled the ten-foot fence carefully. Securing his footing on the other side, a shadow slithered by into the nearby bush. "Snakes, that's just great," he whispered, "all my nightmares are coming to light here."

Quietly making his way down the steep hill, he steadied his footing. Overlooking the city, he recalled the emotions Abbadon spoke of.

Behind the huge letter H was a silhouette in deep meditation crouched over in a gargoyle-like state. Barely visible in the dark, Abraham approached this beast like a lion creeping on its prey. Ghostlike movement inched him closer to the shadowy figure that knew no mercy. Closer now, he could see the gargoyle clearly; deep in thought, he would surely take him by surprise. Only a few steps away, he could catch the madman without confrontation, knocking him unconscious.

Stooping lower, he grabbed a baseball-sized rock. He was ready to strike. *Just a little closer,* he thought. Maneuvering one step forward, he lost his footing. A rock became loose under his shoe and the element of surprise vanished. The size of a tennis ball, the rock bounced up and clanged against the back of the giant H. Concentration broke for both predators. The noise could be heard from down below as the echo rang in the air. They locked eyes on one another, and Abbadon sprang up from his hiding place.

Abbadon rose up from his crouch-like state and faced his former ally. The two combatants were now face-to-face.

"You found me. I knew you would," Abbadon smirked as he spoke, "Only you could've found me here."

He appeared to be at ease. Abraham could not read him, and his actions were unpredictable in moments such as this.

"You are defenseless, as you see I am not." Abbadon waved his handgun in the air, taunting his foe, determined to intimidate him.

Abraham didn't flinch. Adrenaline pumped ferociously through him. Fight or flight was in full effect. Now, he had to choose his tactical method of operation, the fear or the fire.

"Why did you come here? Did they send you to find me?" Abbadon began questioning, "They knew you could find me, right? That's why they brought you…"

"I didn't come here to fight," Abraham interjected, "We came to arrest you…the killing…I didn't think you would go back to that." He tried to reason with his sparring partner, but he knew a fight was inevitable.

"Well, it's too late." Abbadon ran up to higher ground. "You know the frightening truth, don't you? Only one of us will be left standing."

Abraham trailed right behind, sprinting equally fast.

Abbadon searched for an advantage amidst the unlevel plane. "You knew what you were getting into when you came here. It's going to be different, and this time, you will die." He tossed his gun aside. He locked his sights on Abraham, dead in the eye. "Look at you with your Kevlar vest. You're pretending to be a cop, a wannabe cop? Are you ready? Are you willing to take my life because the only way you're going to take me is in a bag. I'm not going down without a fight. I knew it was gonna be just me and you. I could feel it."

Abbadon was ready.

Abraham was hesitant. Images from the first bout came to life and betrayed him. The pain, the fear, slithered into his psyche. *Can I stop him? What if I fail?* Questions panged about in succession. He attempted to reason with him. "Even if you beat me, it's over for you. You can't escape this one."

"What was it that you asked me once, 'How far are you willing to go?' And now, I ask that of you. Are you willing to die for your cause?"

He's trying to psyche me out, make me second-guess. No, Abraham, don't let him. Come on, be strong!

His countermeasures were put to the test as he fought hard on all fronts to keep him at bay.

I've never taken a life before. I don't know what that feels like.

Fear bounced in and out, striking persistently seeking a place to settle in nicely. What if he couldn't beat Abbadon? Worse yet, what if he had to die finding out? Abbadon was challenging him in a way no other human had before. He had to stop thinking and act on instinct and so he commenced the counteraction. "I didn't come here to lose. You took the first bout, but you're not taking the second. I came prepared and if that means that you'll go home in a bag..." Abraham felt unsure saying the words, but he had to stand up to Abbadon and attack him with bold statements as he had done him, "So be it."

"You know, I thought you died back in San Antonio. You almost did, didn't you? How do you think you're going to fare this time? I know you're scared."

Abraham refused to look away. He promised himself that this bout would have a drastically different outcome than the one that came before. "Scared? No. I'm ready to take everything you got."

"Really? Well, after I'm done with you, I'm gonna finish what my dad started…at approximately twelve midnight, San Antonio time, your hometown will have an *explosive* show, greater than any New Year's firework display. Midnight is less than two hours away… and you're over here…about to die. Even if you survive, you won't make it in time to alert your brothers in blue and down goes your beloved tower." Abbadon shook his head in disgust. "San Antonio, LA, and DC will be in shambles by the time I'm through." He scowled intensely. "I'm sure they found the coordinates I left…but the thing is…your police force will run out of time before they find the gift I left behind in the great HemisFair Park…"

"A bomb? It's a decoy to send us on a wild goose chase…tactical warfare to gain the psychological edge. Until I see the Tower go down, then I'll believe it."

"You think I'm bluffing? You severely underestimate me, Abraham. You really don't know what you're up against…twenty-nine degrees, twenty-five minutes, eight point four seconds north, ninety-eight degrees, twenty-eight minutes, fifty-eight point eight seconds west," he said arrogantly.

His presence radiated evil, as he regressed to a dark side that beckoned with no mercy.

Abraham believed him. His chilling confession originally instilled doubt, but now, it was an undeniable truth, foreshadowing a malicious travesty. The speech was evident enough to confirm that a former friend had returned to his old ways.

"You think you've won…but it's not done yet," Abraham spoke with vigor, "I have a little bit of time…my chances are good…and you're forgetting one thing…I have God on my side…"

"God! This is truly a sad story, Abraham! Your faith has led you here to die…and your God has forsaken you…I have only one thing to say to that…fuck you and your God!"

Infuriated, Abraham consumed the blasphemy that his rival reveled in. Abbadon single-handedly lit the fire that Abraham lacked in weeks prior. Previous attempts were sluggish in furthering the flame, but now, a full-blown fire consumed their midst. With the power emanating in his eyes, he spoke with purpose. "I'm here to stop you! You're not gonna hurt anybody anymore…"

Abbadon removed his shirt, revealing a tank top. Preparing for battle, he tossed it aside. "Did they bring you here as a negotiator to counsel me out of this one, a come-quietly kinda thing? You know, as I do, that this is the way it was meant to be…just you and me…" He raised his index finger menacingly, "Just one more time."

"I hoped for another way," Abraham said, calmly taking a deep breath. He closed his eyes briefly and then unhurriedly reopened them, "You're right, this is the way it's meant to be."

Using the steepness of the hill, Abbadon jumped off his left foot, gliding toward the gate and coming back down with his left fist with more momentum and force to strike his opponent. Abraham ducked under, pummeling his brother's midsection and tackling him down. Unloading a barrage of punches into Abbadon's chest and facial area, Abraham questioned his own efforts.

He's strong, not all my punches are landing, he thought. Abbadon, blocking the majority of the assault, kicked him in the stomach, freeing himself. The adrenaline rush had both men hopping to their feet and Abbadon grabbed Abraham by the Kevlar vest, ripping it off him, and punched him repeatedly in the stomach he had just kicked. Abraham slouched over grimacing. Abbadon delivered a series of one-two combinations, scoring several vicious blows to the head. Abraham fell to his knees; his ear, throbbing and cut, reeled to recover. Cocking back his right arm, he released another punch, sending along with it a mighty force filled with anger. Falling to the ground, Abraham felt his cheekbone swelling from the hit.

Abbadon continued punishing his adversary, stomping on his upper body while keeping his balance on the slope. Abraham shrieked in pain.

"You were my friend…I expected more from you. I admired your tactics, but only one of us can win, right?" Abbadon kicked him in the stomach once again.

Struggling to regain his composure, blood seeped from Abraham's mouth.

"This is my chance to get out of here and you're *going* to cooperate!"

Abraham made an attempt to rise up. Despite his efforts, Abbadon sent a swift kick to his face. Abraham collapsed to the ground

Abbadon went for the gun he tossed aside a moment earlier.

Abraham labored to regain composure. *He's gonna kill me,* he thought. He didn't have a choice anymore. He gathered himself for one last hurrah. *"God, strengthen me…in my weakness, you make me strong…"*

He calculated a few precious seconds left to mount a counter-offensive. Sixty seconds to counteract, sixty seconds to stall, sixty seconds of life left if he didn't try to stop him. Abraham coached himself back to life.

What was it that I tell people? What do I always say?

He struggled to remember.

Come on, get up, think.

Abbadon counted on his agility to traverse the hill. Recouping the nine millimeter, he trekked back to where his nemesis lay. Abraham crawled sluggishly up the hill, evading the bushes, in hopes of reaching the fence.

Abbadon heard a crunch under his foot. A rectangular device rested in the dirt.

"Ahh, let's see here…" With one press of a button, the device lit up. "Who shall we call, huh?"

He searched the call log. "How about your precious Liv? Let's give her a ring!"

Abraham rallied his resurgence. The thought of Liv bolstered the roaring blaze. *Remember what you're fighting for? I need to fight for her.*

"Liv! You'll be happy to know that Abraham fought bravely, but now it's time for him to go away. I wanted to give you the courtesy of letting you know…he won't be coming home."

Abraham faintly heard her screams through the phone. Enraged and revitalized, a recollection called to him that defined his trials of late. In the last place he thought he would need it, it arrived at exactly the right moment. The best advice he could ever give to someone in distress.

It doesn't matter how hard you fall, all that matters is how you respond.

His strongest chance of survival, the response mustered up an indisputable effort to live. With his legs a bit shaky, the adrenaline had restored most of his power.

Get up and answer back!

Abbadon dropped the phone. He raised his right leg and, using his boot, forced it onto the device, shattering it to pieces. Holding the gun in one hand, Abbadon clutched Abraham with his left. "Get up…I need you to walk."

Abraham rose powerfully and faced Abbadon. "No, we're not going anywhere!"

Locking his eyes square into his, Abraham snatched the tank top with both of his hands. He swung his head back with as much force as he could gather, striking Abbadon with a head butt that cracked through the air. Upon impact, he reached for his wrist simultaneously. Off balance, Abbadon swung back, his arm flailing backward up in to the air as both combatants stumbled. Abraham reached for Abbadon's arm in hopes of recovering the handgun. They rolled down the hill, grappling with the rocks and bushes. Rather than picking up speed, the terrain slowed their descent down to the metal sign. The gun lay a few feet up the hill from them unbiased to the scuffle at hand. The violent tumble down left both men losing their handle on each other and the handgun. Slowly gathering themselves, they vied to continue the fight.

Picking up Abbadon by the shirt, Abraham delivered retaliatory blows to the head and chest. The momentum shifted on the roll down, and now Abraham was in complete control. Barely able to keep his hands up, Abbadon was at his mercy, as Abraham unleashed a barrage of poundings to the left side of his face. A combination of punches left Abbadon on the verge of unconsciousness. Abraham lit up his brother with a right hook that knocked Abbadon back a few feet. The giant H prevented him from falling over the cliff.

Abbadon froze. His mouth dropped open and his neck swung back violently. Shock swept across his face.

Abraham paused, surprised at the reaction of his opponent. Confused, it took a second for him to understand the moment at hand. He then realized the horrific truth.

The fight was over.

Stunned, Abbadon faced Abraham and pulled himself from the metal beam that protruded through his body. The sharp and jagged beam, jutted out from the H, nearly invisible. The moonlight, unable to give its full potential of luminosity, hid behind the clouds and the darkness fell onto the sign.

Abraham reached out with both arms, helping Abbadon to stay balanced. Blood flowed from his mouth and his wound gushed, spilling over the hillside.

Abbadon plopped down to the ground on his knees.

"Here, just…just relax…I'm gonna, I'm gonna get help…" Hysterical, Abraham had no clue of what to do. His mind went blank.

"Well, you won, brother," Abbadon spoke in a low defeated voice.

"Come on, we gotta hurry. I can save you!" Abraham interjected.

"No…you can't. Not this time." His voice grew faint.

Abraham kneeled alongside him wide-eyed and silent. No matter how much he believed that he would do whatever it took to stop Abbadon, he realized now that was false. Tears welled up in his eyes.

Abbadon hunched over to lie on his back. He reached out for Abraham's hand. Abraham gave his hand willingly. The two hands met and linked in a handshake of brotherhood.

"Not like this…" Abraham forced the words out.

"Help me up," Abbadon requested.

Abraham helped him to his feet. Abbadon put his arm around his brother's neck.

The tears started falling, heavier than he could bear.

"It's all right…you're the one," Abbadon tried his best to reassure his friend.

"I loved you, Abbadon…I loved you like my brother. I would've done…anything…for you. It wasn't…it wasn't supposed to be like this…" His voice shook and tears ran down his cheeks. Abraham tried to speak.

"It's okay, brother…it's okay. It was…meant to be this way…"

"No…we, we have time," Abraham pleaded with him. The area behind the H was not terribly steep, however, the hike back up to the trail was challenging at best. Doubt crept in, and the chances of successfully making it up in time were considerably slim.

"Wait…wait." Abbadon was losing strength with every second. He glanced up at the fence and shook his head slowly up and down. "Abraham…it's all right," he said in a raspy voice.

"No! We're not givin' up!" Abraham demanded, refusing to put him back down on the ground.

"If you love me now…leave me, give me peace," Abbadon, getting weaker in his waning moments, begged his friend for one last favor. "Please, brother."

Struggling to hold on to him, Abraham gently let go of his friend. He left him standing upright, like a warrior wanting to die on his feet.

Tears flooded his eyes, and as he started the upward hike, his vision blurred from the onslaught, knowing his brother cherished his last moments on the earth.

Abbadon hobbled over to where the gun lay. He picked it up, ignoring the pain shooting through his body, but it was going numb already.

"Abraham!" Abbadon yelled as loud as his lungs would let him, for his brother one last time.

Abraham turned to face him. Abbadon held the gun in his hand. He waited for a response and, out of love and respect for the brother he once knew, let him speak his final words.

Abbadon pointed the handgun directly at Abraham, shaking it up and down. "You're the one…you're the one." He then turned it to his temple and pulled the trigger.

It was over. Abbadon was dead.

XL
RESTORATION

"You would've made a great detective, Moreno," Detective Balderama congratulated Abraham with sincerest regards.

"Yeah?"

"We would've never caught this guy if it weren't for your help. Without you, we would've never found the bomb in the Tower of Americas. Luckily, we got to it in time. Excellent work, young man."

"Thank you, that means a lot." Abraham couldn't help himself, he let out a huge smile. He was flattered that the detective realized his potential.

"We could use someone like you on the force."

"I would've made for a good detective…"

"Would've? It's still possible. I could really use you on my team."

Detective Balderama hinted at a possibility for the dream to be alive again. The rush of adrenaline flowed through every corridor of his body. "I don't think so. I'm considered permanently unsuitable, remember?"

"You know, a lot of officers on the force will vouch for you. And not only that, I can pull a few strings here and there, and you'll be back in the academy within the month."

Abraham grinned, shaking his head. The offer sounded tempting. This was his chance to come back. An opportunity to use his deductive reasoning in real-life equations thrilled him, and a badge to back up these skills would definitely differentiate the genius from the psychotic tendencies.

Justice sprang to his thoughts. The way her innocent eyes lit up, knowing he genuinely cared for her, and her smile radiated a warm feeling of safety in his presence. She needed him. She needed a savior in her young life, and he flew in right on cue. He couldn't leave her. He couldn't leave the kids, knowing the difference he was making in their lives.

And then there was Liv. She believed in his gifts. She understood the value of what he needed to do, even when she didn't like it. Her voice shook in their last conversation, and she was uneasy letting him go on the hunt. The look on her face desperately wanting him to come home safely, for this was a one-time circumstance in her mind, and he wanted it to stay that way as well, and in a split second's notice, he realized he was right where he needed to be.

"That sounds good and all, but I think I've accepted the fact that…I'm not meant to be a police officer."

He spoke with a quiet confidence. The plan to be with four-year-olds had been God's call, and in his heart, it was where he wanted to be. It was where he needed to be.

"Well, Moreno, if you ever change your mind, just give me a call."

"All right, I will definitely keep that in mind."

"Abraham, it's been a pleasure."

"The pleasure was all mine, Detective."

"Call me Chris, and don't forget to keep in touch."

"Will do."

The two men shook hands.

"I'm sure God has special plans for you."

"He does."

The detective regrouped with the task force. Abraham staggered through the baggage claim, oblivious to the greetings, reunions, and tears of joy and laughter that surrounded him. His senses were calming, the adrenaline gradually fading. He went on the trip with nothing but the clothes on his back, his tactical gear returned to the custody of the San Antonio Police Department, seasoned from battle. The sliding doors opened leisurely before him. It didn't matter though, he was in no hurry. Tired, hungry, and dirty, he was ecstatic to be home again. He looked up to the blue sky and took a deep breath, inhaling the San Antonio air.

He was alive.

"Baby!" He heard her joyous voice yell across the incoming airport traffic, and it was music to his ears. She ran straight into his arms and kissed him all over his face with urgency.

"Baby, I love you so much! I'm so glad you're home, I was a total mess! When I couldn't get through on your phone, I thought…" The lump in her throat got the best of her.

"I thought…you were…" Before she could finish, her torso jerked repeatedly as she clung to his chest. Her silent cry was heartfelt. Abraham fought the tears coming to life. Liv hugged him tight. Her body shook as her head rested on him, closer to his heart than ever before.

"I'm here…I'm home…it's done…and nothing would make me happier…than to take my soul mate out…for a night of dancing." His decompression was taking place with words, leaving his mouth slower and slower. "I'm with you…wherever you want to be. I don't care, as long as I'm with you."

She did her best to calm herself, but the images of a worst-case scenario were still fresh in her mind. "Anyway, you need to take me to where you promised." She cracked a smile, despite her face full of tears.

"Of course, I will. I just need to catch up on rest…like thirty hours of sleep, at least."

Liv pulled him, her arm around his waist. He rested his right arm around her neck as she trudged him along like a soldier injured in battle. He planted his left hand in his pant pocket for stability. In two days' time, they planned to return to this place, where their next destination was passionately chosen, halfway around the world.

✞

The sand between his toes felt odd and uncomfortable. He had been out of his comfort zone too many times in the last ninety-six hours. This form of unpleasantness, however, he would take any day, over the distasteful date with near death. His spirits were high and his code of recovery within twenty-four hours was now in full effect. Besides, he did not want to disappoint her. He originally waited for her off to the side in the grassy area but then decided to take the plunge with bare feet onto the smooth sandy beach. How bad could it be? He and water were not the best of friends nor would they ever be. However, his soul was linked to a kindred spirit that favored it. His attire deviated little and he was sure that holding a pair of Nikes on the beach looked awkward enough. His black tank top stuck closely like a second skin, just the way she liked. His baggy jean shorts did not blend well with the backdrop of the ocean. He hadn't worn this particular pair of shorts in some time, and when he reached in his left pocket, he felt something peculiar. He pulled out what he thought would be a dollar bill, or a wad of it, at least. Had he known, he would've given it to her to purchase a bottle of water from the vendor. Rather, it was a folded piece of paper. He opened it slowly with wonderment. Liv had planted a love letter in his pants, he thought. She knew how to tug on his heart and as it skipped beats, it was a feeling he welcomed. He opened it giddily, impatient to get drunk off her love. The writing looked all too familiar...

It wasn't the penmanship he expected and definitely not reminiscent of his wife to be...and just as he was about to read the inscribed ink, he noticed it was from an old friend.

Abraham,

I was never genuinely happy. I thought I was, but I fooled myself, and the sickness that you came to witness just drove me to be what I am. Maybe I'm just sick myself. You were the one to give me hope, a somewhat happy life, even if it was temporary. I thought I could be someone special, but it's just not my destiny. I loved you and I'm sorry I couldn't be better...I tried. This sickness, this darkness, doesn't stand a chance because if I can't beat it, I know you will. One way or another, darkness will be defeated because I have the greatest person I have ever known on my side. It's going to be hard, but I know you… and I know you'll find a way. If we ever meet in battle, I hope that you are the victor, for the sake of the world.

Abbadon

Victor? There are no victors, he thought, *and casualties and collateral damage come in different forms.* This particular memory he immediately tried to forget and a definite violation of his twenty-four-hour recovery process. What instantly turned to a dark moment, he transformed back to a light one. Her appearance was too dazzling for him to be consumed by events that took place days before. He stuffed it back in his pocket, deep in the dark corridor where it needed to remain. She walked back to him, and as she did, he wanted to bury everything of his now former life. That story was over now, and it was time for them to begin a new one, together.

* * * * *

The water shined beautifully in the sunset. The brilliant glare provided a pathway to the heavens. The palm trees fluttered in the breeze and the horizon seemed to never end. Liv looked stunning as always. The Hawaiian wrap enveloped her body as she was draped in black with purple hibiscus print. Her lei completed her native look, and her hair was tied up in a tight bun. Time froze, and feelings of adoration flooded his entire being, as his new life flashed in front of him. She was a beautiful Hawaiian queen, his queen. As he looked upon her, nothing more important in the world existed, and there was only one thing he could think about. He spoke gently in her ear.

"You are my love,
my life,
my queen,
my wife…

for all time."

She gazed at the sun dipping its way to the other side of the earth and her power gained momentum, as her precious moon was coming to life. She smiled slowly, knowing that his words came from his heart and soul rather than the flesh.

"I believe in one fine day," she whispered. Her arms wrapped around his neck and his became engulfed around her waist. With sunlight fading, two shadows became one.

"Are you ready?" he asked in a soft tone.

"I'm so hungry…I thought you'd never ask," she smiled.

"No, not dinner. Are you ready to begin…"

"To begin?" She questioned.

"The greatest love story?" His seriousness trailed off to what turned into a huge grin.

She laughed, as she usually did, when she got caught off guard with his humor.

"Baby…" She slipped her hand behind his neck, pulled him close to her cheek, and whispered into his ear, "It already started."

He grabbed her by the hand and they walked along Waikiki together. He raised her arm and twirled her around; she swooped into his arms and he planted a huge kiss on the woman that would be his partner forever. Their lips locked, and like everything else… they fit.

Deep down even the most hardened criminal is starving for the same thing that motivates the innocent baby: love and acceptance.

—Lily Fairchilde

ACKNOWLEDGMENTS

There have been so many people involved in the process of bringing this book to life.

God has always been the foundation in my life. He deserves all the credit, for this story is His. He has taken me to places I never thought I could go. Glory be to God.

To Mom, Buela, and Margie, thank you for being an amazing support system. All my accomplishments would have never been achieved without all of you.

To my beautiful daughter, Maddy, thank you for believing in your dad! There were days when I doubted and questioned, but your excitement about this project and the sight of your eyes lighting up helped me to believe I could make this happen. I hope to make you as proud of me as I am of you.

To the great Jennifer Esparza, thank you for being my editor, work wife, confidant, and friend. You cheered me on, encouraged me, and kept me focused in the home stretch. I would've never made the final push to finish this project if it weren't for you! I can never thank you enough!

Printed by Libri Plureos GmbH in Hamburg, Germany